The Pursuit

Book Three in the Skyy Huntington Series

By Holly Hudspeth

The Pursuit

Book Three in the Skyy Huntington Series

This book is dedicated to my dad. He isn't my birth father, but I am glad to have him in my life and am more than proud to call him my dad. He has supported my dream of writing and publishing my books, and is always there with encouraging words when I need them the most. So thanks Dad, for always making me laugh, supporting me, and helping me along the way. Most of all, thanks for being you!

I'd also like thank my two editors, you guys know who you are and have helped me tremendously!

Books by Holly Hudspeth:

The Lie – Book One in the Skyy Huntington Series

The Countess – Book Two in the Skyy Huntington Series

The Pursuit – Book Three in the Skyy Huntington Series

Guided by Moonlight – Book Four in the Skyy Huntington Series

The Portal – Book Five in the Skyy Huntington Series

One Small Detail

Table of Contents

Chapter 1

I don't remember anything about the transition from human to vampire. The last thing I recall was Aiden telling me he loved me, then I just went to sleep. There were no restless fits or dreams, it was just nothingness. But apparently something went wrong and I was in my death-sleep for almost four weeks. None of my vampire friends had ever heard of anyone taking that long to transition. They thought I might never wake up, Aiden wouldn't leave my side, and my grandfather, Killian Huntington, had one of the Divine Assassins best scientists monitoring me at all times.

Since no Divine Assassin had ever been turned into a vampire, or attempted to turn into a vampire, everyone was at a loss. The best they could come up with was that the magical barriers my grandfather had placed on me when I was an infant to protect me from vampire mind whammy and manipulation, along with the few learning potions I had recently taken, were somehow interfering with the transition. So, everyone kept a close eye on me, and my grandfather had brought in some equipment to keep me alive. I was hooked to oxygen, an IV, and had a feeding tube inserted.

Then, without anything obvious changing from their end, I just...woke up. Jolting up in the bed at Lucius' villa in Italy, I instinctively tried to rip out the tubing by my nose. Aiden was on his feet in a flash, calling out for someone. "Hold still Skyy, don't touch anything, I'm getting someone to help," he said.

Within seconds a middle aged man came running to my side. He carefully removed the feeding tube and oxygen, and then the IV. I wondered what was going on, and got scared. "Why am I hooked up to an IV?" I inquired nervously. Aiden was by my side rubbing my hair comforting me. I could smell the blood of the scientist, and could hear his heart beating. There were six more hearts beating nearby, I could hear them as if they were my own heart beating inside my chest.

The middle aged man answered me, "You've been in your death-sleep for almost four weeks Skyy. My name is Jaime, your grandfather asked me to come and have a look at you. We couldn't figure out what was causing your transition to take so long, and so we needed to keep you alive. Would you mind if I took some blood samples?" His deep brown eyes were kind, but somehow I thought he was judging me. Most of the Divine Assassins were against vampires in general. They had agreed to keep an open mind though when letting me join their ranks.

I could see sweat beading on his forehead, in clear detail, and I could see the tiny pores of his skin move with a life of their own. Every single detail on Jaime was amplified. I blinked and looked around the room. The colors were exploding! I could see dust particles on the dresser across the room, and I could see every single individual strand of hair in my hairbrush that was sitting on top of the dresser. I glanced up to the ceiling and saw a tiny spider hiding in the corner of the room, although it was barely half the size of my pinky nail, I could see his eight eyes and the tiny hairs on his legs clearly.

Jaime cleared his throat, breaking me out of my trance. "Skyy?" he asked me again.

I nodded my head to him, "Sure you can take some blood." I looked up at Aiden, who was smiling at me with his perfectly white teeth. He looked overjoyed. I noticed his light green eyes were glowing very faintly but could make out small flecks of blue and gold in his iris I had never seen before. It was striking and only added to his already handsome features. "So…did I turn, Aiden? Am I a vampire now?"

As I held my arm out for Jaime to take his blood sample, Aiden took my other hand in his. "I am not sure why it took so long for you to turn, but all signs point to you being fully transitioned to vampire now." He didn't take his eyes off me while talking. "Jaime, once you have your sample it'd be best if you took your leave. She shouldn't be around humans for the first few days."

Jaime nodded his head, and I heard his heartbeat pick up a little bit after Aiden made that request. More sweat beaded on his forehead. He was afraid of me. I was staring at his neck, watching his jugular vein move in rhythm with his pounding heart. All I could think about was how quickly I could rip into his neck and taste his blood.

Aiden could apparently tell I was struggling. He called out for his mom, Fiona, to come into the room. Her tiny frame appeared in the doorway within two seconds of him calling for her. A huge smile was on her face as she laid her eyes on me. They were the same lovely light green color that Aiden had. She rushed over to the bed, gently pushing Aiden out of the way and planted a soft kiss on my cheek. Her long, pale blonde hair tickled my face. "Oh Skyy! You look amazing. We're all so happy that you're finally awake!" As much as I loved Fiona, I couldn't get my mind off Jaime's jugular. A feeling that scared the daylights out of me was overtaking my body. I knew it was irrational to attack this man, yet it was all I could think about. I needed to have his blood in my mouth.

"Mother, would you do a favor for me and get some refreshments ready for Skyy?" Aiden asked her, trying not to make it obvious he was asking her to get some donor blood ready for me in front of the human. Fiona nodded and was gone in a flash. Jaime had finished drawing his blood sample and was rushing to get his things packed up so he could leave.

When he looked over at me terror flashed on his face. Mentally I felt as though I was about to lose it, but I didn't think I was physically showing that on the outside with my actions. Aiden stood to shake his hand and quickly escorted him out of the room. Jaime didn't say so much as a goodbye or get well soon to me. The Divine Assassins are used to killing vampires, not being up close and personal helping them, and I guess it was a little more than he was comfortable with.

Aiden was laughing when he sat back down on my bedside. "What's so funny?" I asked him, a little bit pissed off. I was suddenly getting very angry for no reason.

"Well, I think you scared Jaime pretty good. Go take a peek in the mirror and you'll see why," was his reply.

I stood up and walked over to the dresser mirror. My mouth fell open in shock and my eyes became huge as saucers. I had vampire fangs! They were fully extended and quite

9

fascinating. I touched my tongue to the right fang, and I tasted blood rising up off my tongue moments later. I lifted my upper lip up, and touched my finger to one of them with the same result. Putting my finger in my mouth to suck the blood off of it, I began to marvel at my eyes. When I was still a human they were exceptionally pretty, a light aqua blue color. Now they were glowing vibrantly and looked like shimmering water in the Caribbean ocean.

Aiden walked up behind me and wrapped his arms around my upper body, then kissed my neck softly. He stared at me in the mirror, smiling. "I don't think I've ever seen a more beautiful vampire in my life." I was still admiring my new look in the mirror when I heard Jaime talking to my grandfather somewhere in the house. I don't even know what happened, but it happened very quickly. I dashed for the door, flung it open and almost ripped it off its hinges. Aiden grabbed me from behind and dragged me back into the room kicking the door shut. Rage had consumed me.

"Get out of my way Aiden!" I screamed at him. It wasn't like me, and sounded like it was coming from someone else. Smelling Jaime's blood set my veins on fire. It was all I could think about, all I wanted. I had to find a way out of this room.

"Darling, calm yourself down. Breathe deeply. You don't want to do something you'll regret and have to live with for the rest of your vampire life. Fiona will be here any moment with your nourishment. Stay with me until then sweetheart," he said as he tried to approach me again.

I slapped his arms away from me and tried to dash out around him. He was much faster than me though and had me in another hold. Screaming in frustration at the top of my lungs, I bit into his forearm. Aiden didn't even flinch, as I watched blood pour from the gash I had made with my fangs. I put my mouth to the wound, drinking in his salty blood. It wasn't human blood, but it was blood, and it was satisfying my cravings. In the back of my mind I was freaked out, wondering how I could have developed such an immense craving for something that would have otherwise made me gag as a human. I stopped drinking and fell to my knees crying. Aiden kneeled down to be at the same level with me and wrapped his arms around me in an embrace.

"It'll be alright Skyy. We all go through this in the beginning. I won't let you hurt any of the humans, I promise," Aiden said as he rocked back and forth with me in his arms. My emotions were on a rollercoaster right now, I was still enraged that he was holding me back, and also extremely turned on from him holding me close.

Fiona walked into the room, with a large coffee mug. "Come and sit on the bed, Skyy. Drink this and you'll feel much better," she said as she gestured to the bed. Aiden helped lift me off the floor and I sat at the foot of the bed. Fiona handed me the mug of blood, which had been slightly warmed.

I chugged it down in record speed, and glanced up at myself in the mirror that hung over the dresser. I had blood all over my mouth and chin. Wiping it away with the back of my wrist I smiled at my reflection in the mirror. I hadn't done much but smear it around more. Taking deep breaths as Aiden had instructed me before, I tried to calm my nerves down. The blood did help slightly, and I kept smiling at myself and talking to myself, "It'll be ok....it'll be ok....it'll be ok...."

Aiden didn't think I saw it, but I watched as he gave Fiona an odd look in the mirror. He wasn't sure what to do for me. "I think we should get her some more blood, Mother. If you don't mind?" Aiden gently took the mug from my hands and gave it back to Fiona, who nodded her head and disappeared again to refill it.

The breathing exercises didn't really do much to calm me down, and even though my bloodlust was taken down a notch after the donated blood, I could still hear all the human hearts on the property beating. There would be no way I could stay on this property, for the long term. I'd go nuts or kill one of them. "We're going to need to get out of here, Aiden. I can't stay here," I said while still staring at myself in the mirror.

Aiden glanced down at his feet, then put his hands in the pocket of his designer jeans. "Skyy, it would be easier for us to just leave that is certain. But keeping you in the household,

11

separated from the humans will help get your thirst in check much faster. I'm not trying to tell you what to do, but in the long run this will benefit everyone the most." I could tell he didn't want to have to tell me that. I knew he was right, and I knew before I ever went into my death-sleep that this wouldn't be a walk in the park.

Fiona returned a moment later with more warmed blood, and again I chugged it down as if I were dying of thirst. I still wanted more. Turning to look up at Fiona I gave her a half-smile as I held the mug out to her. As if reading my mind she asked, "Would you like some more?" Embarrassed, I just nodded my head yes and she silently left the room for the third time. The undesirable urge to go out of this room and rip into the throats of every human on the property was not fun, and I didn't like the feeling of not being in control of my own body and mind.

"How do you ever get over this feeling Aiden? I feel like I am not in control of myself," I asked him in a soft whisper.

"It takes time, the donated blood will start to move through your veins and work its way into your system and your hunger will slowly dissipate. You'll start to regain control of your mind and senses, and train yourself not to attack humans. It's uncomfortable, and not enjoyable by any means, but it is something you must endure if you want to be fully sustained off of donated blood." Aiden approached me again, testing to make sure I wasn't going to flip out on him, and I let him rub my back as I waited for Fiona to deliver more blood.

"I knew it would be hard, and I wanted this. So I'll try my best to keep it together. I'm sorry in advance if I fly off the handle again," I said. Aiden was the last person in the world I wanted to lash out at. He smiled at me and nodded his head. Fiona delivered my third mug of blood and I was finally starting to feel a little more balanced.

The three of us sat on the large bed in the room, with our legs folded facing each other. Fiona was smiling and cheerful as always. "So, tell me what has happened while I've been asleep," I said. In four weeks a lot could happen. The fact we were still alive, and Lucius' villa hadn't burnt to the ground was a promising sign.

12

Aiden spoke first. "The good news is, there have been no signs of Bathory since we destroyed her book back in Scotland, which also happens to be the bad news too. There have been no sightings of her, or any of her minions since then. Your grandfather and the Divine Assassins think that there is a good chance she could be hiding in The Gloom since she controlled a large force of dark fae. Ridley was staying here at the villa at first but after we saw that you weren't waking up, he has just been checking in with us on a daily basis through his portals. Since we have no way to personally get in touch with the Radiant fae, they were waiting for you to wake up before making any concrete plans on how to proceed, since they'd like the advice and counsel of the light faeries."

After our final showdown with Bathory back in Scotland, my Radiant fae friend Dreamer gave me a rose quartz crystal that was on a necklace which I could use to contact her with. Fiona chimed in before I could ask any other questions. "But before we go making any serious plans we need to make sure you're alright Skyy, so don't go worrying about all of that until it's time, for now let's concentrate on getting you ready for the world. And Ridley will be thrilled to learn you've woken up. As far as Divine Assassins go, no offense, he is a really decent fellow. We've all grown to like him around here."

I was glad to hear that. Ridley Whitmore was my newly assigned partner within the Divine Assassins. This was new territory that we were all treading on. There had never been a vampire in the ranks before me. Ridley had stood by my side and helped me get back to Scotland to fight the war against Bathory when I was told to sit it out. He fought beside me and stuck up for me, insisting that the leaders consider me even if I did turn vampire. Ridley was a fun person to be around, and one of the youngest Divine Assassins at a tender age of seventy-three. He didn't look a day over twenty-one though.

I was happy to hear that Ridley was fitting in with my new vampire family, because we'd be spending a lot of time together as partners. Though it did make me sad that I wouldn't be able to see him at least for a few days, I could however see my best friend Christian Vane, who was also a newly turned vampire. "How has Christian been doing?" I asked them.

Fiona grinned, "Why don't you ask him yourself?" We didn't even have to call for him, he was in the room in a blink of an eye, grinning that huge infectious smile of his.

I hopped off the bed and embraced him in a warm hug. I always felt so tiny when I hugged Christian, he was 6'5" and next to him I was a mere 5'7" but it felt good to see him again. He lifted me up off the ground and spun me around in a circle once before setting me down and holding me out at arm's length so he could check me out. He let out a slow whistle, "Well here we are, two sexy ass vampires. Who would have ever thought this is where we'd be a year ago?"

I giggled and replied, "I know, it's surreal. So how are you doing Christian? Still adjusting fine?" I asked, mostly hoping that he'd tell me things could only get better from here. He hadn't been a vampire very long, two months if that. But according to everything my vampire friends told us, he'd made the transition very quickly and got his thirst under control in no time, and then continued to amaze everyone by grasping abilities such as levitation way before most vampires do.

He nodded, his dark brown eyes shifted and began to reflect and glow like honey in the sunlight. "Everything has been going just fine on my end. Fi's been teaching me some basic mind whammy tactics, which I find harder than the levitation. How are you doing though, that's the question?"

I was amongst my closest friends, and had nothing to hide or be ashamed of, but I felt like a lesser person because I was feeling urges I shouldn't be feeling. But I went ahead and made a joke out of it and opened up to them all, "Well, honestly I want to drain every human on the property, and I really hope you tell me it won't always feel this awful Christian. Because right now, this sucks."

He pat my shoulder to reassure me, "It does get better Skyy, I promise. When I woke up, you were the only human close by. I don't think you even want to know the thoughts going through my mind when you walked down those stairs and I saw you for the first time. But these guys took care of me, and within a few hours I was already feeling a lot better," he said as he flashed a smile at Aiden and Fiona.

Things had been weird between Christian and me for a little while. We have known each other since high school, and while we both crushed on each other at various times during our friendship, neither of us acted on it until just recently. Christian had kissed me and confessed he had feelings for me, but I wasn't sure what I felt. Then I met Aiden and my whole world fell into place. Christian began dating Aiden's mom, Fiona...who also was the vampire that saved his life, and even though I felt like ripping my hair out of my head because I was craving blood so badly, I couldn't be more thrilled that I would get to spend the rest of my immortal life with my best friend Christian, and my new vampire family. Everything had worked out, and Christian and I would be just fine. I longed for things to finally get back to normal, where we could sit on the couch and watch bad movies until four in the morning. Things might never be that simple again, but at least I had my friend by my side, even though I still feel terrible for getting him mixed up in all of this.

I embraced Christian into another big hug. "Thank you Christian. I know I am in good hands with all of you." Thinking of my future, it raised another question. "Do you guys know if I was protected from the sunlight or not?" Before we fought Bathory, my grandfather performed a spell on my vampire friends that allowed them to be out in the full sun, with no consequences. Normally vampires have to bundle up from head to toe, ride in heavily tinted vehicles and keep shutters or shades on their windows, otherwise they will burn very quickly, and if they don't get inside and heal they can die from it. As a thank you for their services, and destroying a good chunk of Aiden's castle in Scotland, the Divine Assassins decided that not all vampires were totally evil and let them keep the sun protection spell.

Aiden answered me, "I am actually not sure about that. But we have taken all the precautions since you went into your death-sleep just in case. No sunlight will come into this room, so you can rest easy until we find out."

Christian offered to go find my grandfather to ask him, and I was starting to feel edgy again. "Would it be weird if I wanted more blood?" I asked shyly to Fiona and Aiden once he was gone. Even though Christian was physically out of the room, he could hear me no matter where he was on the property. Enhanced hearing was both a benefit and a curse to vampires - that part would take some getting used to.

Fiona hopped up off the bed and assured me it was not a problem. "No honey! It's just fine…if you're hungry and want blood, just ask for it. Don't be ashamed. Better to drink the bagged blood than attack a human. I'll be right back with some more."

Aiden smiled at me as I sat back down beside him. Snaking his fingers into mine, he spoke. "I'll go ahead and have Lucius move a freezer and microwave into this room, so it'll be easier when you want to drink." I nodded at him, trying to control my breathing again, because the heartbeats were becoming a nuisance.

Christian returned, even though I had heard that my grandfather informed him I still needed to have a sun protection barrier placed on me. "Grandpa said as soon as you're up to it, they can get you squared away Skyy," he said as he leaned up against the dresser. I could smell Christian's familiar scent from where I sat, and oddly it aroused me. I was 100% in love with Aiden, not that I wouldn't always think Christian was adorable and sexy, but I had not felt sexually attracted to him in quite some time.

I spread my fingertips out over my forehead, pushing up against it. What the hell was wrong with me? I would never, ever be unfaithful to Aiden. And I certainly would never commit murder! Luckily Fiona came back with my fourth mug of donated blood. I stood up and snatched it out of her hands, walking over to the corner of the room facing away from everyone. I took my time on this one, taking large sips instead of gulping it all down. Closing my eyes I tried to focus on the flavor. To my surprise this blood tasted totally different from the previous ones. It was as obvious as going from Coca-Cola to

Pepsi. Maybe it was a different blood type, but this mug satisfied my thirst more than the others had.

"Is this different blood?" I asked, still facing the corner of the room.

Fiona spoke from behind me, "Yes Skyy, the first three were from one donor bag, this one is a new bag. Why do you ask?"

"Because I like this one. It quenches my thirst," I replied shortly. I didn't even know who I was anymore. I knew, rationally that I should not be snapping at my dear friend, and mother of my fiancé.

"It is Type O Negative, I personally prefer it over other types as well, but it's a lot rarer to get," Fiona replied. I finished drinking the blood, and handed the mug back to Fiona. She took Christian's hand and they quietly left the room, giving Aiden and me some privacy.

There was no clock in the guest room we were staying in, and since the windows were covered to keep the sun out, I had no idea what time it was. "What time is it?" I asked Aiden.

He pulled his phone out of his jeans and glanced at it before putting it back. "A little after two in the afternoon."

"And I was out for almost four weeks you said? My parents are probably worried sick about me, I missed Easter I am sure, and with no phone call they must be wondering what is going on. I'll need to give them a call but I don't know what to even tell them," I sighed and began to look through my suitcase for some clean clothes to put on after I showered.

"I know Christian was a little proactive when he saw you weren't waking up any time soon. He sent a text message to Cate to let her know that you guys were planning on staying in Europe for a while longer. Maybe she passed the word on to your parents?" Aiden offered.

"Hopefully. I'm glad he did that, though I'll still have to come up with something to tell them. I don't think they will approve of me running off to Europe with a stranger they have never met, they are pretty religious but I don't know what else to say. I am going to take a quick shower and think about it," I said as I leaned over to kiss Aiden.

He returned my kiss softly, brushing his hand on my left cheek. "I'll go find Lucius and see about moving a fridge and microwave into this room for you while you do that. Love you." I watched his perfectly sculpted form walk out of the room before taking a long overdue hot shower. Being in my death-sleep for almost four weeks had left me feeling quite ripe. I spent longer in the shower than I realized and by the time I had dried off and put clothes back on, Aiden had already moved the microwave and fridge into our guest room.

I was trying to get the tangles out of my long hair, when Aiden pat the bed and motioned for me to sit down in front of him. He took the brush from me and began to gently brush my auburn hair out. "Your hair is so pretty. I think it looks even shiner than before now that you've turned."

"I was thinking that too, but wasn't sure if it was my imagination or not. I am also thinking about cutting it, what do you think?" I inquired.

Aiden stopped brushing my hair for a moment. "Well, I don't think you should. Plus my mother would have a fit." He went back to brushing again, but I could tell he wasn't onboard with the idea of cutting it.

"I guess you're right. I've just kept it so long my whole life, thought a change might be nice." I got compliments on my hair just about everywhere I went, it was down to my waist and a deep auburn color that shined vibrantly. Most people would kill for my hair, so maybe I'd wait before making the decision to cut it off.

After my hair had been brushed out, Aiden leaned back against the headboard and stretched his legs out. I put my head in his lap as I lay sideways on the bed while he rubbed my head. Normally this would put me to sleep, but as a vampire now all it did was relax me and comfort me. I didn't feel the least bit fatigued or tired. I wondered if that would get boring, not having to sleep as often. Aiden said he could usually go a few days without needing to sleep if he had blood daily, but usually slept about two to four hours a day. When I was still a human, I was guilty of just taking a nap sometimes in the afternoon when I was bored. I wondered if vampires got insomnia.

Over the next few hours, I drank six more mugs of blood. I'd drink and feel stable for about a half hour before feeling edgy and aggressive again. Aiden never once made me feel like I was doing anything wrong, and was more than accommodating and sweet to me. I kept listening to all the human heartbeats on the property, whether I wanted to or not. Once it was dark outside I asked Aiden if we could open up the windows and get some fresh air in the room. Shortly after nine that night, I heard the familiar voice of Ridley somewhere in the house.

"Ridley is here!" I exclaimed to Aiden. He nodded his head, but I noticed his body tensed up and he became more alert as his light green eyes began to reflect. He was worried I would make a break for it. Actually I was excited to see my friend, but not to attack him…at least not at this particular moment.

"You'll have to wait a few more days my love, you're not ready to see him yet," Aiden said regretfully while keeping his guard up.

I nodded my head in understanding. "I figured as much. I'd just like to get back to normal soon, I want to catch up with everyone and start the process of becoming a full Divine Assassin."

Aiden leaned over and kissed my forehead. "I know Skyy, just be patient."

Ridley heard that I was awake now, and he had brought some books and documents for me to look over while I was transitioning. Most of it was more information on Bathory, and translated texts that were not in her diary. There was also a report on the box of jewelry I found in Bathory's castle that I had given the Divine Assassins to check out. Turns out three pieces were enchanted in a much smaller fashion as the book…souls from the women she tortured were trapped in the gems of the jewelry.

This news was frightening because if those pieces of jewelry were enchanted, then who knows how many other items or pieces of work might be as well, in locations we have not even discovered yet. When we destroyed her book of black magic, we released what we thought was all of her victims. Since there had been no sightings of her, and no retaliation from her or her army, the Divine Assassins figured that she was in hiding. I hoped that we were right.

Even though the witches who helped her scribe the evil spells that bound those girls to the book were long dead, Bathory herself was a sorceress that was very powerful and dangerous. Her book, which she drew most of her power from, was destroyed...but since she was still alive she'd begin to find new ways to either forge a new one or come up with something even more terrible. We had to find her and kill her, the world shouldn't have to continue to suffer this woman's horrible acts of cruelty any longer.

Thinking of the victims made me think of the girls we had rescued from Bathory's castle in Slovakia. We were lucky enough to save a few girls, who last I heard wanted to open up a center for abused women. "How are the girls from Slovakia doing? Has anyone heard from them?" I asked Aiden.

He smiled at me and nodded, "Actually the girls are doing wonderful. Lucius has been in close contact with them, we set up a bank account for each of them, and a business account for them. They are looking at purchasing a building in Budapest for their center for abused women, and Lucius has been helping them come up with a solid business plan. Personally I think he fancies one of the ladies, but you didn't hear that from me," Aiden said with a wink.

Moments later I heard Lucius call out, "I heard that! Mind your own business Aiden Carrick!"

We both chuckled out loud. "I am glad to hear the girls are adjusting, and I am so thankful that you two helped them out. After what they went through, they deserve a chance to be happy and healthy again," I said as I kissed Aiden on the cheek.

"So if it's nine-ish here, what time would it be back home in New England?" I asked.

Aiden did some counting in his head then replied, "If I am right, we are six hours ahead of Massachusetts."

"Thanks. I should give Cate and my parents a call so they know I am alright. Not looking forward to this!" I decided to have another mug of blood before the phone call that I knew would stress me out and put me on edge whether I was human or vampire.

Aiden asked me if I would like him to leave the room while I called, and I said no. It wouldn't matter if he was in here or not, he could still hear the conversation, but having him near me made me feel better, so I asked him to stay. I grabbed my phone out of my purse, and decided to get the worst part over with first.

My father picked up the phone and right away started in on me. "Skyy! Honey where are you? Your mom and I have been so worried about you. Cate called and said you went to Europe!"

"Hi Dad, I'm sorry if you've been worried but I'm just fine. My phone gets bad reception out here or I would have called sooner," I lied. I heard my mom in the background asking if it was me on the phone.

"Well what are you doing in Europe for so long? Is this because of that man you mentioned to us?" I could already hear the disapproval in his voice.

Rolling my eyes, I figured I should just get on with the inevitable. "Yes Dad, his name is Aiden. He treated me to a trip over to Europe. We've been to Scotland, and now we are in Italy. And before you get all upset, Christian came with us too." They liked Christian and I hoped that maybe me mentioning him being with me might calm him down.

"Yes, Cate mentioned that. He has a job, how long are you two going to be over there?"

I had to decide what to do next. Drop the bomb that I was getting married, and not coming back to New England, or leave that for another day. Putting it off wouldn't make it any easier next time, so I decided to go all in.

"I don't want you and Mom to get upset. I don't think either of us are going to be coming back anytime soon. We're considering relocating here permanently."

"What! You barely even know this man Skyy! And Christian has a good job back home! Are you two involved in drugs? What is going on Skyy?" Although his accusations were unfair, if I were in his shoes I'd probably think it was weird too. I was never one to make huge life decisions like this, they always knew I was level-headed and dependable.

"No, it's not drugs Dad! I just need a change in my life, and it's beautiful over here. Aiden makes me really happy and I know it might seem like it's an irrational decision but what did I have going on in Massachusetts? My life was just on hold, I wasn't setting the world on fire. I really love it over here in Europe. And Christian has met someone as well."

My father sighed dramatically into the phone, and then there was silence for a moment. "I'm going to put your mother on," he said finally, and without another word he handed her the phone.

"Skyy? What is going on with you?" She already sounded like she was crying. Great.

I didn't see my parents very often, only a couple of times a year, but I didn't like upsetting them either. I weighed the pros and cons out before I decided to make the change, and the pros definitely outweighed the cons.

"Mom, calm down. I'm fine, you guys don't have to worry about me. I'm sorry I didn't call sooner."

"We're just happy to hear from you at all Skyy, we were beginning to think the worst. Did I hear correctly, you're thinking of moving to Europe?" she said as if she couldn't believe it.

"Yes Mom, and...well Aiden asked me to marry him, and I said yes. So, that is part of the reason. I'm really happy."

She was always a little easier to talk to than my father was when it came to romance.

"We haven't even met him Skyy! Please tell me you're at least coming back home before you get married! I'd like to be a part of all of this too, help you plan. I know you're an adult now and I won't tell you how to live your life but you're my only daughter, we'd like to meet this man and I'd like to be involved." She sounded panicked, and was sniffling as she talked.

I had not thought about our wedding much, because obviously I had more important things on my mind with Bathory after me, but I suppose that it was something Aiden and I would need to sit down and talk about fairly soon. And to be fair to my parents, we probably should fly back home if we were able to so they could meet him. I would only have maybe fifteen years before people would start to question why I wasn't aging.

"I'll talk things over with Aiden and see what we can do about flying back over there to see you guys, alright Mom? Just calm down, I won't leave you out of any of the wedding planning, I promise," I said, trying to get her to calm down.

"I am happy for you Skyy, but please promise me that you'll call more often. What is Christian doing about his job, surely he can't take this much time off?"

"John was cool with it. Christian is having a great time here as well, he is dating someone now, never thought we'd see that day come." Christian had never really dated anyone before, mainly because he was really shy even though he was very handsome, and because he had a thing for me since high school.

"Well, you tell him hello from us. I don't know what to think about the two of you and all of this, but I hope you'll both stay safe and out of trouble. And you need to call your cousin, she's been worried as well." She was calming down now that I assured her she would be included in the wedding plans. Honestly it went better than I had thought, though I knew they didn't approve of me living with someone before I was married.

"I will call her as soon as I hang up with you," I said. The conversation carried on for a few more minutes, she asked a few questions about Aiden, some I had to lie about like where he went to college and small things like that, but she seemed to be ok with me marrying a rich businessman.

After I hung up I called my cousin Cate, as promised. She picked up on the first ring. "Oh my God Skyy! Where the hell are you?! Your parents are so upset they haven't heard from you!" she exclaimed at me, while talking very quickly.

"I just got off the phone with them, and hello to you too Cate," I joked. My cousin and I were really close, and grew up together so she was like a sister to me.

"So, give me the gossip then! Don't keep me waiting. How is Europe?" she squealed like a teenager.

What I could say and what I did say were two totally different stories. If only she knew I had gone head to head in battle with a centuries-old Countess, and was now a blood drinking vampire. Instead, I stretched the truth a little. "It's really pretty over here. We went to Scotland, and Slovakia, and now we are in Italy. And guess what!" I said, keeping her in suspense.

"What!?" Cate replied, as if she could hardly wait to hear what I had to say.

"Aiden asked me to marry him!" Talking to her made me get just as excited.

"Oh my God! When are you guys coming home so I can meet him? When are we going to start planning the wedding!? I am so happy for you!" It sounded as if she didn't even take a breath in between words.

"We're going to talk about that tonight and make some plans to come back over to the States, I'll let you know as soon as we have a plan. But for now we're just relaxing and enjoying the sights. How are you and John doing?" Cate had started dating Christian's boss, John, a few months ago. The matchup was certainly not expected but they did hit it off much to everyone's surprise.

"He is such a sweetheart, I'm head over heels for him. Of course, no marriage proposal like some people I know…but we're getting along great. He'll be happy when Christian comes back home."

I didn't have the heart to tell her not to hold her breath on that one, but we did chat for a few more minutes and I got caught up on all the latest news back home. She made me promise to take a picture of Aiden and I and text it to her as soon as possible.

Once I was done on the phone, I had Aiden make me yet another mug of blood. After finishing every drop, I sat down in a chair by one of the open windows. "So I guess you heard all of that?"

Aiden nodded his head, as he sprawled out on his stomach on the bed. He wrapped his arms under his head and replied, "Yes milady. It looks as though we have a trip to plan."

I grinned at him. He was so easy going and sweet to me. "I think it'd be the right thing to do. I don't know how many years I'll have left to see them before I should realistically cut off physical contact with them. It's really important to my mother and Cate to be involved in the planning, we both spent hours talking about our future weddings when we were teenagers."

"I suppose I should have asked your father's permission before asking you to marry me. I hope he'll forgive me. But I agree it would be nice to have them involved as well, whatever makes you happy milady. I will stand by your decision."

"What did I do to deserve someone as wonderful as you, Aiden? Now if I can get over the urge to rip people's throats out, maybe we can plan a quick trip home before we get wrapped up in everything else with finding Bathory." I stood up and gathered up some more documents that Ridley had dropped off for me and plopped down on the bed. Aiden rubbed my feet for me as I worked.

A few hours had passed, and Lucius knocked on our door. His huge muscular frame entered the room. I had nicknamed him Lucius the Lurking Shadow a while back, though he didn't know it. He had his arms crossed, which was his usual stance. His long dark brown hair was back in a ponytail and his violet colored eyes were reflecting very faintly. His face was unreadable for the first few seconds, then he broke into a slow smile as he eyed me up.

"I think that had to be the longest transition from human to vampire in history, girl. You had us all terrified. But you look fantastic." Lucius walked into the room and closed the door behind him, and I jumped off the bed to give him a hug. He wasn't used to physical contact and wasn't a very emotional or talkative guy for the most part, but I have seen the softer side of the huge man before and knew he wasn't as tough as his exterior let on to be.

"It's good to see you Lucius," I said as I stepped back from our hug, still smiling.

"And you as well, Skyy. I came over here to ask if you'd like me to bring Cupcake to see you."

My eyes lit up at the mention of my dog's name. "Is it ok? I mean is it safe for me to be around her?" I asked.

Lucius and Aiden both nodded, and seemed to think it was alright, so I waited for a few minutes until Lucius came back with my darling little Boston terrier. She jumped right up on the bed and began to lick my face. I picked her up and hugged her as she wiggled excitedly in my arms. "How has she been getting along with the other dogs here?" I inquired.

"Oh, they are inseparable. They play all day long out in the fields, and she has taken up swimming now as well," Lucius said as he chuckled.

"Swimming! Wow Cupcake it sounds like you're having a great time here girl," I said as I put her back on the bed.

"My dogs love her, and Miss Abby has been fattening them all up with her table scraps. I keep telling her they'll get fat, but I still catch her sneaking food to them." I had never pegged Lucius as a dog lover, let alone a dog owner before, but it was nice to see that Cupcake was well cared for while I was unable to do it myself.

"I'll be sure to thank her as soon as I can for taking care of her both back in Scotland and here. And thank you to you too Lucius for letting us stay here with you."

"Of course my girl. If you need anything just give a holler. I'll leave you three to yourselves now." He gave a slight bow before he turned and left the room, closing the door behind him. I spent the next few hours snuggling in bed with my dog and my fiancé, until the sun came up and we had to shut the blinds.

Chapter 2

Day two of being a vampire was going a little better than day one had. I'd had close to thirty mugs of blood in the last twenty-four hours, and was starting to go stir crazy from being secluded in the guest room. The rage and bloodlust feelings were happening about once an hour now, as opposed to once every ten minutes yesterday. Ridley brought a few more things for me to read today, including a book on herbalism, and a book about basic alchemy that he said I should start memorizing right away.

I tried my best to concentrate and study them, but kept getting distracted by Robert and Luke, who were two of the humans we'd moved here from Aiden's castle in Scotland. They were outside working on the grounds of the villa, and their accelerated heartbeats from the physical labor were driving me insane. No matter what I did, I could still hear them. I put the radio on, the television, took a shower. Thankfully they stopped their work after about three hours of torture, and I finally started to calm down.

Reading the books got boring after a while, so I decided to start thinking about wedding plans with Aiden. "So, what are your thoughts on a wedding date?" I started out.

Aiden looked up from his laptop that he was clicking away on. He owned several businesses and invested in multiple companies, and it was always a safe bet if I couldn't find him that he'd be on a computer somewhere. "I think a fall wedding would be nice, but I've already been advised by certain people that the wedding planning is something men should stay out of," Aiden said as he laughed.

I frowned for a moment. "Honey, I want you to be a part of it too, it's our special day, you should have just as much of a say as I do." I knew a lot of women who wouldn't dream of letting their future husbands even have a say in the wedding, but I was of the opinion that a wedding should be about love and not how much money you can spend.

Aiden continued to smile at me though. "I wouldn't even know where to start with the planning. Things like that aren't as important to men as they are to women darling. I'll give you my opinion if you ask, but I'm leaving the planning to you ladies. My mother is anxiously awaiting the green light to get started."

"Hmmm. Alright then, what are your thoughts on a location?" I asked.

"I know it's not a realistic option, but when we talked about getting married in The Lucent that idea just really sounded neat. But I don't know if they would let us, and even if they did your family couldn't attend it there."

"My parents will be disappointed no matter what I chose if it's not a church, and I have no intentions of getting married in a church. I'd like them to be there though. I guess we'll have to think about it. But an outdoor wedding is what I'd like." I had no idea where to even start with planning.

"You have another laptop I can use?" I asked Aiden.

"Sure," he said as he hopped up and produced one out of a backpack. He handed it to me and I waited patiently as it booted up.

Just for the heck of it I started to search for outdoor locations in Italy. Not even fifteen minutes in, and I was blown away. "Wow, maybe you should think about investing in wedding planning honey. These prices are just crazy!"

Aiden put his own laptop on the bedside table and came over to check out what I was looking up. He didn't even bat an eye at the prices though. "Don't let the prices discourage you. Find the place you like, and we'll book it. The sky is the limit my love, whatever makes you happy," was his reply. I wasn't sure how I felt about blowing this kind of money, no matter if we had it or not.

I kissed his cheek and clicked on another venue to check its prices. "Aiden, I know money isn't an issue but I don't even know how these people can have the nerve to ask these prices. It's robbery."

He chuckled and replied, "It's a huge industry Skyy, and people will pay those prices. I bet if you check their availability they are booked months in advance. It seems like it's a lot of money, and to most people it is but people splurge for weddings."

"That is true, but I still don't see the point of us blowing a lot of money on our wedding. It's going to be very small, and most of the guests will be vampires anyway."

I continued to look at venues, then moved on to cakes, and finally dresses, and I have to admit after about two hours of looking I was beginning to get wrapped up in the wedding fantasy myself. I was starting to see how people managed to blow thirty thousand dollars on the event. Aiden assured me that no matter what the price tag was, if I wanted it I'd have it.

If we wanted a fall wedding, I'd have to start actively planning this thing soon. Fiona would be able to help me get it started, but I wanted to make sure I saved some of the important things for when I visited my mother and Cate. Dress shopping was a traditional thing to do with your mom and sister, and since Cate may as well be my sister I would save that part for when I saw them.

I sat the laptop down on the bed and went to warm up another mug of blood. I was feeling agitated again, and couldn't wait to get out of this room. "Do you think we could go for a walk outside tonight? I asked Aiden.

He nodded his head. "Sure, that would probably be fine. You seem to be going longer between drinks today and if we wait until all of the humans are in bed you should be fine."

I really hadn't seen much of Lucius' villa or the grounds because I chose to turn almost immediately after coming here, and have since been isolated. We waited until just after midnight until we ventured outside. It would have been much nicer to see the grounds during the day but I still needed my sun protection. I did find that my night vision was drastically improved though. I could see birds nesting in the trees, and all the leaves on the trees.

Lucius owned a huge chunk of land, and I couldn't wait to see it in the sunlight. There were rolling hills as far as the eye could see, and he even owned a small vineyard. Aiden and I walked hand in hand until we came to a small lake. It had a dock with some canoes, a small boat for fishing, and several jet skis. We wandered over to a covered gazebo and sat down. It was so quiet and peaceful, far away from the main house and the beating human hearts. Now all I could hear was water lapping on the shore from the lake, and Aiden's heart slowly beating.

I sat down on Aiden's lap and wrapped my arms around his neck. Aiden told me when Christian had turned that newly turned vampires have enhanced emotions, whether it's anger, happiness, lust; they feel everything much more intensely than normal because their bodies are adjusting. Much to everyone's dismay, Christian could hardly keep his hands off Fiona when he had first changed. Aiden wanted to wait until we were married before we had actual intercourse, out of respect for me, and because he was very old, and old fashioned. His mother apparently outgrew the old days, but Aiden still stuck by certain things.

I'd gotten used to that fact before I changed, though we did fool around a couple of times, but still had not had actual sex. Sitting this close to him and smelling his intoxicating scent was making me very turned on. Much like the anger and rage I felt when I needed blood, I was quickly starting to get the urge to rip Aiden's clothes off. He was rubbing his hand slowly up and down my back. I could see his eyes faintly glowing and reflecting, and knew he was also feeling aroused. He was still a man after all, even though he was a respectful one.

I wondered how I was going to wait until the fall...months from now...to get married and finally be with Aiden. Adjusting myself on his lap, I began placing soft kisses on his neck, which only turned me on even more. I knew my fangs had extended when I tasted blood in my mouth from nicking my lip with one of them. Tasting the blood amped me up another notch. Aiden turned his head and began to kiss me on the mouth, which quickly turned into a groping fest.

I couldn't control myself and was starting to take Aiden's shirt off. We were kissing hard and fast at this point, and I was rubbing his crotch with my other hand, feeling his erection through his jeans. He pulled away from me, his eyes now glowing very intensely. "Slow down Skyy, I know you're feeling things very strongly right now, but if we keep this up I might not be able to control myself either," he said while breathing heavily.

"And? What is the problem with that Aiden? I've already told you waiting until marriage doesn't matter to me. I love you, you love me…what is the problem?" I said in between kissing him on his neck again.

He gently broke away from me and stood up, running his fingers through his light brown hair. "I just feel like it's the right thing to do milady. But either way, doing it here in an uncomfortable gazebo isn't the way I imagined our first time to be. How about we go swimming? The weather is nice, the water should be warm," he offered as he held his hand out to me.

I sighed and took his hand. We untied our shoes and left them in the gazebo before walking down to the water. Testing it out first, we stepped in at the very edge. The water was warm and comfortable. "You'll find that as a vampire your body won't feel the heat and cold as drastically as it did as a human," Aiden said as he began to unbuckle his belt.

I moved closer to him, smiling. "Here, let me do that for you," I said. He returned my smile as I took over for him, and proceeded to unbutton his jeans. As usual, when I pulled them down I saw he was not wearing any underwear. Trying my best to control myself I took my eyes off his large erection and began to pull his shirt off of him. He lifted his arms up and I tossed it aside before running my hands over his lovely six pack abs.

Aiden kicked out of his jeans and flung them up into the grass then proceeded to lift my own shirt off of me, then slid my pants off. Standing in only my bra and panties now, he took my hand and we stepped into the clear water of the lake. The moon was only half full tonight, but with my enhanced vampire vision it reflected off the lake brightly enough that I could see Aiden clearly.

We walked out until the water came to just over my shoulders. I was still able to stand here, and wasn't sure how much deeper the water would get. I had nothing to worry about, it's not like I could drown, but I was still trying to grasp the fact that I was pretty much indestructible. I kicked off the floor of the lake and dove under the water. It was amazing that I could actually see under the water! I could make out tiny fish swimming in the crystal clear water, even at night, and see plants swaying back and forth gently. The colors weren't as vivid as they would be during the day, but it was an amazing sight.

I came up and swam back over to Aiden, who was floating on his back looking up at the night sky. "Wow, I can see fish swimming under there," I said as I came to a stop next to him. He put his feet back down and stood up, reaching out for me. I wrapped my arms and legs around his body.

"I forgot how amazing everything looked to me when I first transitioned as well." Aiden was roughly 6'0" so I was able to rest my head on his shoulder as we floated in the water. I know he wanted to take it easy but he was irresistible to me, newly turned vampire or not. His skin was slick with water and the muscles in his upper arms were bulging out as he supported me. I raised my face to his and placed a kiss on his lips. And that is all it took before the fire inside me took over.

We locked lips like two horny teenagers in the backseat of a car, hungry and devouring each other. The last time I had blood was probably two hours ago and not only was I filled with lust and desire, but I was also starting to go into a bloodlust. My fangs were extended once again, and I accidently bit Aiden's tongue. The second I tasted his blood, I lost control of myself. I moaned out in ecstasy as we kissed, mixing the taste of his blood around in our mouths.

Panting and moaning I moved to his throat, and could not control myself. My fangs slid into his jugular vein and within seconds I felt the warm rush of his blood fill my mouth. Aiden also moaned out loud, seemingly enjoying it. I sucked on his neck, gulping down his essence. Moments later I felt his fangs sink into my neck as well. Unsure if he was projecting thoughts into my head or not, I felt better than I ever had in my life. The act was almost more intimate than sex, and produced feelings in much the same way. Both of us were breathing heavily and drinking from one another's neck before we broke away and our lips collided again.

This was probably the most passionate kiss I had ever shared with someone. Our mouths and chins were covered in blood, but it made it even more intimate. Aiden tried to unlatch my bra and ended up just ripping it to get it off me and threw it into the lake, then slid my panties aside underneath the water and inserted two of his fingers into my fold. I was climaxing within thirty seconds as we continued to kiss and mix our blood together. Grabbing on to his erection I returned the favor and we were both spent in record time.

The vampire blood did not quench my cravings quite like the human blood did, though I did feel much better, and the euphoria I had from the sexual interaction had me on cloud nine. I was still wrapped around Aiden as we silently floated back and forth with the waves of the lake. After a few moments he broke the silence. "Well, that was definitely something I've never experienced before. I didn't hurt you, did I?"

I looked up into his eyes which were glowing on fire. "Oh my God no! That was unreal Aiden."

He smiled at me in the moonlight. "Unreal is one way to put it. Absolutely amazing is another way."

I laughed out loud and kissed him again. I could see my bra floating on top of the water a good distance away. "I liked that bra by the way," I joked to Aiden.

He kissed my forehead. "Don't worry, I'll buy you a new one." We lingered in the water for a while longer before making our way back to the shore and then stretched out on the dock to air dry before climbing back into our clothing.

We took our time on the walk back to the villa. It was nice to be out of earshot of the other vampires and away from the temptations of the humans while we were out on the lake. Lucius asked to speak to Aiden when we got back inside the house, and I wanted to take a shower, so Fiona and Christian got to babysit me while I was in the bathroom. They lounged on our bed and watched television until I came out.

Feeling as though I could use more blood, I made myself a mug. It wasn't Type O Negative but it'd have to do. I sat down in one of the chairs in the room and Cupcake jumped right up in my lap. Sipping on the blood made me feel better, and I was finally relaxed and feeling balanced for the first time since I woke up from my death-sleep. After I felt a bit more stable I figured I could chat a little with Fiona about the wedding.

"I've been looking at some stuff on the Internet for the wedding, and Aiden and I are going to see if we can take a couple days to fly back home so he can meet my parents," I said as I pet Cupcake.

Fiona sat up on the bed at hearing this, and a huge smile appeared on her beautiful face. "I was wondering when we'd start the planning! Christian can you go to our room and get me that silver binder I have on the desk in there please?" She didn't even wait for Christian to answer she immediately grabbed Aiden's laptop from our bedside table and powered it up. Christian left the room silently and Fiona pat the bed and motioned for me to come sit by her.

Within minutes she had pulled up several different websites for cakes, and themes. Christian brought back the binder she had asked for, and when she opened it up I almost laughed out loud but figured it would hurt her feelings. "Wow Fiona. How long have you been at this project?" Inside the binder were neatly organized sections for wedding planning, everything from dresses, colors, cakes, venues, tuxes for the men…you name it she had it in here.

She waved her hand in the air, "Oh not very long. I've just thrown together a few things that might work for your wedding." I was impressed with her skills, I couldn't have put something together like this even if I had wanted to.

Fiona began flipping through the binder, and Christian looked incredibly bored. I smiled at him and threw a decorative pillow off the bed at his head. He grabbed it with lightning fast reflexes and grinned back at me. "Hey! I'm outta here ladies, wedding planning and flying pillows are my cue to exit. Have fun!" He leaned over to plant a quick kiss on Fiona's forehead then left us to our planning.

I'll give her credit, she was very good at wedding planning. I really had no idea where to even start, so having her help was really great. We spent the next hour and a half looking at venues all over the world. I drank three mugs of blood as we browsed.

"It's so nice that we are not limited to a wedding at night now that you all have the sun protection," I commented absently.

Fiona nodded her head in agreement. "It sure opens up a lot of options for you." We had looked at everything from New Zealand to Hawaii, Italy to Alaska, and pretty much everywhere in between. Fiona also offered up her chateau in France, and showed me some photos. It was gorgeous and definitely an option.

After a while, even I got bored. "So how did you get so interested in weddings? Have you ever planned one before?" I asked Fiona.

She shut the binder and stood up to stretch. "I planned a few weddings here and there over the centuries, but nothing major. I love the whole process, the colors, the flowers, the planning, seeing it all come together."

"I really had no idea this much went into a wedding. I've only been to a couple small weddings in my life, and none of them were very impressive," I admitted.

"Well, I have been waiting my whole life for my Aiden to find the perfect woman to settle down with. This has been a long time coming, and I am so thrilled to help you with it. He couldn't have picked a better bride, and you'll be so beautiful," Fiona said with sincerity.

I blushed at her compliment. "Thanks Fiona. I never thought I'd be getting married, at least not anytime soon. Then Aiden just came into my life and everything changed. I couldn't be more proud to be his future wife."

Aiden replaced Fiona a few minutes later, leaving me with a lot to think about. She suggested I pick a venue first before deciding on colors. Many places booked up months in advance, so if I wanted something fancy I'd have to choose soon. Or we could go with a simple beach wedding. All of the planning and thinking had me thirsty again, and Aiden made me another mug of blood.

I felt stressed out and wished that I was tired enough to sleep. I sighed loudly and flopped down on the bed. Being in this room for so long was getting old. "I wish I could just sleep," I said out loud.

Aiden came and sat beside me, rubbing his hand over the top of my hair. "It's easier than you think. You'll be able to sleep at-will eventually. Humans sleep too much at times, more than they need to. Some people sleep to escape life. You're going to feel so much better and energized as a vampire, and once you start working with the Divine Assassins you'll be so busy you won't even miss sleeping on a daily basis. Now you'll have the time, and money to do whatever your heart desires, and fully enjoy it without fatigue."

I suppose he did have a good point. But I was still in my human frame of mind. "You're right, as usual. It's just so incredibly boring here in this room."

Aiden smiled at me, with his perfectly straight, white teeth. "I think tomorrow we'll let you have a visit with your grandpa and Ridley. They aren't normal humans, since they are trained to kill vampires. It's a start at least."

At the mention of that, my face lit up. I sat up and wrapped my arms around Aiden. "That sounds like fun!" I gave him a small peck on the cheek and then laid my head in his lap.

It was close to sunrise at this point, and Aiden suggested that we try to get a couple hours of sleep. "Come on and lay down with me milady. I'll share some of my techniques with you," he said as I snuggled up into his arms. Before long I did indeed drift off to a dreamless sleep.

Chapter 3

I'm not sure if I felt better or the same when I woke up from my slumber. As a human when you slept you usually felt refreshed and rested. As a vampire, I just felt…the same. I hadn't felt "tired" yet at all. But the good news was that it was now the next day and the sun was up, meaning that I could visit with Ridley and Grandpa soon.

Aiden settled in with his laptop to check on his businesses while I took a quick shower. I did feel less aggressive today, which was a good sign. The human heartbeats on the property were also less of a nuisance as they were the past days. They were still tempting, but I was beginning to think clearly instead of out of instinct and bloodlust. I knew right from wrong: attacking a human for their blood was definitely wrong.

I dried my long hair, which is always a project, and put some light makeup on. Not sure why I was even bothering but it felt nice to do something normal again, and getting into my old routines might help. I put on some slim fit jeans, and a plain light blue baby doll shirt and slid into some cute flip flops. Satisfied with how I looked, I went back into the bedroom to wait patiently until Ridley came through his portal.

Aiden whistled at me when he saw me. "You're looking back to your old self again, my love. Very nice." I smiled at him and sat in one of the chairs in the room, clicking on the television. Aiden worked silently and the hours dragged by. I watched a show on the ancient pyramids, followed by one about sharks, the local news, and then a movie. By the time it was all over, it was afternoon.

My grandfather had been staying at the villa for the most part ever since I went into my death-sleep and they found out I wasn't waking up. He'd go back to the Divine Assassins headquarters a few times a week though. I was surprised he'd willingly stay in a house full of mostly vampires. I knew Ridley had arrived because I could hear the two of them talking across the property.

I had to wait agonizingly for another fifteen minutes before they came over to my room. Aiden opened the door and let Grandpa and Ridley in. My initial instinct was to rush over and hug them both, but Aiden had advised me earlier to keep my distance from them for this first visit. He gave me a glance that reminded me of that as I stood up to greet them.

Grandpa was the first to enter. His snow white hair was neatly combed and he was wearing casual clothes; cargo shorts and a Hawaiian shirt with busy red and white flowers all over it. He'd always loved Hawaiian shirts for some reason, and if you were ever in doubt of what to get him for a birthday or Christmas present, that was always a good standby.

He was smiling at me, which lately was a rare thing. Once I discovered that he wasn't really dead, and that he belonged to a secret organization with the purpose to find and destroy Elizabeth Bathory, he had become grouchier by the day. But he had a lot on his mind and many things going on at once, since he was one of the head decision makers in the Divine Assassins.

"Skyy, you're looking nice. How are you feeling?" he asked me sincerely. I wasn't sure if Grandpa was totally onboard with me being a vampire or not, but he had agreed to let me become a Divine Assassin on a trial basis.

"I'm feeling much better each day Grandpa. It's really great to see you though, I am going stir crazy locked up in this room!"

Before he could reply, Ridley made his way into the room, smiling from ear to ear. He was carrying a backpack and a stack of books, which he set down on the dresser. Ridley was a cute man, though he dressed like a total dweeb, and today was no exception. He had on khaki dress pants that were hiked up way too high, and a button up plaid shirt that was tucked into the pants which were tightly bound by his unstylish belt. He combed his hair in a drastic part and smoothed it down so flat on his head that it looked comical. Nevertheless I was thrilled to see him.

"Ridley! It's great to see you, thank you for coming to check in on me!" I exclaimed with joy.

"I've been checking in everyday Skyy, they just wouldn't let me see you until today. You look fantastic though. I hope you're ready for some more reading and studying," he said as he gestured to the books he placed on the dresser.

I rolled my eyes to tease him, but was actually excited to continue to learn more about the Divine Assassins. "Can't wait," I replied.

Ridley went to shake Aiden's hand, and not wanting to be outdone, Grandpa followed suit. I wasn't sure how he felt about Aiden, but he was at least tolerating him now, which was a huge step from when we first started.

The two men took seats in the chairs that were in the room, and once everyone was comfortable, Aiden offered them drinks, which they refused. Aiden proceeded to take his laptop and blend into the background while I had my visit with the men.

"So how long until you think you'll be ready to go out into the world, Skyy?" Ridley inquired.

I sat on the edge of the bed, not too close to them. I wasn't feeling aggressive with them near me at all, which was a good sign. "I feel better every day, right now I don't want to rip into your neck so that's a good sign, right?" I laughed.

Ridley laughed with me, but Grandpa stayed neutral, his face unreadable. "Yeah, that is a good sign, for me anyway!" he joked.

"I think in a couple more days I should be fine. If Aiden will let me, tomorrow I'd like to try to mingle around the villa, see how I do around the humans here." I obviously directed it towards Aiden, who just smiled at me and winked.

Grandpa was fidgeting with a thread on the arm of the chair, but finally spoke up. "When you think you're ready we'll need to have you come in to headquarters and get some security details out of the way, as well as train you for portal usage and give you your own portal signature."

I nodded, but had no idea what I was in store for. The Divine Assassins could open up magical (at least I assumed they were magical) portals to travel between locations, and even to send objects from one location to another. We used what I liked to call a breadbox to communicate with Grandpa after I first discovered his lie.

"Well, speaking of training and all...I was wondering what your thoughts were on me taking a few days to fly back home to see Mom and Dad, so they can meet Aiden before the wedding? I know it's bad timing but Mom got really upset when I told her and she wasn't a part of anything, and you know how religious they are," I let the end of the sentence linger, so he'd get the point.

Grandpa cleared his throat, but didn't speak. Ridley spoke instead, "I don't see why that would be a problem Skyy. Right now we don't know Bathory's location but we're working hard uncovering clues and preparing teams to go into The Gloom to search for her. But that is still a few weeks off."

Grandpa shot him a look that said he wasn't happy, and Ridley shut up immediately. "Last time I checked I was in charge of the decision making Ridley. Don't get too big for your britches son. As for your trip back home, I don't see why it would be a problem, but you need to get it out of the way sooner rather than later, because there are quite a bit of things we need to brief you on Skyy."

I nodded at him, and had to cover up a smile when I glanced at Ridley because he was rolling his eyes at my grandfather's scolding of him. "Alright Grandpa, if I am able to I will try to fly back there within the next week or two. I wouldn't even ask, but you know it's important to Mom."

"I know dear, and you've got yourself in a pickle now with the vampire ordeal, you won't have much time left to spend with them before you'll need to cut off communication. The potion we take slows down aging but we do age...you'll never age and they'll start to wonder what is going on. I miss your father though, I wish I could go with you, but alas life moves on." Soon I'd be in his shoes, either faking my death or making up excuses on why I couldn't visit anymore. It couldn't be a fun thing to do.

I wasn't sure what to say to that, so I didn't say anything, and then there was a few moments of uncomfortable silence. "Is Christian going back with you guys as well?" Ridley finally asked, breaking the silence.

I hadn't even thought of asking Christian to come, but it'd make sense. I am sure his parents wondered what the hell he was doing, and he could tie up loose ends with John and his job. "We haven't talked about it, but it's not a bad idea. Speaking of which, it is safe for me to go visit my parents, right?"

Grandpa nodded, "It should be as safe as it can be. We've had no sign of Bathory or any of her vampire brood since the showdown in Scotland, but we've had agents outside your parents' house since way before then keeping an eye on the situation. I'd not suggest going to your house while you're there, but visiting your parents should be safe."

I'd need to get the rest of my belongings out of my house soon. "What should we do with the house now that neither of us can live there anymore?" I asked.

"We'll keep it. I have my underground office there and I have no intentions of moving it after all the work that went into constructing it. I'll have one of our agents go there a few times a month to make sure everything is cared for, but we should get your things boxed up and shipped or stored as soon as you're able."

"I'll start looking into it then. I'd like to have some more of my clothing at least, living out of a suitcase sucks. Fiona did some shopping for me, but I still miss my clothes." Thinking about seeing my parents made me wonder about certain vampire traits. "What am I going to do about my eyes? They tend to glow...a lot. If I get excited or hungry, or just about anything really...they glow. My parents won't miss that one."

Ridley answered, "Oh, I am sure we can come up with something for you before you leave. Sounds very simple actually! I'll start on it as soon as I get back to headquarters tonight."

"Thanks Ridley, I don't want to have to mind whammy my folks because they freak out on me," I said as I laughed. Ridley was an incredibly smart guy, and was head of security operations for the entire Divine Assassins until recently, when he broke his orders to watch me and instead opened a portal so we could join the epic fight with Bathory. As a punishment, he was stuck with me as his partner, and removed from his position for the time being.

We chatted for a while longer, before Grandpa said his goodbyes and promised to check in with me tomorrow. Ridley wanted to discuss some more things with me, but I could tell he was unsure if he should stay or not. "Are you alright, to visit for a little while longer?" he asked shyly.

The last five minutes or so I was feeling a little edgy, but not to the point I would attack someone. "Honestly, I'd like to take a minute if you don't mind. I'll be quick I promise."

Ridley excused himself from the room, while Aiden made me a mug of blood, which calmed me down immensely. I was back to feeling totally in control of myself, and told Ridley to come back inside. Once we were all settled back in, he began to tell me more about some of the documents and diaries we had found in Bathory's castle.

"I didn't want to overwhelm you when you first woke up, but I did find some things that alarm me," he said as he shuffled through his backpack and began pulling out papers.

"Like what?" I asked, not sure I wanted the answer.

Ridley began to lay the papers out on the bed for me to look at. I picked one up, and glanced over it. The general outline was that Elizabeth Bathory had several different ways to resurrect herself in the event that she was killed. My mouth was open in shock.

"I know. Not good news," Ridley said, reading the look on my face.

"So, this applies to her in her vampire form? This wasn't written before she was turned in reference to her being mortal?" Somehow I knew the answer before asking, but thought I would ask anyway.

Ridley shook his head no. "I don't know if she had something like this in place when she was still mortal, but as a vampire she writes in several of her diaries and documents that she has more than one phylactery in place in the event of her death."

I had no idea what a phylactery was, so I just asked. "And a phylactery is…?"

"In this case, it is an object that will capture her soul and preserve it for eternity, until someone can resurrect her. The way she describes it, she used her own blood, flesh, hair, breath, and black magic to enchant an amulet that her soul will flee to if she is killed. There is no description in her writing as to what it looks like either, which is even more frustrating. And she has created more than one of these amulets, which makes it even better," Ridley said as he sighed in frustration.

"Shit. So even if we do find her and kill her, she could resurrect herself, maybe not anytime soon, but she could do it, and then we'd be back on the hunt again? Like her book wasn't bad enough, now this…" It was very frustrating to say the least.

"Yep, and I am sure she has several people in place with knowledge of how to resurrect her, and they would certainly be guarding these phylacteries. She has always been a smart and cunning woman, very educated even in her mortal life, so this doesn't shock me. One step ahead of the game, as usual," replied Ridley.

I started to feel very angry, out of nowhere. I think Ridley knew it, because he began to gather his papers up. Aiden set his laptop down, and came to my side. "You're alright Skyy, just breathe. It's good for you to be angry in front of Ridley, he's human and if you can control yourself here, you'll learn from it." He looked at Ridley, and I saw his face go from slight panic to controlled and confident in the blink of an eye.

Ridley nodded back at Aiden, getting the message that he was the guinea pig. "I know how you feel Skyy, remember Bathory is responsible for my mom and sister dying, it pisses me off too. We'll get her one way or another though. It might not be in our lifetime, well…in my lifetime, but she'll go down for good," he said, then I heard him whisper so soft a human couldn't possible hear it, but I could with my enhanced vampire ears, "She has to…"

Without realizing it, I had made fists so tight that my fingernails had dug into my palms and I was bleeding. Aiden's eyes began to glow as he smelled my blood. After our night on the lake where we shared blood, we found out that it was a very intimate experience and turned both of us on greatly. But Aiden, being much older than me in vampire years, was more in control of his actions than I was.

"Ridley, we probably should wrap it up for the day. We made great progress with your visit today though, and if you'd like to come again tomorrow I am sure Skyy would welcome it," Aiden said as he helped Ridley gather up the rest of his paper and books.

"Of course, I'll come around tomorrow about the same time if it works for you guys?" he said, as if things hadn't just gone from weird to weirder.

Aiden spoke for me, because I was losing it quick. I wanted to jump Aiden's bones and was beginning to go into bloodlust which wasn't safe for Ridley, even though I knew he could kill me in a split second if he wanted to.

"Tomorrow will be great Ridley, we'll look forward to seeing you," Aiden answered kindly. He was always so polite and nice.

Ridley hoisted his backpack up onto his right shoulder and gathered his books up before giving me a little wave. "See you tomorrow, Skyy. Feel better." And with that he walked out and shut the door behind him.

I was in Aiden's arms within seconds, pressing my mouth to his. We kissed for a brief moment before he pulled away from me. My fangs were fully extended at this point, and I was not thinking clearly. I nipped at his shoulder blade, drawing blood. The second it hit my tongue I relaxed, as if Aiden and I were one again. Suckling at his shoulder for a moment I moved back to his mouth, Aiden seemed to be trying to control his lust, but I couldn't even begin to. My lips touched his, but he pulled back from me again.

"Skyy, I know it's difficult but you need to get in control. Not just with humans but with your emotions too,"

Aiden said, breathing heavily. I knew it had to be great control he was exhibiting to pull away from me since his eyes were glowing brightly.

I didn't like hearing what he had to say, and got angry again. I closed my eyes and started to breathe slowly trying to calm down. Aiden made me another mug of blood. I snatched it up and gulped it down in the blink of an eye.

Aiden gave me a cute smile and winked at me. "You really did make a lot of progress today Skyy. And tomorrow it will be even easier.

I spent the next twenty-four hours trying to kill time, bored out of my mind locked in my guest room. Since Aiden thought I did so well with Ridley and Grandpa yesterday, I decided to test the waters, asking him if I could walk around the villa a little today. "What are your thoughts on me leaving the room for a bit today?"

Aiden thought on it for a moment. Finally he answered, "Why don't we see how your visit with Ridley goes today, then we'll go from there?"

I sighed but knew he was right, again. It felt like years had passed waiting for Ridley to finally show up, but he entered the room all smiles with more books as usual. "Hello!" he said cheerfully.

Aiden had informed me last night that I should try to make physical contact with Ridley today; a handshake or hug, something besides keeping my distance. So I strode over to him and embraced him. I felt his entire body tense up, and I wasn't sure if it was because a female was in contact with him, or a vampire was in contact with him, but assumed it was a little of both. He gave me an uneasy pat on the back and then I stepped away from him. He straightened his collar and cleared his throat, regaining composure, "So I am to be the guinea pig then?" he said as he laughed, totally grasping what had just happened.

I swatted at his arm playfully, and Aiden was laughing along with Ridley. "Well, I passed the test! You're still in one piece!"

He nodded at me, then went to his backpack and pulled out a small box, handing it to me. "What's this?" I asked curiously.

"Open it up," was all he replied, as he grinned at me.

I opened the box and found some tiny glass vials inside. "What are these for?" I inquired.

"You've never worn contacts before I guess. I made them for you guys, for your trip back home. They will conceal any glowing or reflection and your eyes will look totally normal at all times. Let's pop them in and give them a try," Ridley suggested.

It took me about ten minutes to get them both in, and get used to the idea of touching my eyeball. It freaked me out when I put the first one in, but wasn't as bad as I attempted the second eye. My eyes were watering and burned slightly, but I blinked a few times and everything was fine. Everything looked the same, it didn't alter my vision at all. "How do I look?" I said, batting my eyelids for drama.

Ridley gave me the thumbs up, and Aiden did the same as I looked his way. "Now let's leave them in while we have our visit, and see how they do. There are a few pairs in there for both of you, in case they tear or you lose one or something."

We settled in and Ridley began to update me on the progress with the green lizard-like humanoids we had captured during our battle back in Scotland. They were the same size and had the same arms and legs as a human though their hands had huge claws on the ends of the fingers, their skin was scaly and green, and their eyes were lidless and pale yellow. The scariest thing about them was their ability to produce poisonous mucus that melted the flesh off of anything it touched. I got a close up demonstration of it, and boy did it hurt.

"We think our best place to start looking for Bathory will be The Gloom. The lizard beings assured us that they would never let Bathory into their homeland. They helped her because she was trading resources with them, but that was where they drew the line. She did not control them or summon them like she does with the demons."

47

"Where do they live? Here on this planet?" I replied.

Ridley nodded, "Yes, according to what they told us, The Noxious is another plane or dimension here on our planet, like The Lucent or The Gloom, though this place is filled with poisonous gasses, air, earth, vegetation, even their water…pretty much everything there will kill you if you touch it, but the air alone will kill you if you breathe it. At least that is the story they are telling, whether it is true or just a fib to keep us out is unknown."

"Well they sure did a number on us in battle. I still cringe when I think back to the pain I felt when that poison hit my side," I said as I thought back to the battle.

"Now, we also have a few dark fae, and some demons trapped, but neither of them will talk. We've tried every kind of torture there is. We could really use the Radiant fae to loosen their lips again. The logical assumption though, is Bathory would be in The Gloom. Her dark fae were the majority of her forces outside of her coven of vampires she made."

I went over to my suitcase and pulled out a small bag I kept my jewelry in. Taking out the crystal necklace that Dreamer had given me, I showed it to Ridley. "I can try to get in touch with Dreamer later today and see if she and the Radiant fae can help us out."

He smiled at me, "Sounds like a plan. Now I have another idea, that may be a shot in the dark but, if we can get in touch with Alina again maybe she can find out where Bathory's other castles may have been from the spirits of the girls that were released from that book. They could all lead to dead ends but I'd feel safer if we explored every possibility."

"That's not a bad idea at all, though I have no idea how I would go about getting in touch with Alina. Other than swinging by the castle in Scotland and hoping she'll appear."

Aiden chimed in, "We could do that on the way over to see your parents. Take a quick stop by the castle."

"Alright, sure," I replied.

"You know...I'd have to clear it with Mr. Huntington first, but we could just portal you over to Scotland, and to America and back. Be a lot faster than flying would be," Ridley offered.

I hadn't even thought about that before now. "You make a good point. It would get me there and back faster too so I could get to work with the Order sooner."

We continued to go over some more topics, before Ridley had to take his leave. He packed up all his papers and books into his backpack and I gave him a quick hug again. He grinned at me this time as I pulled away. "You know what? You touched me twice this time, and you never even had to stop for blood during the whole visit. And those contacts seem to work perfectly, your eyes never looked odd to me. Great job Skyy," he said.

I hadn't noticed it myself, but I was totally in control, it had felt like a normal conversation and visit with my partner. "Wow, you're right. Thanks for being my lab rat Ridley."

He rolled his eyes and said his goodbye before leaving the room. He was barely out the door when I turned to Aiden. "Soooo...does this mean I can wander the house for a bit today?"

He grinned, "Yes, we can give it a try. But first let's get you some blood and take a small break." I agreed and we spent about an hour relaxing and I had two mugs of blood while we did.

Just as we were about to leave the room, the fact that I hadn't gotten my sun protection spell yet hit me like a ton of bricks. Aiden and the other vampires were so used to it by now, they didn't even think about the sun. But I wouldn't be able to go out in it. "Shit! I can't go out of the room because it's still daylight!" I cussed out loud.

Aiden apologized to me about ten times, saying he was sorry for forgetting, but we'd have to wait until dark now for my free roam of the house. I pulled out my phone and sent a message to my Grandpa letting him know we needed to get the sun protection on me as soon as he was able. He replied saying that he'd come get me tomorrow and bring me to the base for the ritual since I was feeling much better and capable now.

Once it was dark I charged out of my guest room like a horse out of a gate at a race. Aiden zoomed up behind me and gently took my hand in his. "I know you're excited, just try to act as normal as possible. I don't want to have to mind whammy anyone because you freak them out," he said as he winked at me.

Overall it went really well. Having the contacts in hid my eyes from glowing. I visited with Miss Abby for about fifteen minutes. We had come up with the story that I had a bad case of the flu that just took me a really long time to get over. She was enjoying her new life in Italy but confessed that she was a little homesick for Scotland. After the meeting with her, Aiden and I went outside to one of the terraces that overlooked the little hills below. We relaxed on two big lounge chairs, staring up at the night sky, when I heard the sound of a basketball.

"There is a basketball court here?" I inquired.

Aiden nodded and smiled. "Yes, there is a tennis court, basketball court, a swimming pool, stables with horses and grounds for riding, an indoor racquetball court. Plenty of activities to do here."

I thought I heard Christian's voice, so I got up from the lounge chair and grabbed Aiden's hand to boost him up out of his. "Let's go check it out," I said excitedly. We walked on the outside of the huge villa around the house, passing by some beautiful landscaping and archways. Finally we came up on the basketball court and sure enough Christian was there, along with Luke and Robert.

Christian had a big advantage over the two humans because of his natural height of 6'5" and I could tell he was holding back even more because of his vampire endurance. To my eyes it looked like the equivalent of an adult trying to play with a small child going easy on them, but Luke and Robert had no clue.

We walked to the edge of the court and I shouted out, "Got room for two more?" to the men.

They all smiled and nodded at us. Christian walked over to us, with a concerned look on his face. "Are you sure you're ready for this?" he whispered in a low voice.

I shrugged, "I feel like it, but I guess we'll see," I said as I flashed him a smile.

Christian bounced the ball a few times and then jogged back out onto the court as I pulled my long hair up into a messy bun. Aiden gave my shoulder a reassuring rub and we joined the men in the game.

Everything went well...more than well actually, for the first half hour or so. The humans had to stop every once and a while to grab water from a large cooler by the court, and we all followed their lead so we wouldn't seem out of place. I found that I wasn't sweating at all, which was actually very nice. Just as we were about to end the game, Luke tripped and scrapped his knee on the court. I was nowhere near him, on the opposite side of the court, but could smell the blood the instant it happened. My fangs extended immediately.

Aiden was next to me and turned me away from the humans, who were thankfully too concerned with Luke's knee to notice the threat of a vampire attack. He picked me up, like a groom carrying his bride over the threshold, and informed them that I had twisted my ankle and we were done. The second we were around the corner Aiden flew at vampire speed with me in his arms and into the villa, plopping me softly onto the bed. Before I could even make a peep, he was getting some blood ready for me.

I sat silently on the bed, trying to calm myself down, until Aiden handed me my blood. "How do you feel?" he asked.

After taking a sip of blood and licking my lips, I smiled at him. "Honestly, that wasn't as bad as it could have been. I smelled Luke's blood the second it happened, and my fangs extended but I was able to control my thoughts and knew attacking him was the wrong thing to do. I wanted to, sure, but knew I shouldn't." I slammed the rest of the blood and asked for more.

Aiden complied, while smiling at me. "I'm very proud of you. You're doing better each day. It never gets to the point where being around blood won't affect you by the way. Even I smelled it, and reacted to it. You just have to control yourself, and you're already doing a great job of that Skyy."

I drank the second mug of blood he had made for me, and felt loads better already. Within twenty minutes I was back to normal. Deciding that I should probably call it quits for the day, satisfied with the overall outcome of my mingling with humans, Aiden and I settled in together for the night.

Chapter 4

Sleeping was obviously a thing of the past that I was trying really hard to get used to not doing, so sometime in the middle of the night I decided I should probably try to contact Dreamer. Ridley and Grandpa could use the help breaking the dark fae they had captive, and truth be told I kind of missed Dreamer's bubbly and warm personality. I wasn't quite sure how this necklace she gave me worked – she told me if I needed her to just rub it and she'd know how to find me. I changed out of my comfy pajamas and into a casual sundress, before pulling the necklace out of my jewelry bag.

"I don't know if she'll know the exact location we are at, but I hope all the humans are asleep by now, we don't need them having a heart attack if she appears somewhere random on the property," I said as I laughed.

Aiden, on his laptop as usual, chuckled with me. "I'm sure she knows how to avoid being seen by humans. The Radiant fae have been around a lot longer than civilization."

I took a deep breath while holding the pink quartz in my hand, and rubbed it softly between my thumb and pointer finger. "Well here we go." I sat down on the edge of the bed, and within seconds I saw the stone start to faintly glow a soft pink color. "Oh! Look Aiden, its glowing!" I exclaimed.

Aiden set his laptop down and came over to check it out. "Neat," he whispered softly.

A few moments later we saw a tiny pink light outside one of the windows in the guest room. We usually kept the windows open at night, because the weather was nice this time of year. Dreamer was hovering outside the window waiting for the signal that it was ok to come on in. Aiden went over to the screen and popped it out so she could fly inside our room.

Once she was inside, she materialized into her humanoid form, tucking her big translucent wings behind her. She was a tiny little thing, four feet tall or so, almost childlike in appearance. Her long, rose colored hair was pulled into a cute ponytail high up on her head. She was smiling from ear to ear, and dashed right over to me to give me a hug.

I was also smiling as I embraced her. "Dreamer! Thank you so much for coming. We've all missed you!" I said to her.

She hugged me tight for a few seconds before stepping away and giving me the once over from head to toe. "Omigosh! You did it! Look at you, Miss Vampire! So sexy!" Dreamer had a way of talking very fast and mashing her words together, but she was always upbeat and happy.

I laughed at her statement. "Yep, I went through with it. Took longer than expected to transform, but here I am." I did a little twirl, with my hands up and out for drama.

Dreamer glanced over at Aiden, and then went to give him a little hug, which he returned awkwardly. "And Aiden, still as gorgeous as ever. Good to see you both again!" Dreamer exclaimed.

"Nice to see you as well, Dreamer," Aiden replied.

Her eyes, which were the same color as her hair, were sparkling and bright, and though her skin was about the same shade as a humans might be, it shimmered with light on the surface ever so faintly. Her race thrived in the light, and Aiden and I got to see her home world, The Lucent, once before. Rainbows, nature, color, life, light…that was the Radiant fae's realm.

"How is Crimson doing?" I inquired. One of their friends had been captured and experimented on at Bathory's castle. We found her in bad shape, and her wings had been ripped out from the root, a wound so deep they weren't sure she would ever be able to fly again.

Dreamer's adorable face got sad for a moment. She shook her head back and forth, "We had hoped that she would grow her wings back, but it hasn't happened. It doesn't look like they ever will. Other than that, she has fully recovered, but without her wings she is a sad little faerie indeed."

My heart broke just hearing the story. I didn't know Crimson like I knew Dreamer, but when we found her she was in bad shape. I knew how close the fae were as a community of beings, and this had to be hard on all of them. "I am so sorry to hear that Dreamer. Tell her hello from us when you see her again. It really is a shame," I said sincerely.

"I will. So how have things been since you turned? What have you been up to?" she inquired.

I plopped down into one of the chairs in the room, and Dreamer took the one beside it. "Well, other than trying to control myself around humans, not much. I've been locked in this room ever since I woke up from my death-sleep for the most part. We're thinking of heading to see my parents in America soon though. But the real reason I needed to see you, is because the Divine Assassins have some of the dark fae captive and they won't talk. We're trying to get information out of them, to see if Bathory is hiding in The Gloom. Do you think you'd be able to help?"

"Sure, I can probably help with that. I figured that she'd be hiding in The Gloom too. If it comes down to it, I am sure we can gather some Radiant fae to go into The Gloom with you," she offered.

"That'd be fantastic, I doubt the Divine Assassins would turn down that offer. If we can get any information out of those captive fae, we'll be able to act a lot faster. I'll get in touch with my grandfather once the sun comes up, and tell him you'll help. He'll probably bring the dark fae to another location for you to interrogate them, they are pretty secret about their base and all," I said, hoping she wouldn't be offended that she couldn't go there.

She giggled, but nodded her head. "Psssh It's not like I don't know how to find them, their portals are a dead giveaway. They suck energy up like crazy. But yeah, just let me know what the plan is, and I'll melt some dark fae brain for ya!"

I didn't know what she meant by that, but I was sure that I'd find out soon enough when I got my crash course for the Divine Assassins. "Great Dreamer, you're the best, thanks again."

Dreamer left after a short visit, and the next day Grandpa showed up at the villa with some items for me. He handed me a small, plain ring that was dark and shiny. "Go ahead and put that on. Since our bases are protected from vampires, you'll need a way to get past those security systems. You'll have to have that ring on each time you want to portal into the base, we've designed it to override security for you to be able to enter safely."

I slid the ring on to my right ring finger. It was a slender band, kind of like a very plain wedding band, and it was very cold on my skin. But it was plain enough that I could just keep it on at all times. I wouldn't want to find out what would happen if I forgot it. Grandpa also gave me some books to read, and placed a small box of potions in glass vials on my dresser. Inside the glass I could see faint purple and pink colors swirling around slowly.

"Now, we'll take you to the headquarters and get your sun protection on you, then we'll set up your portal signature, but when you come back here you'll drink those bottles in the order they are marked. They will teach you everything you need to know about using the portals," he said as he pointed to the vials.

"Alright," I replied, half nervous and half excited at the same time. Aiden was nervous about me leaving his side for the first time since I turned, but I assured him being with the Divine Assassins was the next safest place for me. They knew how to control and handle vampires, which should scare me to death, but I trusted them and knew they would take good care of me. After a quick hug and peck on the cheek I said goodbye to Aiden, and Grandpa opened up the portal right there in our guest room to the headquarters.

Having already gone through a portal before, it was easier this time, and I figured I better get used to it real fast because it was going to become my number one form of transportation very soon. This was the same base I was at last time, though Grandpa took me down a different hallway. I also noticed a lot of hushed whispers and weird looks from certain people. I knew not all of them were onboard with a vampire joining their ranks, and this proved it.

First we went into a big area that reminded me of a cafeteria but without a bunch of tables, and Grandpa called for his men to come perform the sun protection ritual. They held hands, chanted, and it was over within a minute. I felt warm and safe, but couldn't visibly or physically notice anything different about myself.

Then Grandpa took me down another long hallway to a large room that had a bunch of computers and what looked like medical equipment in it. He motioned for me to have a seat at a table, and thankfully Ridley walked in the room not too long after that. He tousled the top of my hair as he walked by in a wordless greeting, and had a seat behind one of the computers in the room. Grandpa sat down across from me, and passed me a bunch of papers. "We'll need you to fill all of these out, then we'll need to run some tests on you, to make sure you're healthy enough to continually use the portals."

"Well, I'm sure that I am healthy enough, my body repairs just about anything that's wrong with it. But, whatever you need me to do Grandpa," I said as I reached for the pen on the table and began filling out the mountain of paperwork. It was mostly health related questions, much like you'd see the first time at a new doctor's office visit, but it was a lot and took quite some time to complete.

Once all the paperwork was done, Grandpa moved me over to the computer desk Ridley was at and I sat down on the other side of it. "We need to get your fingerprints scanned," Ridley said as he pushed a few keys then slid a fingerprint scanner towards me on the desk. "Put your two thumbs up there first," he instructed me. "Now put your four fingers on the scanner flat, then the other hand." I did as I was told again.

Then Ridley told me that we'd run a CT scan, and an MRI, draw some blood, do a glucose test...all kinds of things, when I stopped him mid-sentence. "Honestly guys, I really don't think you need to waste your time on all of this with me. My body isn't normal anymore, not like yours. I'll repair any damage I take, I don't require 'food' like you do to survive, so I don't see how these tests will be relevant. I'm not saying I won't do them, I just don't think it's necessary." Ridley glanced at my Grandpa for an answer.

After a moment of contemplation, he finally spoke his thoughts. "I do suppose you're right Skyy. We've never had anybody in our ranks that wasn't human before, and we have to keep up with testing to make sure our bodies can handle it. The blood draws Jaime took from you when you woke up certainly had some different results than a humans would. Alright, well I guess we can skip all the tests, but you better come to me immediately if you ever start to not feel right."

I nodded at him eagerly, "I promise I will."

Satisfied with that, he went over to a drawer in the room and got a device that looked like a large screwdriver. He handed it to Ridley, and he hooked it up to the computer he was on for a few moments. Grandpa put some medical gloves on, then came over to me again. "This is a microchip, it's got all of your information in it. It just goes under your skin, it's very tiny and painless. This way we can find you or track you at all times in case something goes wrong while you're out in the field. It'll also communicate with our systems while you're using a portal, so we know who's got an active portal open and where they are heading to."

The thought of having something under my skin sort of creeped me out, but given all the other weird things I have seen and been though recently, on top of being a vampire, I just sucked it up and nodded at Grandpa. "It goes in the fatty part of the palm of your hand, by your thumb. You won't even know it's there, and with how fast you heal, the pain will be over in minutes."

I extended my hand, and he wiped the area clean with a sterile wipe, and then shot the microchip into my hand. It stung, and a minimal amount of blood rose to the surface. Grandpa gave me a piece of gauze to hold over it for a few moments. After about five minutes I started to feel the area stinging uncomfortably, so I moved the gauze away to check it out.

"Uhhh, guys? This can't be a good thing," I said nervously. The microchip was forcing its way out of my skin and body. My vampire healing was protecting my body, and wanted nothing to do with a foreign object in it.

Ridley and Grandpa came rushing over to see what I was talking about. Grandpa rubbed his hand over his mouth and sighed deeply. "Guess I should have expected that. Well, now we'll have to come up with some sort of external way to keep the chip with you. We could probably just make you a new ring, with the chip inside and the security overrides, but it'll take a day or two."

"Sorry guys," I said as I picked the microchip out of my skin, and handed it to Grandpa.

Ridley gave my shoulder a little reassuring squeeze. "Don't worry about it Skyy, we'll get you setup either way. You're in the database now, and have your own portal signature so once we get the ring remade, you'll be all set." I smiled at him, and thanked them both for being patient with me.

"We should probably get you back to Italy, Skyy. I'm sure you're needing nourishment, and we've had you here for a few hours now," Grandpa said.

"Actually, I wanted to ask Ridley a few things, if you have the time? Maybe he can give me a lift home when we're done?" I asked.

Grandpa nodded and smiled, "Sure, just don't over exert yourself dear, you're still new to the vampire thing." He gave me a hug and left Ridley and I to talk.

Once he was gone, I sat back in the chair across from Ridley's computer desk. "So, I got in touch with Dreamer last night. She's more than happy to help interrogate the dark fae, and even thought that some of her people would help us with our sweep of The Gloom."

Ridley's face lit up with the news. "Great! I'll talk to the people in charge about how they want to do the interrogation."

"I'm also letting you guys know, she made a comment about knowing where our bases are, because of the energy the portals drain. So it's not like this place is a secret, she knows where we are, so bringing her here probably wouldn't hurt anything," I said.

Ridley chewed on his bottom lip while he thought that over. "Hmm I am not sure if I should even mention that to the others or not. They are very protective of everything. I'll see what your grandfather thinks before anything else." I agreed with him on that one.

I smiled at him and rose from my seat. "Alright, well I guess I should be heading back. Don't want to push it too far without having blood. Just get in touch with me as soon as you figure out how they want to do the interrogation and I'll have Dreamer ready."

He stood up and came to stand by me, "Sounds like a plan. You ready to go?"

I nodded, Ridley took my hand and before I knew it I was back in my guest room at the villa in Italy. Aiden wasn't in it, but I felt confident to be there without him for the moment. Ridley glanced at the books and vials that Grandpa had left me. "Don't forget to take those, there should be instructions in the box."

"So, you guys took my fingerprints and tried to microchip me, but how does it all work actually? I mean, how do these portals function? Is it magic?" I asked him.

"It's a combination of magic and manipulating the energy and space around you. All the dimensions, or planes, that coexist on this planet are an example. Except we are just moving within our own dimension, from point A to point B. From Italy to Missouri. All the species that live on this planet, including humans, have been doing it for centuries. You'll understand it once you drink the learning potions, though," he tried his best to explain.

"Fair enough. There is a lot to learn, and I think we're both learning from each other, since you've never had a vampire in your ranks before today," I grinned at him.

"Are you going to be ok here alone if I take off?" he asked. Before he even finished asking it, Aiden was coming through the door, having heard us arrive. Ridley smiled at Aiden, and shook his hand. "Scratch that thought," he said as he laughed.

I slipped the ring that Grandpa had given me earlier off my finger. "Not sure if you guys need this back or not, but here you go," I said as I plopped the ring into the palm of his hand.

"Hopefully we'll have something ready for you again by tomorrow, but I'll be in touch either way. Have a good night you two." Ridley gave us a wave and opened another portal back to the base and disappeared into it.

Aiden gave me a welcoming hug, and then prepared me a mug of blood, figuring I'd need it after my trip. "So, how did it go," he inquired.

I took the warm mug from his hands and sipped it. "It was…interesting."

Chapter 5

That evening I read the instructions that came with the potions, which basically just told me to drink them in a certain order. The little vials glowed a soft purple that illuminated my whole hand as I held each one. Like the learning potions I took last time, these also tasted strange. They tasted bitter and sweet at the same time, and they left my tongue feeling tingly for a good twenty minutes after I was done. Ridley was right, once I was done drinking them, I understood how to open and use a portal. It was just a matter of manipulating the space around you.

I placed the empty vials back in the little box they had arrived in and had a seat next to Aiden. "Once they finish modifying that ring for me, we should be able to head over to Scotland, then to America. Do you think that is alright?" I inquired.

Aiden smiled at me, then his brow furrowed. "Skyy, go look in the mirror. Your eyes look very strange, are you feeling ok?" He stood up, very concerned about me, and guided me over to the mirror.

I took a peek and saw that my irises were glowing purple, like the portal potions I took. They were softly swirling, like a lazy whirlpool, in a circular motion. I touched my hand to my cheek, in shock. "Holy....crap," I whispered, to nobody in particular. It looked really cool, that's for sure, but I had no idea if this was a side effect, if it was normal, or what was happening, so I dove into my purse to get my phone out to call Ridley.

He picked up after three rings. I didn't even let him get out a "hello" before I blurted out, "Ridley, you need to come over here, like right now! Please! Drop whatever you're doing!" The words had barely left my lips before I saw a portal opening up in our guest room.

Ridley stepped out of it a minute later. I didn't even have to say anything to him, he saw my eyes immediately. "Whoa," was the only thing he said, which didn't comfort me.

"So, I take it this isn't normal?" I said with a bit of sarcasm in it.

He shook his head no, as he moved closer to me to inspect my eyes. He seemed mesmerized by them. "No, I've never seen anything like this. Do you feel strange?"

I shrugged my shoulders. "No, not really. I feel fine. My tongue was a little tingly after I drank them, but that went away."

Aiden just kept staring at me, and I knew he was very worried. Ridley suggested we get my grandfather over here, so he made the call and within ten minutes he was also standing in my room.

Grandpa inspected me as well, asked the same questions Ridley had. "Well, we've never seen this reaction in anyone else. But then again, we've never given a portal potion to a vampire before now. We have a few more bells and whistles to add to your ring, but as soon as it is done I'll bring it over and we can see if you can actually open a portal. It may just be a side effect that will fade, it could be harmless, but make sure you tell us right away if you start feeling any different."

After some more discussion, they took their leave and Aiden and I were alone once more. A soft knock came on the door moment later, and Aiden opened it to find Christian standing there. He let him in the room and I saw the worry on his face as well. "I overheard the conversation with Ridley and Grandpa. Are you alright?" he asked.

I stood up and walked over to him, looking him in his eyes so he could see mine, "I don't know, to be honest. I feel fine, but obviously my eyes look a little nuts right now."

"I know I shouldn't make fun, but I think it looks pretty cool", he said as he kept staring at my eyes checking them out.

"Yeah it kind of does, huh? I hope it's nothing serious though." I plopped down into a chair and put my head into my hands. Just one more thing to add to the craziness of the past few months. I blew out a big breath of air I hadn't realized I was holding, then looked up and smiled at Christian again. "We're going to go visit my parents in a couple of days, and I was wondering if you wanted to come with us, to tie up your loose ends as well?"

Christian scrunched up his mouth in a funny angle. "I don't know Skyy. I know I should go home and tie up my loose ends, I just dread the confrontations with everyone. I suppose I'll have to get it done sooner or later, and I really would like to pick up some of my belongings, so count me in I guess."

I nodded at him, and stood up. "I know the feeling. We'll be using portals to travel, so it'll be much faster than flying. Just be ready to go with short notice, it should be in the next few days."

Christian and I had a short visit, and once he left, Aiden was looking after me with extreme care and worry. We went for a walk around the grounds, and I honestly felt perfectly normal. Of course I was curious as to why I had this reaction, but I wasn't going to worry myself sick over it. There was nothing to do but wait and see what happened.

The next day, Ridley and Grandpa came back with my newly designed ring. They wanted to test and see if the portal potions had worked, so they gave me coordinates to the base in Missouri. The system was based on longitude and latitude coordinates, and once you knew them or the general area at least, you could travel anywhere in the world. I opened a portal there and back again without a hitch, and it was one of the most exhilarating things I had ever done. Ridley tagged along with me, and said I did fantastic.

So the portal potions had worked, and the base got all of my information via the chip in the ring when I opened each portal, and had my location as well. Everything was on track, except nobody knew why my eyes were still glowing and swirling purple. The following days, Aiden had me mingling with the humans in the house as much as I could, and I was adjusting just fine. I was down to only need a few mugs of blood per day now, and thankfully the contacts that Ridley had invented for us covered up my crazy purple eyes.

Aiden thought I was prepared to make our journey to America, and I called my folks to let them know the good news. I told them we'd see them in about five days, giving us sufficient time to stop by the castle in Scotland to see if we could get in touch with Alina. They pestered us and pressured us to stay at their house, but we politely refused and booked a hotel instead because we needed our privacy.

Fiona also wanted to come along with Christian. They planned to stay the majority of their trip in Salem, Massachusetts at his house, and the other vampires thought that this was safe enough for them. Bathory and her coven knew where my house was, but the only vampires who knew where Christian lived were dead now. We'd need to make multiple trips to move everyone through the portals, and Ridley had offered to help me since this was my first big adventure with portals on my own. The Order asked me to contact Dreamer before I left and inform her that they would bring the dark fae to Aiden's castle in Scotland while we were there, because they had a way to easily dispose of the bodies in the event they ended up vegetables like the last time the Radiant fae interrogated them. Aiden had an incinerator on his property for garbage, which also doubled as a crematorium after the huge battle with Bathory.

Once everyone was packed and ready to go, Ridley came over and helped me move Aiden, Christian, and Fiona through the portal. We had to make three trips total to get us all to the castle in Scotland, since we can only carry one extra passenger with us at a time.

The castle was eerily deserted. Images of the battle on the grass and hills outside flashed before my eyes. The vampires did a great job of repairing the wing that had burnt down before we left for Italy, but the land outside the castle still showed the signs of battle. The grass was still burnt and black from the demon-fire that devastated several acres of land.

Once we were settled into our rooms, I wandered over to the guest room that I had originally encountered Alina in. Hoping that she would make an appearance, I called out her name a few times, and sat on the bed for over an hour with no results. We'd stay here a few days before moving on to my parents' house, so I'd just keep trying.

Fiona and I spent the afternoon talking wedding stuff, which bored the men out of their minds. Aiden asked Ridley and Christian if they liked to fish, and the three of them went off to a small pond on the property to fish and do "manly things" as

Christian had joked. Later that evening we found them lounging in the living room, watching the news. Fiona and I joined them, asking how their fishing excursion was.

Half listening to the news and trying to listen to the men at the same time, my stomach dropped as I turned my attention fully on to what the news reporter was saying. "Guys! Shhh! Hush for a minute, I need to hear this."

"For the last two months, horrible and brutal murders have swept the London streets. Investigators are at a loss, and are calling this case 'The New Ripper' because the murders resemble those of the still unsolved case of Jack the Ripper in the late 1800s. Officials are advising that you don't go out at night alone, and to keep your doors and windows locked, as there have been two cases reported that took place inside resident's homes. While it's still too early to make an official statement, investigators are saying that the latest murder scene has an eerie resemblance to the Mary Kelly murder scene on November 9th 1888. All of the victims so far have been prostitutes. Do we have a copycat Jack the Ripper roaming the streets of London? More to come at eleven."

My mouth was hanging open so far that it could have touched the floor. I was speechless for a good thirty seconds. Nobody else in the room had any idea why I was so interested in this. Once I found my voice I stood up and looked at Ridley while wringing my hands nervously.

"Ridley, I really, and I mean really, hope I am wrong about this. But do you remember those letters I found at Bathory's castle that I had you take a look at?" He nodded silently, and I continued, "Well, it had never occurred to me until just now, who this mysterious 'J' person was. This might be a far-fetched theory here, but hear me out. The time line matches perfectly, if Bathory was in London in the late 1800s and came in contact with Jack the Ripper, of course she'd be enraptured with him because he is just about as bat shit crazy as she is. Whoever this 'J' person was, she stalked him for a long time before making an introduction, she had a small romance with him, and an infatuation with him after it ended. It would make sense that the great, noble, egotistical Elizabeth Bathory would want to befriend another person who shares her sick and twisted mindset. What if she turned him into a vampire?"

I paused to gather my thoughts before continuing, and it made more and more sense the more I talked. "Think about it. Whoever 'J' was, Bathory obviously had people watching over him, cleaning up his 'messes' which could mean he never stopped killing at all…her vampires just covered it up. Now, fast forward to a few weeks ago, Bathory goes into hiding, and a huge chunk of her vampires are dead or also in hiding. 'J' no longer has anyone to clean up his mess, so it's coming into the limelight now. No matter what, 'J' is someone she has kept in close touch with over the decades, and he's not happy about her having him under constant surveillance."

All eyes were on me. After I had laid my theory out, I could see Ridley mulling it over in his head. He slowly nodded after a moment or two. "It's not as far-fetched as you might think Skyy. Anything is possible, and the timeline does indeed fit."

"Aiden, can you get us a laptop? I'd like to look up more information on both Jack the Ripper, and this new case," I said. I ran up to my room to grab a pen and a pad of paper out of my backpack and by the time I got back Aiden had fired up his laptop for us.

Everyone was interested, and we started throwing ideas around left and right. After looking up the old letters that Jack the Ripper supposedly sent to the police back in the 1800s it fit even more. "The handwriting is identical to these! And the spelling is just as terrible. Oh my God. This is crazy. Ridley, portal with me back to the villa in Italy so I can get the letters and we can all have a look."

A half hour later, I passed around the box of letters from 'J' to Bathory. Letters from as early as 1891, to 2010 were in the box. It didn't take everyone else very long to come to the same conclusion as me. "Ok, so the possibility of Jack the Ripper being alive and well is pretty real. The question is, what do we do about it?" Ridley asked us all.

"Well we can't let anyone else get murdered, so my vote is we go to London and see if we can hunt this psycho down," I said, without thinking twice about it. "Bathory is in hiding, so right now she isn't an immediate threat to humans. We'll still work on finding her, but I think we should focus on 'J' first, perhaps he might even have some idea of where she might be hiding."

Ridley had a huge smile plastered on his face, he was ready for action. "We have to report this back to the Order first Skyy, its protocol. And they'll probably be pissed off you didn't bring this information to them earlier."

"I know, but I was kind of busy being in a coma for four weeks. I wanted to go over the letters on my own before handing them over, and well…things kind of got crazy and now here we are. I didn't mean any harm by not handing them over."

I glanced over at Aiden, "Well it looks like our trip to see my parents is on hold indefinitely, I will have to give them a call."

He gave me an encouraging smile, but I could tell he was nervous about me potentially going out in the field on my first mission as a Divine Assassin. "Do what you have to do, my love. I'll be here when you're done, and we can head off to see your parents whenever you're ready."

My God I loved that man. He was the sweetest, most selfless person I had ever met. Not to mention the most handsome man on the planet. I ran over and wrapped my arms around his neck and gave him a soft kiss. "I love you, Aiden."

He returned my sentiment with a kiss of his own. "I love you too, Skyy. Just be careful."

"Christian, if you and Fiona still want to head to Massachusetts we can portal you over before we head to the base," I offered.

He waved his hand in the air dismissing my offer. "That's ok Skyy. We're in no rush to go. I'd rather wait and head over there when you guys do."

"Alright, well I don't think any of us should stay here in the castle for an extended amount of time, since every single person in Bathory's network knows where it is. So where do you want us to drop you guys off?"

"You can take me back to Italy," Aiden said. He was already packing his laptop back up in its carry case, then disappeared up the stairs to get the rest of his luggage.

Fiona and Christian looked at each other for a moment, then Fiona spoke up. "I wouldn't mind heading back to France for a little while. Check in on my house, and show Christian around. Would that be too much trouble?"

Ridley and I both spoke at once in unison, "No not at all!" then proceeded to giggle like two school kids who just jinxed each other.

Twenty minutes later, I was dropping Aiden off at Lucius' villa in Italy and saying my temporary goodbyes. "I might be back here in a few hours, or they might send us out into the field. I'll let you know as soon as I do. I love you," I said as I kissed him. He packed me a small knapsack cooler of blood for my trip, and handed it to me before I left.

I met up with Ridley at the base, with the box of letters in tow. We gave each other a look that pretty much said "who knows what'll happen" and proceeded to walk to my grandpa's office.

Chapter 6

Grandpa was mad at first, just as Ridley had assumed, but he got over it pretty quick once he started to go over the letters from 'J' to Bathory. He told us that he'd need to discuss this with the others, and led me to his private quarters to relax while he did so. I had packed a small bag with a change of clothes and my toiletries in case we had to get on the move fast. I wanted to wash my face, so I plucked my contacts out of my eyes and got my face soap out of my bag. After that I felt refreshed and just kicked back on Grandpa's bed with a book until they came and got me.

His office was big enough, but the moment I walked in it felt cramped and crowded. There were about twelve Divine Assassins, including Ridley and Grandpa, in the room, and with nowhere left to sit I just hovered by the doorway. But Grandpa quickly demanded I move to the front with him by his desk. He introduced me to those I hadn't formally met yet. It was a mix of smiles and frowns as I looked across the room. A few of them weren't sure about me being a vampire.

"What the hell is the matter with her eyes, Killian?" one gentleman said, as if I weren't present in the room.

An uncomfortable pause came from Grandpa, and I was regretting that I hadn't put my contacts back in my eyes after washing my face. "It happened after she drank the portal potions. We're not sure what is causing it exactly, but she isn't under any physical or mental distress," he replied professionally.

Two of the men who had the frowns on conversed, then came the outburst. "This is just one of many reasons why a God damn vampire has no business in our Order!" one of them shouted. Wow, way to make a girl feel welcome...

My grandfather slammed his hand on his desk, and that shut them up real fast. "Keep your thoughts and opinions to yourself, McCoy. If you can't work with and be civil to my granddaughter, then you can leave. This is all new territory, and having her in our ranks, and the help of her friends and the Radiant fae, is a huge benefit to all of us. So, anybody else have anything to say about it?" Silence. "Good, then let's get on to the point, shall we?"

He had briefed them all on the 'J' letters and findings, and they had all come to a unanimous agreement that we should head to London to see what we could find. "Ridley and Skyy, since you brought this to our attention, you'll be heading to London, along with another team. So go ahead and get your stuff together, we want to get you out there before the end of the day."

I went back to his quarters and gathered up my small bag of stuff, and gave Aiden a phone call to let him know I'd be coming by the villa to pack a more suitable bag for the field. After going through a small briefing, the others were given potions with information pertaining to the Ripper cases, both new and old, as well as maps of London and its surrounding areas, Underground maps, and likely places to start the search. I noticed I was not given a potion. Unable to keep my curiosity at bay, I finally asked, "Why don't I get a potion?"

I heard the asshole McCoy give a little snicker, but he didn't say anything. Ridley spoke up, "Since we aren't sure what caused the side effect from the last round of potions you drank, we figured it would be best if you hold off on drinking anymore."

"I can't be much help to you guys in the field if I don't have the same information as you do. I don't feel any different, except for having purple eyes. I'll take the risk, let me have the potion too," I said in an upbeat tone.

My grandfather just nodded to Ridley, and he produced a vial for me. It was the same size as the portal potion was, except the liquids inside this bottle were brown and green, and the green parts were glowing faintly. As with the language potions I took, I could see tiny letters and numbers floating around inside the liquid. I took the topper off of it and slammed it in one gulp. It tasted disgusting, as usual, but this time my tongue didn't tingle at all. I bat my eyelashes at Ridley, "Well, how do I look? Are my eyes looking like a box of crayons now?" I joked.

He shook his head no. "They are still purple." I shrugged and didn't dwell on it. I felt perfectly normal, and soon after we were all set and ready to go. Ridley and I would travel together, first to his house, then to the villa to get our luggage before meeting up with the other team in an abandoned warehouse, and from there we'd hop on the Underground to our designated hotel.

The other two Divine Assassins we were working with were named Logan and Keith. They both looked to be in their mid-forties. Logan was very fit and in shape, with chestnut brown hair, some freckles, and a crooked smile. Keith was an average looking, average sized man, with hair so dark it was almost black, and had an annoying habit of chewing his gum very loudly. They were both very friendly towards me, which was a positive thing.

We checked into The Royal Horseguards hotel, which blew my mind. This place was fancy, with amazing views of the city. We each had our own suite, and once we were checked in and settled, we met back in the lobby to get started. I don't know who was footing the bill for this business trip, but it couldn't be cheap. I'd never been to London before, and once again found myself visiting a place I'd love to check out under better circumstances, as a normal tourist.

Aiden had arranged for a delivery of blood to my suite later that evening, and I hoped that I would be ok until then. He was very unsure about me being out and about in an unknown city without another vampire accompanying me. Ridley and the others knew how to restrain and kill vampires, but knew nothing about what I was going through as a newly transitioned vampire. I knew they all had gadgets and tools on them at all times in case they came across hostile vampires, and I also knew they wouldn't hesitate to use them on me if I flipped out.

We decided to start by visiting the locations of all the recent murders to see if we could put together any kind of clues or piece together motives. There had been six females murdered in the last two months, but unlike the Ripper cases from the 1800s which all took place in Whitechapel, these were spread out all over London. One of them however did take place in Whitechapel, so we decided to start with that location.

If you took into account the generally accepted victims of Jack the Ripper, his first kill would have been Mary Ann

"Polly" Nichols. Her body was found in Buck's Row on August 31st, 1888. Oddly enough, the first victim of the new case was found in the same general area, inside a flat on Durward Street. We couldn't access the building so we couldn't see the crime scene, but the news reports had said that the murder was inside an unoccupied flat.

With this crime scene so close to the first murder in 1888, it would almost be silly to not take this as a sign. The media was touting that it was a copy-cat murderer but we knew there was a chance it could very well be the same Ripper.

We had spent about two hours traveling from the hotel on the Underground to the scene and then looking around the area, and I was starting to feel on edge, needing blood. I'd have to wait a few more hours, and at this point I wasn't sure I wanted to be out in the public. I pulled Ridley aside and talked to him privately. "Would you mind if I went back to the hotel? I'm not feeling so hot, if you know what I mean?"

Ridley got it immediately. "Of course, I'll accompany you back there so you won't be alone. Logan and Keith can scout out the next crime scene." He relayed the information to the men, and they seemed fine with it, so after our goodbyes, Ridley and I headed back towards the Whitechapel Underground station.

The subway ride was almost unbearable for me. My sense of smell was heightened as a vampire now, and when my bloodlust was satisfied I didn't notice the smells of everyday human life as much. But now, since I was on edge and needed blood, I was to the point that I was questioning if me being on the subway was safe or not. I could smell that the guy three seats down from me had eaten oysters for lunch. The mixed scents of the numerous different kinds of perfume and cologne drifting inside the stale air of the subway car were sickening, but worse than that was the smell of body odor that people were trying to cover up. And much to my disgust and dismay, I could tell which ladies were menstruating. The dead blood and stench all around me was too much for me to handle. I was about to rip into someone's throat if I didn't get off this damn subway.

I started to make my way towards the doors, and Ridley followed my lead. I had no idea where we were in relation to the hotel, but I had to get off, so when the car stopped at the next station I was the first to jump off, shoving two people out of the way who weren't happy about it. If they only knew how close they were to pushing my last button and getting more than they bargained for. Once we made our way back up to the surface and the fresh air, I started to feel slightly better, but I needed to get blood.

Taking my cell phone out of my pocket, I called Aiden to check on the delivery. He answered right away. "How are you holding up?" was his greeting.

I was pacing back and forth on the sidewalk, while Ridley stood close by with his hands in the pockets of his lightweight jacket. I wondered if he had them wrapped around some device to stun me in the event I attacked someone.

"I'm not doing good Aiden. Do you think that guy could make the delivery sooner? Like now?" I inquired.

"Why don't you just portal back here and drink?" was his reply.

"I'm not in a place I can do that right now. We were on the Underground and I had to jump off, I have no idea where I even am right now, but I'm standing on a sidewalk in a very busy place. I'll make my way back to the hotel and call you back, but please call the guy and see if he can come by earlier." I blurted all of that out very quickly and I knew I needed to get back to the hotel immediately.

I hung up the phone, and we determined we were nowhere near our hotel, so walking wasn't an option. We hailed a cab, and even though being around the human driver wasn't fun, it was better than being on a subway with dozens of potential humans to drain. I covered my nose with my hand, which did little to mask the smell of the man's blood, and practiced the breathing techniques Aiden had taught me to calm myself down. Before too long we were up in my suite at the luxurious hotel. Aiden had made the call to the delivery guy, and he was on his way. I paced and paced while we waited for him to arrive, and if Ridley was nervous or scared, he never showed it. He sat on one of the couches casually, flipping through the television channels.

Soon, the front desk called to confirm that I was expecting a guest and they sent him up. I opened the door before the poor guy barely even knocked the first time, scaring the shit out of him as I grabbed the box out of his hands. He was a human, but I had no idea if he knew what I was, or even if he knew what was inside the box. I thanked him, tipped him, and slammed the door. It was packed in a plain cardboard box, and inside were several bags of blood, packaged nicely in some Styrofoam and dry ice to keep it cold.

I probably looked like a crazed madwomen, but at this point I didn't care. I grabbed a bag, ripped open the cabinet door to get a mug out and poured the red liquid inside it, shoved it in the microwave for a few seconds and then gulped it down in two huge gulps. I could already feel the blood working its magic on me, but knew it wouldn't be enough so I prepared another mug full. I sighed and sipped it like a person thoroughly enjoying their first cup of coffee for the morning.

Ridley had gotten off the couch and leaned against the doorway to the kitchen area. "What's it taste like?" he asked me, though I caught a hint of embarrassment in the question.

I rinsed the cup out and put it on a paper towel to dry, and took the now half empty blood bag and placed it in the small freezer. "Well, each blood type tastes different. I noticed that I really liked Type O Negative. To me, I'd compare it to the most satisfying, juicy, delicious steak dinner I've ever had. The others types are good, just different. And you can also taste certain differences in the blood too, like if the person smoked or drank alcohol, if they were on drugs or prescriptions, herbal supplements. Things like that, it's very slight but it is noticeable. Aiden tries to always get pure blood, people who don't do any of those things, and it tastes much better."

Ridley laughed, "You make it sound almost good. So it doesn't taste revolting to you like it would have if you had been a human? Iron-like?"

I shook my head no, "Not at all. I was shocked the first time I took a sip of blood, because that is what I expected too. I was craving it, my body knew it wanted and needed it. It's weird for sure, but I am glad that it doesn't taste bad because then I'd be even more miserable than I already am," I said as I laughed with him.

I called Aiden back to thank him, but he was still overly concerned about me. "Skyy, if you don't think you're ready for this, you don't have to do it. I'll admit that what you're doing is more than I think any new vampire is ready for. Going to visit your folks is one thing, and you'd be in the company of other vampires who could help you. But you're out in a major city that is busy and filled with many temptations, with nobody to guide you. I'm sure your grandfather would understand." I knew he wanted me to come back home, and truth be told I sort of did too, I missed Aiden already and I hadn't even been gone that long.

"I know Aiden, and I'll consider it. I'll give this one more try before I give up though. Now I have blood here for when I need it, and I'll be sure to drink before I go out." We chatted for a while longer before hanging up, but I knew Aiden wasn't happy with my decision.

Ridley and I spent the rest of the afternoon watching television. Logan and Keith came back a little after six that evening, and the three humans went out for dinner. I stayed in my suite and had a mug of blood by myself. When they came back we decided that we'd go out later that night to see if we could find anything. Four of the murders happened in the same area, which was known as a high prostitution area, so we suited up and hopped on the Underground to King's Cross.

Nothing eventful happened but we stayed in the area for a few hours. Most of the murders happened late in the wee hours of the night. We wandered the more populated areas early in the night, trying to blend in as best as we could. Once the stores and restaurants started closing down we walked over by Argyle Square. There was a small park that had a public garden and basketball court, but it closed at dusk, so we just casually walked around the block. There were a lot of homeless people in the area, but none of us were the least bit afraid of anyone approaching us.

It was just after two in the morning when we decided that'd we would call it a night and try again tomorrow. Walking back to the Underground station, I heard faint screams in the very far distance. I knew that Ridley, Logan, and Keith would not be able to detect it with their human ears. It was a female being restrained and it sounded like muffled screams and words, probably someone holding a hand over her mouth. It could be a domestic dispute between a husband and wife, since there were dozens of hotels and homes in the immediate area. But I wanted to investigate.

"I hear someone screaming, it's coming from that row of buildings over there, let's go," I said as I took off running. I hadn't had any vampire training on how to flash or teleport short distances like the others could do, but I knew I could already run way faster than the other men, and had to work at keeping a pace they could keep up with.

As we got closer I started smelling blood. A lot of blood. It was coming from a small alley behind a row of buildings. I raced over the small brick wall like an Olympic athlete, no longer caring if my partners were right behind me or not. The lighting was dim but I could make out a male figure in the distance, hovering over a body that lie limp on the ground, no longer struggling. There were a few very small brick walls separating yards for the residents and businesses of the building that I had to jump over, and as I got closer the man stood up and I heard him say "fuck" before he flashed out of my vision. He was a vampire, no doubt about it.

Once I reached the body my bloodlust kicked in. The smell was intoxicating, it was fresh, live blood, flowing out of this poor woman's body. Her throat was slit, and her clothing was ripped in the front, revealing a huge incision from her pubic bone to her sternum. Her insides were spilling out. I wasn't prepared for this, and could feel my fangs extending. I knew I had to chase after the man who did this, but I physically could not force myself to do it. By now, Ridley and the others caught up to me and were panting heavily from the run.

I tried, I really tried my best to control myself. But I failed. Being around Luke when he cut his knee was nothing compared to what was in front of me. The last glimmer of life was fading from this woman, and I grabbed her wrist and put my mouth to her vein like some rabid animal. Her blood was tainted with drugs, but I didn't care. It was nothing compared to drinking bagged blood. This was the most amazing feeling I had ever experienced in my life. I could not control myself, I didn't care if she lived or died.

I heard Ridley whispering loudly, trying not to alert any of the buildings occupants to our presence. He was begging me to stop, begging me to not have to make him use silver on me. I didn't care. The next thing I knew I felt my body jolt with pain. It was as if every nerve ending in my body was being ripped out. I was paralyzed and could not move. The pain was unbearable. I knew I'd just been silvered. And I also knew I'd just royally fucked up our mission. We had to get out of there before we were discovered by an onlooker, or worse the police, and with me being paralyzed and unable to move, the men decided they'd risk opening a portal in the alley. It was dark enough and if we did it fast enough we'd be gone before anyone could realize what was going on.

Ridley picked me up in his arms, and then we were traveling through a portal back to our hotel room. He placed me on the bed of my suite to recover. I knew from experience watching Aiden go through the same thing when I accidently nicked him with my silver enchanted ring that I'd be like this for several hours.

Ridley also knew that he was in way over his head with me. Once I had my mobility back there was no telling what I would do. "Skyy, I don't know what happened tonight. I'm scared for you, and we don't know what to do to help you. So I have to go and get Aiden to come here and watch over you. I hope you're not mad at me," he said apologizing me to. I wanted to scream out how sorry I was, how much I hated myself for ruining everything. We had the murderer at the tips of our fingers!

He opened a portal and several minutes later Aiden stepped out of it with him. He ran to my side immediately. His eyes were filled with concern as he looked me over. Then he went to the bathroom and came back with a wet rag and began to wipe all the blood off my face, hands, and arms.

"Skyy, my dear Skyy. What happened?" he whispered.

Chapter 7

Ridley, Logan, and Keith had left immediately after retrieving Aiden for me. I was dying to know where they went, and being paralyzed I couldn't ask. It was probably for the best that I was though, because the varying range of emotions and impulses running through me would have probably gotten me into more trouble. I was a wreck, craving more fresh human blood, seemingly back to stage one of my bloodlust. I was also fuming mad at myself for losing control and having played a part in an innocent woman's death.

Aiden was as gentle and as caring as I knew he'd be. He understood completely what I was going through, a secret that only I was let in on. He had attacked and almost killed his own mother the night he was turned, though he didn't have to live with the guilt of murdering someone like I now had to face.

He lay my head in his lap after he had cleaned me up, and stroked my hair for what seemed like hours. My body may have been paralyzed but my mind was sure going a mile a minute. Guilt, anger, sadness, bloodlust, and the murder scene with the fleeing vampire kept going through my mind. Hours later I began to feel my limbs tingling as the sensation came back to them, and soon enough I was sitting up on my own, shaking out my hands trying to get full feeling back in them. Aiden was right by my side, encouraging me to take it slow and easy.

The first words out of my mouth were: "I need blood." Aiden was quick to oblige, making it in record time. He helped me sip the blood from the mug, and went to make another one as soon as I had drained that one. I was on edge and angry, feeling like I had flushed all my progress down the toilet that I had made controlling my bloodlust. I knew what it tasted like to drink live, fresh blood from the vein now, and I had to settle for this bagged, stale version of it. Five mugs in a row, and I was only just starting to feel calmer.

Ridley and the others had returned at some point, but had not bothered us, giving me privacy to get myself together. Now that I had my voice back, the questions were about to fly.

"Go get Ridley please," I asked Aiden. He gave me a look, but didn't say anything. Moments later Ridley entered my suite.

I couldn't even look him in the eyes, I was so ashamed of myself. I sat Indian style on the bed, fiddling with my hands that I had folded in my lap. "I'm really sorry Ridley. I lost it out there, I am sorry I put you in that situation," I said in almost a whisper.

Seemingly unaffected by my savage attack on the woman hours earlier, he strode across the room and sat at the edge of the bed. Placing a hand on my shoulder, he spoke, "I can't even imagine what you're going through right now Skyy. It was probably not the best idea to have you out in the field so soon with us. But I know you're strong and you'll work past this. I haven't reported this to anyone yet, I asked Logan and Keith to keep silent and they agreed. I wanted to talk to you first."

I hadn't expected that. I thought for sure my grandfather and the others would be arriving any moment to rip into me. McCoy and his friend would come at me with pitchforks and torches when I went back to base, at least that is the scene I had conjured up in my mind.

Finally I looked up and met Ridley's eyes. There was nothing but compassion and concern there, no judgment, which surprised me. "Thank you Ridley," I said. Then, nervously added, "What happened to…the lady?" My eyes were back on the bed again, I couldn't look at him when I asked.

"We took care of it," was his reply. My head shot up, wondering what he meant by that.

"What do you mean?" I inquired back, as I nervously grabbed a piece of my long hair and began to twist it around my pointer finger.

"Aiden let us take the body to his house, to the garbage incinerator. We cleaned up the scene without being seen or heard, so everything is all good," he said as he grinned, obviously pleased with himself.

I was shocked, and I tried to stand up too soon, quickly realizing that I wasn't ready for it. I sank back down to the bed, feeling my legs tingle slightly. "You took the body, and destroyed evidence the police could use for the investigation!?" I exclaimed. I pointed to Aiden, "And let me guess, it was your idea?"

Aiden put his hands up to begin to defend himself, but Ridley was the one to answer. "Skyy, you attacked that woman. Your saliva and DNA were all over the body, along with who knows what else. The last thing any of us need is for you to be involved in a murder investigation, especially with your newfound lifestyle. Think you could last long in prison without blood?" he said, challenging me to argue his logic.

He was right, but I couldn't help but feel so sorry for that poor woman. She was brutally murdered by not one, but two attackers, and her family and friends would never even know what happened, she wouldn't have a final resting place because her body had been disposed of in the ever popular garbage incinerator.

Aiden tried to comfort me, "I know it's not easy Skyy, but it's for the best. There is no way I would leave evidence of you being at a crime scene, no matter if it helped the police or not. Your safety, and the safety of vampires not being exposed to the public, are more important to me than the crime scene."

They were both just looking out for me, and deep down I appreciated it, but I was not ok with the situation. I was doubting everything about myself, and that was not a good feeling. "So, now what? I blew it...we had the murderer, Jack the Ripper or whoever it was, right at our fingertips. I didn't even get a good look at him. Do you even know who the victim was? Did she have identification on her?" Did I really want to know?

Now it was Ridley's turn to look down at his hands. "She didn't have ID on her. The murderer either already took it, or she didn't have any to begin with."

I couldn't decide if this was for the best or not. I couldn't put a name on the woman I helped kill. What good would it do if I could? It's not like I could waltz over to her home and tell her family I was sorry.

Ridley spoke again, "Skyy, I know it's not much consolation...but there was no way that she would have lived.

With or without your involvement, even if we had stopped to try to help her, she wouldn't have made it. Don't blame yourself for her death, it wasn't your fault."

His words really didn't console me, in fact it made things worse. It felt like the room was closing in on me, and I couldn't catch my breath. I put my head in my hands and inhaled deeply. The tears had already started though. "This is all so fucked up!" I shouted, which startled Ridley slightly.

He began to speak, "I know but --- "

I cut him off mid-sentence, "No you don't know! The past few months have been insane for me. I don't know how to deal with so much so fast! My entire life, literally my entire life, has changed! And I know I brought some of it on myself, but Christian made it look so easy when he turned, I thought it would be simple. And look at me now, I am a train wreck."

Ridley stood up and took that as his cue to leave, since I was drifting onto more personal things he had no part of. I went to the mini fridge and grabbed all the bottles of booze that were stocked in there. I had no idea how alcohol would affect me but I was about to find out. All I wanted to do was get plastered and pass out, to forget for a while.

Aiden spoke softly, not sure how to approach the situation. "Skyy, don't judge yourself based on how Christian transitioned. He is something of a prodigy, and it's definitely not a common thing for any vampire to pick up all the things he did so quickly. Most of us struggle, like you are doing now. It's very rare for vampires to not drink directly from humans Skyy. It's a lifestyle choice for our family. Most newly turned vampires do drink from humans, and if it is something you'd rather do, I can arrange for donors for you. You won't have to kill anyone to feed."

I had slammed five of the mini bottles of booze, my throat was on fire. I did feel the alcohol working though, much to my surprise. "So I can be the fuck up of the family? The reject who can't handle it?" I snapped at him nastily. "You're all so perfect, you all make it look so easy."

I could tell I hurt him, and a small part of me didn't care. I opened another bottle of booze and slammed it down, then tossed it on the floor with the others. Aiden glanced down at the bottles but didn't say anything about it. "Well trust me, we might make it look easy but we all struggle as well, and speaking for myself it took me quite some time to get to where I am today. It doesn't happen overnight, as much as Christian makes it look like it does."

"And what if I do want to drink from a donor? What then? Will you still love me?" I asked him, still with venom in my voice.

He didn't even have to pause to think about his answer. "Skyy, of course I will still love you. I'll love you no matter what. I know what you're going through – what you went through – hasn't been easy. You've kept on moving forward as if nothing happened, but I told you I was always here for you if you needed to talk, and I meant it."

My anger vanished and I ran into Aiden's arms. I wrapped my legs around him and he lifted me up off the ground in a bear hug. "I wish this was all over, Aiden. All of this bullshit and trouble because of one crazy woman. I just want to be with you, marry you, and live a simple quiet life."

"We'll get there one day. And if you feel like this is all too much to handle right now, being a Divine Assassin and transitioning, just tell them. They have plenty of people who can continue the search and the fight until you're ready. They did just fine for centuries without you, I am sure they'll live a few months until you're back."

"A huge part of me wants to do that. To just run off with you somewhere remote and forget about everything for a while. But there are so many people's lives at stake, every minute Bathory is in hiding, and every minute this murderer is on the streets more people are at risk. He's a vampire by the way…that much I am certain of. But maybe I should take a few days off," I said as I put my feet back on the ground.

Aiden kissed the top of my head, but stayed silent. My head was spinning now from the alcohol, and I needed to sit down. "So vampires can get drunk?" I said while laughing.

"Yes, we can, but it leaves our system much faster than a humans. You'll be sober again in about an hour."

"I do want a donor, Aiden," I said very seriously. I knew it made me weak, I didn't care. I'd tried it his way and it didn't seem to get me anywhere. The bagged blood was like drinking a virgin margarita instead of the real thing. I had to down so much of it, and it barely even settled my bloodlust.

He nodded at me, but I knew he had to be slightly disappointed. "Alright, I'll arrange for it to happen. I just want to warn you though, once you start drinking from the vein, it will be even harder to stop and drink bagged blood if you ever decide to do it. Much harder than it is for you now to control your thirst." He put major emphasis on the word "much".

I did consider what that meant for a few moments, but decided that I would go through with it anyway. If drinking a small amount of blood directly from the vein would get me feeling like a normal, functioning part of society again then I was ready to accept that. "I still want to get a donor," I said.

Aiden nodded again, but chimed in with some more wisdom. "I'll support you no matter what your choice is, but I want to tell you that you were making progress with the bagged blood Skyy. It may have seemed like you were drinking a lot, but you were decreasing the amount and the length between drinking each day. You running into a human who was bleeding out and dying is not a normal scenario, and it would test even the strongest of us."

He was right, and I knew he was. I was taking the easy way out. I was quick to throw away my progress with the bagged blood. But why should I feel guilty for wanting to feed off of humans? It's how we were meant to feed. "Well, you're probably right, but given the line of work I am in now, this type of thing might happen more often than you think."

"And coming across it, whether you drink from the vein or bagged blood, won't make it any easier to deal with. You're still very new to this, if I were to have come across that scene it would have taken immense self-control to not do the same thing you did. I just have more practice, but it doesn't make it less tempting. Right now you're feeling remorse and guilt because you think you played a part in her death, but I'll tell you that vampires who do drink from humans tend to lose that respect for human life that you're feeling right now. It's one of the reasons we choose to drink bagged blood." Aiden was putting up a good argument.

"You mean I'll feel less attached to humans in general, and just see them as a food source?" I asked.

He nodded, "It can happen. I am not saying it will happen to you, because you'll be in close contact to humans on a daily basis working with the Divine Assassins, but a good number of vampires do begin to feel that way. I am not trying to talk you out of your decision Skyy, I just want you to be aware of what can happen."

"Will I be able to go longer between feedings and cravings?" For me that was probably the most important part. I was sick of feeling like I was a slave to the blood.

"Yes, if you're on a regular feeding schedule, you should be able to get by with feeding only once every other day," he replied.

My head was starting to hurt from the alcohol, and I needed to lay down. "Lay with me for a while Aiden. My head is killing me from the booze already. Quickest hangover of my life. I'll think over what you said, and let you know what I decide." We both got under the sheets and snuggled up together for a short nap.

When I woke up my head felt better, but of course I was craving blood. I made myself three mugs of bagged blood and still felt edgy. I wasn't sure how the Divine Assassins would feel about Aiden being here with us on the job. Ridley probably didn't care, and was probably glad he was here to calm me down. Aiden was still relaxing so I went into the large luxurious bathroom to splash my face with some water. I still wasn't used to seeing my purple eyes when I looked at myself in the mirror. Would they ever go back to normal?

I knew I should take some time off from the Divine Assassins, but knowing that the murdering vampire was out here on the streets somewhere pissed me off. It was personal now, and I wanted to help find him now more than ever. Ridley was right, I knew that poor woman would have died even if I hadn't attacked her, but I couldn't get her image out of my mind. Nobody should die like that, and I had a feeling hundreds of women already had suffered at his hands. Bathory may be in hiding and still a threat, but this vampire on the streets of London was greedy and craved attention, that much was obvious from his letters. He'd slip up again and would be easy to catch.

I stared at myself in the mirror for what seemed like an hour, deep in thought. Everything Aiden had said to me about drinking blood from humans was fresh in my mind. Did I really want to lose touch with humanity? He was right, I barely even tried. I was basing my cravings and failure on thinking it was an easy thing that took no effort. I'd be nothing more than the equivalent of a junkie who fell off the wagon if I gave up now. I had to believe that I was stronger than that. And it wouldn't be easy.

Heading back out into the bedroom, I sat down beside Aiden and took his hand into mine. Stroking it softly, I finally spoke. "I guess you're right about the blood. I don't want to ever become anything like Bathory, or any of the other vampires who have no remorse or feeling for human life. I'll try my best to stay strong and continue to drink donated blood. And I am really sorry for letting you down. I cracked under the pressure, these last few months have been harder than I guess even I realized." I kissed the back of his hand and smiled at him shyly. I was still embarrassed and angry with myself.

Aiden propped himself up onto his elbows and flashed me his killer smile. "You didn't let me down Skyy. As I said, most vampires do drink from the vein. You're trying very hard, even if you don't see it. You were put in an unusual situation, and at this stage in your transition I think just about any other vampire out there would have done the same thing as you. You'll struggle the next few days and need a lot more bagged blood, but I know you can do it." He stroked the side of my cheek softly with his hand.

I glanced over at the mini alcohol bottles I had thrown all over the room. That was the quickest binge I had ever had, and I didn't see me becoming an alcoholic vampire anytime soon. I had to get my head right, because there wasn't any time to feel sorry for myself when other people's lives were at stake. I kissed Aiden's hand one more time before I got up and started cleaning the room up. We took the rest of the day and evening to relax and for me to get my act together. I drank so much of the blood that Aiden had to call for another delivery. The next morning I called a meeting with Ridley and the guys to let them know where I stood.

We gathered in the living room area of my hotel suite, which was plenty big enough for the five of us. I could tell that Logan and Keith weren't as comfortable in the presence of two vampires as Ridley was, after watching me go feral on that poor woman. They sat on the couch nervously and I could hear both of their hearts beating faster than usual with the tension. Logan had some sweat forming on his brow, even though the room temperature was more than comfortable. Ridley on the other hand was busy sipping from a steaming cup of coffee, sitting in a big comfortable chair, legs crossed like he didn't have a care in the world.

I paced around the room back and forth, deciding how I should begin. Ridley made some small talk with us, which I appreciated. I was so thankful to have such a great partner. Finally I found my voice and let them know what I had decided.

"I'd like to apologize to all three of you for what happened yesterday. It's unforgivable and I know that you must all be questioning how safe it is to have me on your team for this investigation. I messed up, badly, and I also put our mission in jeopardy. I promise to do everything in my power to make up for that and see to it that it doesn't happen again. Thank you for acting so quickly and getting the situation under control," I said as I continued to pace and fiddle with my hands.

Ridley was blowing on his cup of coffee trying to cool it off. "Don't mention it Skyy. I'm sorry we had to silver you, but given the options we thought it was the quickest way to get you under control and get out of there."

I nodded in agreement. "You're right, it was and you're smart to have done it. Now, I don't know if you've relayed the information back to headquarters or talked to my grandfather, but from my standpoint I'd like to continue on this investigation with you and see it through to the end. We know this murderer is a vampire, and I think I can provide a special edge to the team because of it. Of course, that is if I am still welcomed on the team," I said and flashed them a smile that I hoped would lighten the tension in the room from Logan and Keith.

Neither of them spoke, but they at least looked at me and acknowledged me. They had every right to be uneasy around me, but it still felt like shit to be feared by your colleagues. Ridley had a devious smile on his face as he set his coffee down on an end table and leaned forward in his seat. "I know it's not protocol, but I think we'll let this incident stay between the four of us. I know you Skyy, and know you wouldn't ever do something like that on purpose. So as long as you can play it cool and keep it together, I don't see why anyone back home needs to know about this. Logan and Keith agreed to keep quiet too, so don't prove me wrong," he said as he winked at me.

I let out a huge breath I had no idea I had been holding and smiled. I ran over to Ridley and embraced him in a bear hug that caught him by surprise. "Thank you so much, all of you. I promise it won't happen again."

Once I let him go, he stood up and looked over at Aiden. "Now, it would probably make all of us feel a little more at ease if Mr. Carrick stuck around for a few days to help you out. No offence, but we know you're still new at the vampire lifestyle, and I think having him here to make sure things go smoothly would be good for everyone. That is of course, if you have the time Aiden?"

Aiden smiled at the gentlemen in the room, "Of course. I'd be happy to help in any way that I can. And I'd never say no to spending time with Skyy." Everyone in the room, including me, looked a little more at ease knowing he would be sticking around.

Ridley nodded at Aiden in thanks, and wasted no time in getting to our plan of attack. "Alright then, with that covered let's talk about our next move. We've got two options the way that I see it. The murderer seems to have a pattern of where he likes to kill. Our theory on him murdering in order based on the old Jack the Ripper murder sites seemed to have been accurate, or maybe it was pure luck. I vote that we go stake out the same area again, and see if he comes back."

I agreed with that statement. "I think that is the best plan as well. And now that we know he is a vampire, we'll be more prepared for him when we do encounter him again. How do you two feel?" I asked Logan and Keith.

They both spoke in unison agreeing that it was the best plan. So it was decided that we'd venture out again this evening in search of the mysterious vampire who could very well be Jack the Ripper. If only we knew how spot on we were....

Chapter 8

Jackson Ripleigh stood in the shadows at the end of the alleyway he had been interrupted in earlier that night. Staring down the long corridor of businesses and residential homes, he became angrier by the second. Fisting his hands into tight balls, his fingernails began to cut into his palms drawing blood. He didn't even flinch. This was the area he had to kill in next, there was no other location that would work. He had to find another prostitute to kill, and it had to be soon.

At a quick glance, the passerby might think that Jackson Ripleigh was a normal, middle aged, handsome man. He had chestnut brown hair that fell in soft waves to just above his shoulders, which he usually tied back into a ponytail. He had a well-kept moustache and goatee, and sparkling hazel eyes. Though rather on the short side, his body was very muscular under his clothing, which was usually much fancier than most people this day and age would wear. The passerby might think he was a rich gentleman, instead of the devious murderer that he was. He rarely ever smiled, but if he did you'd instantly see the madness behind it.

"How dare you interrupt me," he whispered into the night, clenching his fists even tighter than humanly possible. He knew that the girl was a vampire. He had caught her scent and he would do everything in his power to find her, and make her pay.

There was no humanity left in Jackson. It's probable that there never was any humanity in him to begin with. Though highly intelligent, he was just as mad as he was smart. A veterinarian by trade, he was also a self-proclaimed, self-taught surgeon. His love of torturing and dissecting human females, consumed him totally. Abandoned by his mother at a very young age, he was put out onto the streets to fend for himself. He placed full blame on his mother, and his hatred for her grew into hatred for all women. His birth mother was a prostitute, and Jackson was never wanted.

He learned how to steal, blend into the shadows, and stay out of the reach of the police by age eight. When he was nine he had sweet talked his way into the home of a widowed man in his forties. He stayed with this man for three years, who was also a veterinarian, and it was there that he became interested in anatomy in general. The gentleman wasn't well off, but he didn't hurt for money either, and little Jackson settled in and was thankful for the roof over his head. The man taught him how to read, and once he knew how he got his hands on every book he could find about medical procedures. He was fascinated, but not for the reasons most people are. He wanted to learn how to remove female organs. Often times the gentleman would take him on the job with him, and Jackson would sit quietly observing every move that the man would make.

He watched the man spay female dogs enough times that he figured it couldn't be that hard. Thinking his caretaker was asleep, Jackson snuck out of the house and found a female dog one night. He took her into the basement and bashed her in the head several times with a club to knock the poor dog out. On a makeshift table he tried to emulate what he saw the gentleman do as a professional vet. He failed miserably and became frustrated, yelling out in rage at himself and at the now dead dog that lie limp on the table. The man woke up and found Jackson covered from head to toe in blood. His mouth dropped open in shock when he saw the scene before him. Scolding him, but not realizing the extent of the madness inside this poor young child he said "You ripped her to pieces, Jackson. If you want to learn how to become a veterinarian let me teach you the proper ways."

That one sentence stuck in his mind, and from then on Jackson took on the alter-ego Jack the Ripper. What a clever twist on his own surname, he thought! The man stayed true to his word, and taught Jackson everything he knew in the short time before he died. When he was in his presence he had to be professional, but when the man was sleeping Jackson continued to sneak out and let his anger and rage out on innocent female dogs. He'd rip them to shreds removing their female organs.

Once the man had passed away, he left all his belongings, finances, and property in Jackson's name. Now twelve years old, he was once again on his own and the man of the house. He kept a low profile, and was amazingly good with finances. The house was paid for, but Jack made sure all the proper taxes were paid for and that he had plenty of food and supplies each month. The man had appointed his lawyer as a guardian until Jackson was 15, but the man never came around, and the only contact from him was when he sent Jackson his money each month.

Left to his own devices, Jackson was now totally unsupervised and became more and more wild as the years passed. At the age of sixteen, not yet totally corrupted, but not far from it, an event happened that marked his true descent into madness. He met a young lady who was only two years older than him walking home from the market one day. She looked like a middle to high class young lady, well dressed. Playing the shy young maiden part to a tee, she lured him in with her smile and innocent flirting.

Thinking that he was immune to feminine charm, it sparked something inside him he had never felt before. Instead of seeing her as something he hated and loathed, he felt attracted to her and wanted to feel her touch on his skin. He would walk to the market and back each day whether he needed something or not, just for a chance to run into the young lady.

Finally after weeks of flirting and talking, he convinced her to have a date with him. Not knowing it was not at all normal for a woman of that era to come home with a man on the first date, he invited her back to his house. Once inside she wasted no time in getting physical with him. Jackson loved the way she smelled, and the way her hands felt on his body. She was very aggressive once they were out of the public eye, initiating his first kiss and quickly moving on to unbuttoning his shirt. It happened so quickly he barely had time to process it all, but one thing was for sure: he loved the way she made him feel.

They were upstairs and undressed within twenty minutes of entering his house. Jackson was still just an unsure, inexperienced young man having never been with a woman before. But this lady definitely knew her way around a man's body. If he had been older, he would have known something was amiss from the start, but with raging teenage hormones he just lay back and let her work her magic.

He didn't bat an eye when she suggested that she tie him up to the bedpost. Quite fond of torture himself, he couldn't possibly see what could go wrong. Once his legs and arms were secure, he was naked and vulnerable lying on the bed. She teased him for several minutes, smiling deviously as she did so. She enjoyed the teasing and torture, which turned the young man on even more. Slowly and deliberately she fondled his erect penis in her delicate hand. Just when he was on the brink of explosion, she'd stop. He begged her to continue but the more he begged the more she would draw back, giggling the whole time.

Finally she gave in to his requests, after what seemed an eternity, and let him have his way. She stroked his penis for a few moments before taking it into her warm, soft mouth. Jackson had never felt such bliss in his entire life. Just before he came to completion she took it out of her mouth and finished him with her hand. Her eyes lit up as she watched him ejaculate all over his stomach and chest. Jack's heart was beating out of his chest as he tried to catch his breath. He felt like a million bucks. The girl then bent down like an animal lapping up water, and began to lick up the semen on his belly. She was giggling and writhing around with her backside in the air as she leaned down over him. Then she started rubbing her hands around in it. "You're so innocent," she whispered to him before straddling him.

He felt her wetness dripping down onto him, and just when he thought he couldn't handle any more, she slid her soaking wet fold down onto his still erect penis. He cried out in joy as she rode him, slow at first then faster and faster. There was no mistaking that she was enjoying herself as well, as she screamed out obscenities and started gasping and squealing. Her fingernails tore into Jackson's chest, tearing him apart and he glanced down to watch the blood rise to the surface. Usually he was fascinated by it, but seeing the young girl on top of him surpassed his love of blood. He longed to have his hands untied, so he could touch her beautiful breasts.

She rode him for over ten minutes before he finally came again inside her. Shortly after that she screamed out even louder than she already was with her orgasm, and then climbed off of him. They lay there both breathing heavily for a few silent moments. Jackson's hands and feet were starting to go numb from the bonds. When he asked her to please remove them, she turned towards him and stroked his face with a sad look in her eyes.

"I hate to have to do this to you, you're so handsome and young. It's not personal," she said as she got up and went to her clothing. She came back with 2 small rags, one she balled up and shoved into Jackson's mouth, the other she used to tie around his mouth behind his head. His eyes were lit up with fear and rage at the same time. He struggled as much as he could, but it didn't get him anywhere. She kissed him on his forehead before gathering up the rest of her clothing and putting it back on. Taking a quick peek in the mirror above his dresser, she winked at herself and went over to Jack's pants. Removing all his money from his wallet, she tossed it to the floor before ransacking the room for anything valuable.

He lay there, infuriated while she did the same to each room in his house. Before long he heard two male voices in his house. They had come to move the heavy stuff. She was kind enough to come say goodbye to him after cleaning him out. "Sorry this couldn't work out between us, handsome. No hard feelings?" she said as she giggled. She threw a small knife down beside him on the bed. "Good luck if you can reach that." It was the last words out of her before she left him lying there, naked and tied up.

He struggled for hours on end, his limbs had long ago gone numb and purple. His wrists were bruised and bloodied from trying to wriggle free of the bonds. His feet came loose first, which did him no good. It took him over twenty-four hours to loosen the bonds on one of his hands. He had urinated on himself twice by then, and was dehydrated from all the struggling. With his ripped up chest, and battered ankles and wrists he made his way downstairs to survey the damage.

Something dark and sinister crawled into Jackson's mind that day. Any tiny bit of love or emotion he may have begun to feel for that young lady died. Pure hatred replaced it. He cursed at himself for being so stupid to get close to a woman like that. She had taken anything worth value in his home, as well as cleaning out his wallet. Thankfully he had plenty of money in his bank account. He vowed to find the bitch who did this to him, and when he did he was going to let Jack the Ripper out.

It was four years before he ran into her again. Jackson had enlisted in the British Army under a false name, and was assisting in the medical field. He soaked up all he could from there before growing bored and finally leaving. Stupidly enough, he saw the young girl who had robbed him of his heart and possessions in the same spot he had met her years before. She had changed her hairstyle and color, but it was no doubt her.

Once he saw her, he devised a plan. He saw her blood spilling out of her in his mind, and he smiled at the thought. "You stupid whore. You never should have come back here," he whispered to nobody in particular as he walked back to his house. Hoping that she would remain in the area for a while longer, he visited a costume shop and picked up a wig and moustache. He dug out the old glasses that the man he lived with used to wear. Dressing up in the best suit he had, he tucked the man's surgical kit into the medical bag he used to carry around with him for his veterinarian calls, and glanced in the mirror at himself.

Satisfied that he didn't even recognize himself in the reflection he set out into the late afternoon sun to see if the girl was still there. To his surprise she was, and she gave him that familiar shy flirtatious smile he remember from years ago. This time it had no effect on Jackson, all he felt was rage and the need to rip her throat out. But he played the part of the interested young gentleman perfectly, and it's here he first learned the art of acting to attract his prey.

"Good eve to you ma'am. How fare you?" he inquired. She smiled at him and moved closer. He knew her tricks.

"Very well, sir. Off to the market this eve? Such lovely weather," she replied as she softly touched his arm.

"Indeed. Would you care to walk with me?" Jack asked, flashing her a smile of his own. His costume must have fooled her because she didn't think twice or hesitate before saying yes.

He offered her his arm, and she took it. They walked for a moment or two before he faked forgetting his wallet. Feeling in his coat pocket he said, "Looks like I have forgotten my wallet. My home is only a half a block from here, would you mind if we took a small detour ma'am?"

"Certainly," was her reply, keeping her innocent smile plastered on her face. She followed him down the street while they made small talk, never suspecting what was to come. When he stopped in front of his house, a flash of recognition came over her face. Jackson had already taken a knife out of his pocket and quickly put it to her side, hidden through his jacket.

"Don't make a peep. Walk inside, and do it as if you want to be here," he threatened. Any trace of niceness was gone from his voice. The young girl looked into his eyes, finally realizing who he was. She did as he said though, and entered quietly without a struggle.

Once inside the house, he quickly presented some cloth, the same ones that she had used on him years ago in fact, to gag her with. He shoved one into her mouth, and tied the other around her face. She was struggling against him, kicking him trying to get away. He yanked her by the arm so hard he heard a "pop" and figured he had dislocated her shoulder. She tried to scream out but the gag muffled her voice. "What goes around comes around," he said to her as he yanked her back to her feet.

Dragging her into the basement, he secured her arms and legs and forced her to sit in a chair. Not thoroughly thinking the whole thing through, Jackson had to improvise. He pulled out the old table he had used years ago to dissect that female dog. The girl's eyes were lit with terror. "You remember me, don't you? At least you were kind enough to fuck me before robbing me."

Tears were streaming out of her eyes now. 'I suppose I can thank you for ridding me of any lingering love of females. See my mother was just like you…a whore. You don't deserve to breathe the same oxygen as I do. You are worthless; scum. A disease to this planet." Jack was losing it, going out of his mind with the thought of the kill.

He got his tools ready, then yanked the girl onto the table. Looking back on it, he wished he could remember it clearly, but it was all a blur. What was left of the poor young girl was unrecognizable. He started with her throat, slicing it across and watching the blood flow out and onto the floor. He began to spew hateful words at her as he stabbed her repeatedly in the chest and stomach. Then he took out the tools to perform a hysterectomy, which he had never before attempted on a human. Blind rage hit him as he ripped into her flesh. When he came out of it, he stood in a puddle of blood, covered from head to toe in flesh, blood, and human insides. A huge smile was plastered on his face.

He had thrown all of her female organs in different directions, spewing blood and guts all over the basement in the process. Some of them hit the walls splashing blood all over them before sliding down to the floor. He had stabbed her eyes out, and cut her nose off, along with her tongue which he shoved up her anus. As he was coming down off his high, he stared down at her chest. He ripped into her breastplate and removed the heart, squeezing it as hard as he could in his bare hand, watching the blood ooze out of it.

Reveling in the beauty of his first human kill, he felt better than he ever had. Even better than when the whore had fucked him for the first time. Once he came down off his adrenaline high though, he looked around the room and suddenly realized he screwed up. "How the hell am I going to clean this up?" he said out loud. It was then that he vowed to never dirty his own home up, and began his rituals of finding the perfect locations to kill at. Jack the Ripper was evolving.

. . . .

Jackson stood at the edge of the alleyway for only a short time that night, before he was on his way. He was on edge and irritated not only because his kill was interrupted, but because that meddling annoyance of a woman, Elizabeth Bathory, had contacted him. He was beyond elated when he realized that her coven were no longer following him and covering up his murders. While she did have a point that keeping a low profile would keep him out of trouble, he craved the

98

attention that the spotlight gave him. The last thing he needed was her coming back to England to bug him.

He first met Elizabeth back in the 1800s. He knew from the start that there was something different about her. Even a heartless, woman-hating man like himself had to stop and recognize her other-worldly beauty. With her long, silky, jet black hair and porcelain skin she was just as sexy as she was deadly, and he hated to admit that he was a little turned on by her. Little did he know she had sought him out and stalked him for the last few months because of his twisted mind.

There was never a choice for him, if he wanted to associate with her or not. He was a human, and she wasn't. Plain and simple…she forced her way into his life. In the beginning, he liked it. He couldn't believe what she had told him at first; that she was a centuries-old vampire, and a countess at that! But he soon realized that she wasn't lying, and then he began to crave her power as well. If he were immortal, he wouldn't ever have to worry about anything. It was his lust for more power that kept him at her side. She was obsessed with him, and they would sit for hours on end sharing their twisted stories. She loved him, in her own sick and perverted way, but Jackson was incapable of love. He pretended, for his own gain, but after the newness of her company wore off, he began to see her as a pain. Elizabeth was always around, always wanting to be close to him. Always wanting to touch his body. He associated sex with bad memories, and hated the act of it. It didn't help that Bathory also loved to torture him while they made love, which only brought up the memories of his first time.

But she assured him that she would never leave him, and that she could offer him the world if he'd let her. She tried to help him cover up his murders, but he wanted no part of it. She relayed her story to him, of how her greed and ego led her to her capture, and would have been her final death had she not been turned vampire. Jackson just brushed it off, and told her to mind her own business. But she was persistent, and he was still a human and at her mercy which made him even more infuriated. She kept stringing him along with the promise of turning him. Bathory wasn't stupid, she knew that Jackson didn't care for her as she did for him, but she was so intrigued by him that she didn't care. It was the only way she knew how to keep him close to her.

Their affair continued for a few years, until Jackson had finally convinced her to turn him. He didn't want to age in human years anymore and wanted to retain his looks. She agreed and turned him. He had dropped out of the spotlight at her request, and his murders took a backseat in the public eye finally. He traveled around the world with Elizabeth for a few more years, killing when the urge rose up, before returning to London. Elizabeth hung around for a while longer before she finally left him to his devices. She would write him frequently and stopped by a few times a year. Once he began his killing again, she had him followed, for his own safety of course, and her vampires would clean up his messes. There was nothing he could do about it, because even though he was her equal now in immortality, she was an immensely powerful sorceress. She had told him what would happen if he ever crossed her, and she was one of the few things in the world that he feared.

But now, Elizabeth sounded desperate. Reaching out to him in fear, she wouldn't explain what had happened, just that she needed his help and a place to hide. One of her vampires had delivered the letter the night before. He read it and rolled his eyes, as usual. But knowing there was nothing he could do about it, he told the vampire that she was welcome to come stay with him. There was some huge secret that they were keeping.

He'd find out soon enough what it was. Little did he know he'd soon be plotting to rid himself of her for good.

Chapter 9

Staking out the alley where we first encountered the murdering vampire the next night proved to be uneventful. But we'd keep trying, at least for the next few nights in a row before deciding if we should come up with a Plan B or not. We also had a probable spot for his next kill based on the old Jack the Ripper murder scenes. It had paid off the first time, and I was pretty certain we were on the right trail.

Since we knew whoever it was wouldn't be killing in the daytime, we had some spare time during the day to go over the other loose ends. We still needed to get Dreamer and the dark fae over to Aiden's castle for interrogation, and see if we could get Alina to make an appearance while we were there. Ridley contacted my grandfather, and the Divine Assassins moved their hostages over to Scotland that same morning.

We didn't need the entire London team going over there with us, so Logan and Keith stayed behind at the hotel, while Ridley opened up his own portal, and I took Aiden through one of my own. Stepping foot back in the castle always brought back a mixed bag of emotions for me. I loved the place, because it meant so much to Aiden. It was beautiful and historical, but it also brought back memories of the huge battle we had on the rolling hills outside. We'd almost killed Bathory, and so many of our friends and colleagues died that day. Not to mention the flood of ghosts that were released on the property, some of which still hung around. The place was both beautiful and eerie at the same time.

My grandfather had already arrived on the property, and his men had secured the dark fae in the cellar that we had used last time to interrogate them. I joined them in the library, which was my grandfather's go-to meeting room in Aiden's castle. He manned the large desk in there like it was his own, but Aiden didn't seem to mind. He was used to Killian's prickly personality, and as long as it wasn't harming anything he usually let him do as he pleased. It was easier than a confrontation that usually led nowhere.

Since there were other Divine Assassins in the room, I wasn't sure how to address my grandfather. Usually I called him Grandpa, but I wasn't sure he would appreciate that in a business setting, so instead I just smiled at him and waved, taking a seat on a small sitting couch along a window. Aiden was right behind me, nodding at the gentlemen in the room and then shaking my grandfather's hand before joining me on the couch.

Grandpa took the lead as usual, bringing us up to speed. "We've got the dark fae ready, all we need is for you to contact Dreamer, Skyy. They won't talk to us, no matter what we try and I am afraid they won't last much longer so we need to act quickly."

I nodded and pulled out the pink crystal Dreamer gave me to contact her. "I'll see if I can get her here right now." I gently rubbed the crystal, and it lit up in my hands. Moments went by before we saw her cute little face peeking at us through one of the huge library windows. I saw her and waved, and her face broke into a huge smile.

One of the Divine Assassins started to move towards the door, "I'll let her in through the front," he said. I waved him off and told him there was no need.

"No need for that, she can come in right here." I gestured at the window as I got up from the couch. Once I went over there, I saw she had some of her friends along with her, but they were in their tiny fae form barely noticeable flying behind her. I opened the huge window, and they all flew inside. As it turned out, we knew all of the Radiant fae that accompanied her. It was Spring, Holland, and Pacific – the green, yellow, and blue fae. Also joining them was one of their elders, Solara. She was a beautiful Radiant fae that had pale yellow and bright orange hair and wings. They all materialized out of their tiny light forms into their equally small humanoid forms, smiling and holding hands. The room lit up with beauty and happiness instantly. Dreamer ran over to hug me, and then I shook hands with the other fae.

"Thank you all so much for helping us again," I said as I moved aside for my grandfather to fill them in on what we needed. They had no problem at all with performing the interrogation, which would be extremely painful for the dark fae, most likely resulting in their death. They would mesmerize them with their bright rainbow colored lights, which was extremely painful to the dark fae who thrived in darkness and shadows. Last time they kept one watching while they tortured the others, and I assumed the same thing would happen here. Honestly, I didn't even want to know what took place, I just hoped that we got the answers we were looking for.

They wasted no time in getting down to business, the Divine Assassins showed the Radiant fae to the cellar they had the hostages in. Aiden went with them last time, but I noticed he didn't move this time. "Not going with them?" I asked him.

He shook his head no. "I trust that they know what they are doing. It wasn't pleasant to watch the first time around." I took his hand into mine and kissed the back of it.

"I understand. All this death and fighting is hard to get used to. Even though the dark fae are our enemies, it still isn't easy to think about what will happen to them."

Aiden nodded back at me. "I agree. You have to remember, I led a pretty simple, quiet life before you came into it." He grinned at me and winked.

I swatted his arm playfully, "Hey!" I said, pretending to be hurt. Aiden just chuckled at me and kissed my forehead.

"I wouldn't have it any other way," he said.

All the Divine Assassins and Radiant fae had left the room by now, and I had a proposition for Aiden. "Let's go upstairs for a minute, I have something I want to run by you," I said as I stood up and offered him my hand. He took it and we went up to the second floor of his castle.

We were also hoping that our ghostly friend, Alina would appear while we were upstairs. I took Aiden into the room that I used when I first came to his castle, which was the first place that she made an appearance. Though I used to sit in graveyards and try to seek out spooky things like ghosts, I wasn't quite prepared for it once it really happened. It scared me pretty good the first time I saw her, unlike vampires who are unnatural but still retain human form, ghosts are unsettling. They are shells of a former life, stuck wandering the planes of earth for eternity.

The extreme sadness that radiates off of them is heart wrenching. They don't want to be here, and there is nothing they can do about it.

I moved Aiden over to the edge of the bed and we sat down. "I wanted to bring this up to you in private, while we had Dreamer and her friends here. I know that Fiona, and my family are all really excited about a big wedding. Your mom has been emailing me and messaging me on an hourly basis with ideas for decorations and all this crazy stuff. And while I appreciate all of it, I can't seem to get into it right now. We have our hands full with some pretty serious stuff. And I just keep thinking 'what if something happens to one of us?' I don't want to wait any longer than we have to just for the sake of pleasing everyone else with a fancy wedding. I just want to marry you, and I was thinking of seeing if the Radiant fae would perform a small, simple ceremony in The Lucent for us. We can still have the big shindig for everyone else once things calm down, and we can keep it a secret until then, but I just want to be your wife already…make things official."

Aiden was smiling at me as I talked, and could barely wait until I finished before giving me his thoughts. "I think that sounds wonderful, darling. Though we will need someone to sign off on a marriage certificate for us, I can have my lawyer do that. I want to make sure everything is legal paperwork wise in case anything should happen to me, so you can take charge of my money and properties. I just want you to be happy, I don't care where or how we do it, as long as I can call you my wife at the end of the day," he said as he caressed the back of my head.

"I'll talk to Dreamer then before she leaves. I'm not sure when we'll find the time to get away for a few hours but I hope we can do it soon. I love you, thanks for being so understanding and so supportive." I wrapped my arms around my soon to be husband and kissed his cheek. I never knew what could happen from one moment to the next in this new world I had become a part of. I hoped that one day everything would settle down, and Aiden and I could go back to living that peaceful, simple life he spoke about. But for now we had huge problems, and I wanted to be united with Aiden in every way possible.

He returned the hug, wrapping his strong comforting arms around me. "I love you too, darling."

We ended up just lounging around on the big comfortable bed for twenty minutes, snuggling in each other's embrace. I had no idea how long the interrogation would take, but the Divine Assassins knew where the garbage incinerator was, and Aiden gave them instructions to clean up when they had finished.

Lost in thought, we both lay there in silence together. Without knowing how much time had passed, we both got startled back into reality when we heard soft humming coming from the corner of the room. I recognized Alina's sad song immediately. I was relieved we were able to get in contact with her while we were here.

She sat crouched in the corner, humming to herself, and running her fingers through her long hair. She looked the same as always, filmy and transparent, wearing an old fashioned nightgown. Her behavior was usually erratic, and she wasn't always coherent when we saw her. Unsure if it was a side effect of being a ghost, or if something happened to her while she was alive that mentally damaged her, we didn't always get what we needed out of her.

I sat up slowly, and Aiden did the same. Very softly I spoke a greeting to her. "Hello, Alina."

She didn't acknowledge me at all, just continued to stare into space combing her hair. I tried again, "Alina, do you remember us? It's me, Skyy…and Aiden, who owns the castle now."

Without looking at us, she replied in her hushed whisper of a voice, "Of course I remember you. I am dead, not a dimwit." Wow…ok then. Apparently Alina was having a bad day.

Figuring that we shouldn't waste any time with her, I got to the point. "Alina listen, I know we have already asked so much of you, and we all greatly appreciate the help you've given to us. But I'd like to ask another favor. If there is any possible way you can find out where Bathory's other castle or places of residence might be? We've learned some frightening news about her, and we need to search her properties, so that other girls don't suffer the same fate and get trapped by her black magic." I hoped using the ghosts being trapped angle would encourage her to help.

She didn't reply for quite some time. I let it all sink in without pushing her, knowing that she had heard me. Alina tugged on the arms of her nightgown angrily, and began lightly punching the wall. After about five minutes of this, she finally looked at us. I preferred when she didn't look at us, because the otherworldly stare went right through to my core. "There are many spirits I can contact. Many that were released still wander this area. I will see if I can get you the information you need, so no others suffer."

Before I could even say thank you, she was gone. Aiden and I just looked at each other, both feeling uneasy after her visit, but relieved at the same time that we could possibly find the locations of Bathory's other homes. We had no idea what the phylacteries might look like, but if we could find and destroy even one of them it would be a start. Knowing if we killed Bathory and that she could still be resurrected was something I never wanted to face.

Aiden and I stood up and stretched, and he made me a mug of blood from the stash in the mini-fridge hidden in the closet. We had no reason to continue lounging around, and decided to go see what the others were up to. Grandpa, Ridley, and two of the Divine Assassins were in the library, but the others were nowhere to be found. "Dreamer and the fae haven't left yet, have they?" I asked hoping they were still around.

Grandpa shook his head no, while popping a piece of gum into his mouth. "They are just finishing up now. Shouldn't be too much longer. The dark fae broke, Bathory has been in The Gloom, but also in The Umbra. We obviously won't go into The Umbra, but we're working on getting a team ready to enter The Gloom. Solara has also agreed to send some of her fae in with us."

"That's great news. I am glad someone was finally able to get the dark fae to talk. Is this something you're going to want my help on, or should we stay on the trail in London?"

"You and Ridley are going to stay on in London. I think you're on to something huge there, and if this other vampire is somehow connected to Bathory then maybe we will have better luck catching him and getting him to talk. Just keep in touch, and we'll do the same. Are you holding up alright, my dear?" The Divine Assassin in him relaxed as he inquired about my wellbeing as a grandfather.

I nodded, but kept my secret to myself about the run-in with Jack the Ripper and the dead woman. If Ridley thought it was a good idea to keep it between us then I was alright with that. I just hoped it would never come out, because the two of us were already in enough trouble with the Order that we didn't need to be caught lying and covering up evidence on top of everything else.

"I'm adjusting well. Each day is easier for me. Keeping my mind active and busy is certainly helping me as well, now that I am not trapped inside a room 24-7." I smiled at him to add some reassurance behind my statement, though I am not sure if it was more for me or for him. Truth was, I was thinking about blood just about every five seconds.

Grandpa nodded, buying it. "Good, I am glad to hear it. Just let me know if there is anything we can do to help you out." I thanked him and gave him a quick hug.

"Also, while you guys were with the dark fae, Aiden and I got in touch with Alina upstairs. She agreed to look around and see if she can get any information out of some of those ghosts who we released from the book."

A smile crept on Grandpa's face at hearing the news. "Good, good. The sooner we can figure out where those phylacteries are the better. All of this will be for nothing if we can't."

Dreamer and the fae came back into the library, smiling and cheerful as if they hadn't just melted the brains of some dark fae. There was some serious hatred between the two races. The dark fae had been kidnapping Radiant fae for Bathory's experiments for centuries. Not to mention they were the true definition of light vs. dark. The dark fae sought out to ruin and destroy anything that nature created and were cruel by nature, while the Radiant fae were the complete opposite.

Once they had relayed all of their information to Grandpa, I asked Dreamer if we could have a word in private with her. I took the little fae out to the gardens on the castle grounds. They were gorgeous and I figured she could use the uplifting surroundings after what she just had to do in the cellar.

We sat on a stone bench facing a small fountain. I wasn't sure if me asking this of them was overstepping my boundaries or not, but I thought there was no harm in trying. "I know that this might be too much to ask of you Dreamer, and it'll be perfectly fine to say no. But Aiden and I were wanting to get married really soon, and in private without the big wedding my soon to be mother-in-law was planning with or without my help. We can't think of anywhere more beautiful than The Lucent, and were wondering if you'd let us do it there?"

Before I was even done asking her, she was bouncing up and down on the bench excitedly and her mouth formed into a huge O. The second I was done speaking she blurted out her answer all in one fast sentence. "Yes yes yes, I am sure it would be fine!" She took my hands into her tiny child-like hands. "I'll ask Solara right away, how exciting!"

She began to get up but before she flew away I grabbed her arm. "Remember, this is a secret for now. Aiden and I don't want anyone else to know. We'll have a real ceremony with all of our family when time allows, but for now please keep this quiet."

Dreamer nodded her head, smiling at me. She was gone in a flash, and I didn't even make it thirty feet before she and Solara appeared again before me. They transformed out of their tiny light form to their humanoid form. Though Solara was more mature than Dreamer, being an elder and having responsibility within the race, she was still just as excited and animated as Dreamer at times.

"Dreamer just told me the news. We'd be happy to bring you both back into The Lucent and perform a ceremony for you!" Her crystal necklace she wore was sparkling in the sun like diamonds, almost blinding me.

I didn't expect an answer that fast, but was thrilled to hear it. "Wow that was fast. I'll let Aiden know and we can plan from there. As I am sure you both know, things are a little hectic around here, but we'd like to try to find the time as soon as possible. Do you need a certain amount of time to prepare, or can we do it anytime?"

Solara was waving her hands about, dismissing my question about planning. "Oh anytime, anytime is fine dear one! You will see that the Radiant fae love to celebrate just about any occasion we can find at a moment's notice. Just contact Dreamer when you're ready, and we'll have a great time!"

Once that was settled, I thanked them both and we joined the rest of the people in the library again. After a short summary of events and plans for our future missions, I opened a portal for Aiden and me and we followed Ridley back to London. Grandpa didn't know, or need to know, that Aiden was staying with us, but I didn't think he'd mind if he did.

Back in the luxurious hotel suite, we had a few hours to kill before sunset. I relayed the good news to Aiden about the fae agreeing to us marrying in The Lucent. Thankfully Dreamer and Solara weren't part of the Radiant fae who would be going on the mission to The Gloom. We decided to go out and browse wedding bands while it was still sunny outside.

Aiden still looked like a kid in a candy store every time we walked in the sunlight. For me, it wasn't a big deal because I was a newly turned vampire. But for him, he had been hiding in the dark for centuries. We strolled hand and hand down busy streets. After browsing through the selections at two small jewelry shops, we found a platinum matching set that was perfect for us. Aiden wanted to get my band engraved but the owner told him it'd take three to five business days. It's amazing what an extra thousand bucks can do for those time restrictions. The man had the bands ready and engraved within the hour.

We didn't need the certificate immediately to get married in The Lucent, but Aiden wanted to get the paperwork started for it so that we could file it as soon as possible. It was a lot easier to file in the United States than to deal with the paperwork and wait times in the United Kingdom, so as soon as we could get some time we would portal over to Massachusetts and file using our home address there. Aiden told me in order to keep things legal over the centuries we'd have to do this once every 50 or so years with new identities. I guessed he knew what he was talking about, since he'd been living the vampire lifestyle much longer than I had.

Being out in public and around humans so much today was hard on me, and once we were back to the hotel, I had five mugs of blood in a row. We were also bringing a blood pack with us for the night out on patrol. It couldn't be heated but it was better than nothing. I also was strapping on my enchanted sword that Lucius had loaned me a while back. It was now even more dangerous for me to wield it because I was a vampire. One nick from the silver pommel and I'd be paralyzed again. Aiden suggested I wear some leather gloves to protect my hands, and I took him up on that advice.

Just as we were about to leave to meet up with Logan, Ridley, and Keith, Aiden grabbed my hand gently and turned me towards him for a hug. I wrapped my arms around him, breathing in his scent. "Skyy, I don't want to sound like a parent scolding a child, but I just want to remind you not to try anything crazy tonight if we do encounter the murderer. We don't need you getting hurt."

I could tell that he didn't want to say it, but given my track record with not listening to what people tell me, he had every right to. I squeezed him tighter for a second to reassure him, "I promise I'll stick to the books tonight Aiden."

He kissed the top of my head and that was the end of it. We met the others and headed to the Underground towards our destination, like five normal, everyday citizens. When we reached the Argyle Square area, it was just after nine. We took a quick peek at the alley where the murder had taken place. I reluctantly glanced down it with the others, shame and guilt plastered all over my face. Ridley noticed and gave me a pat on the back.

Everything in the area looked untouched and normal. Since it was a mix of buildings converted into hotels, residences, and businesses, we tried to blend in as best we could without making it obvious we were up to something or loitering. Aiden and I could hear things from a good distance away, but the Divine Assassins had to rely on human hearing. Once it got past eleven we were pretty much the only people in the area, and we stuck out like a sore thumb because there were five of us. Ridley suggested that we use an invisibility spell to cloak us.

After that was in place, we could wander around as much as we liked, and nobody could see us. Things stayed pretty quiet all night. I had to sip from my blood pack several times, and Aiden was right – it was disgusting when it wasn't heated.

Just after three in the morning we heard some muffled screams, a female struggling. Aiden and I both heard it immediately, and with a hand gesture we alerted the others. We bolted in the direction of the noise. Not sure if I should be shocked, or if I was expecting it, we saw the vampire in the same exact location as last time. He couldn't see us because we had the invisibility spell on still. I couldn't believe the balls on this guy.

Trying to be as quiet as we could, we hopped over the first small brick wall that was separating the buildings in the alley. He was instantly alerted, dropping the now limp female on the ground looking in our direction. Though he couldn't see us I was sure he could hear us breathing and hear our movements. A moment went by where I could tell he was thinking about whether he should bolt or stay.

Ridley was removing a crossbow and loading it with silver arrows as we moved closer. We couldn't use guns because they would be too noisy, and we couldn't use the silver dust anymore because Aiden and I were there and would be affected by it as well. I removed my enchanted fire sword from its sheath. It didn't take but a few split seconds, but the vampire knew something was wrong and he took off in a flash.

"Go!" I said to Aiden and we were both off like lightning bolts in pursuit after him. There was no way Ridley and the others could keep up on foot, but I glanced back and saw

Logan and Ridley trying, while Keith stayed behind to see if the victim was alright.

Aiden was obviously much faster than I was, and he was teleporting short distances ahead of me every now and then. At some point our invisibility spell wore off. I wasn't sure if they had dropped it or if we lost it because we had left Ridley in the dust a while back. Aiden didn't get too far ahead of me at any time, which I appreciated but I also knew he was the only one of us who would have had a chance at catching the vampire.

I decided to shout out to him, "If you've still got his trail, just go! Chase him!" One second I was running, trying to keep pace with Aiden, and the next second I was clotheslined and knocked on my ass. I was back on my feet in moments, and though the area was dark I could see the vampire plain as day with my enhanced vision. Aiden saw it too, and turned around but he was too late. The vampire had a gigantic knife in his hands and he ran it across my throat so quickly I didn't even have time to process what had happened. In the blink of an eye he was gone, without uttering a word.

I felt warmth pouring out of my neck and down onto my chest through my shirt. I knew I was gushing blood. Moments later the pain kicked in, and I was grasping my throat desperate to try to stop the bleeding. Aiden came to my side instead of chasing the vampire, which I expected. I couldn't talk but if I could have I would have yelled at him to follow him instead of stopping for me. Once I realized that this wouldn't kill me, even if I lost a lot of blood, I started to calm down.

Aiden had taken his shirt off and tied it around my neck to try to stop the bleeding. "Don't worry Skyy. I know it hurts like hell but you won't die." Thankfully nobody was out on the streets at this hour, and we weren't near any buildings.

Ridley and Logan caught up to us, and Aiden informed them of what happened. I could tell Ridley was pissed off that we once again missed the killer, but he was more concerned about me than that at the moment. "Well, the idiot was stupid enough, or egotistical enough, to come back to the same spot again. Chances are we'll get another shot at him and the third time will be the charm. Aiden, I hate to ask you this but the victim he grabbed wasn't harmed. Keith subdued her to keep her from screaming, but if you could mind whammy her that would be fantastic. We can portal Skyy out of here back to the hotel room if you're alright with that."

Knowing that Aiden didn't want to leave my side, I reached out for his hand and have him a reassuring pat to let him know I was ok with it. He bent over and picked up my enchanted sword for me that had fallen out of my hands when I was clotheslined, and put it back in the sheath on my belt. "I'll be back at the hotel right behind you milady." He kissed the top of my head and then flashed out of my sight.

Ridley and Logan gently lifted me to my feet, each taking my weight under one of their arms. "I'm going to move us over to that area there behind the big tree to portal us out of here, just to be safe. I know it hurts Skyy, just hang in there."

We hobbled along to the tree, and then we portaled out of the area back to my hotel suite. True to his word, Aiden wasn't far behind. The men moved me to the couch after putting down a few towels. The shirt that Aiden had wrapped around my neck had long been soaked through with blood.

I was starting to crave human blood, and not in a good way. I could hear the heartbeat and pulse of all three of the humans in the room, and it was calling to me. Tempting me. Reaching out to me like a sirens call. My body began to tremble and shake, but thankfully Aiden knew what to do. He straddled me and held me down, informing Ridley that he needed to get some blood heated for me.

"Logan, Keith…you two are better off going back to your rooms. If we need you I'll send Ridley, but you being here is too much of a temptation for Skyy. She's lost a lot of blood and her instincts are kicking in, telling her body to get it by any means possible." He didn't have to tell them twice, they both left in a hurry leaving us alone with Ridley.

I wanted Aiden off me, and I was getting pissed off. I couldn't talk, all I wanted to do was rip into a human. My body was convulsing by now, and he tried to keep me as still as possible. "Skyy, honey. Try to stay as still as possible. We don't want you to lose any more blood than you need to."

He was only doing what was best for me, but I was deep into my bloodlust. Ridley came with the blood, and Aiden informed him to continue to heat more of it and keep bringing it. He had me sit up a little and put the cup to my mouth. I drank it down quickly, but it hurt like hell. The asshole vampire had severed muscles and tendons in my neck, and I wouldn't be surprised if the blood was just flowing right back out as I drank.

Ridley kept bringing the blood, and Aiden kept feeding it to me. It seemed like hours had passed but I did finally start to feel better. The wound was closing up, and it was a very strange feeling. It itched like crazy, but Aiden held my hands away from it. The convulsions stopped, and I was starting to feel like my old self again.

Once Aiden was confident that I wasn't going to tear into Ridley's jugular vein, he finally got off of me and helped me sit up on the couch. I wanted to talk so bad, but I still wasn't able to. The wound had sealed and stopped bleeding but it was still very painful.

Aiden and Ridley didn't say much of anything, and at some point one of them turned on the television. I was itching to know if they got the victim out of there, and if she was ok. And I was madder than hell and wanted revenge on the vampire now more than ever.

Eventually I was able to speak, though it was a whisper. By now it was almost midafternoon the next day. I hoped that I'd be ready to head back out again tonight with the team. The first thing out of my mouth was, "Is the woman alright? Did you guys get her to safety?"

Aiden smiled at me. "Yes, she is safe. He didn't have a chance to harm her, other than a few bruises. Nothing that won't heal. I altered her mind, and for good measure placed the idea in her head that she shouldn't come back to the area, and that she should look for a new line of work."

Ridley, who was sitting in the big comfy chair again, chimed in. "We know for certain now that he is targeting prostitutes, which fits in with the Jack the Ripper theory perfectly."

I nodded and whispered out, "And the idiot was dumb enough to come back to the same spot. I think we should place invisibility on us and camp out in the alley next time...already be in place without moving or making noise. Maybe then we'll be able to catch him."

"While that is a good idea, you know that he would hear our hearts and breathing, even if we were invisible. That would notify him and he'd take off again," Aiden reminded me.

"Well, the Divine Assassins do have traps we can set in place to catch them. Now that we know where he will be and that he'll be coming back. We can set a spell in the alley that will paralyze him," Ridley offered.

"Yes, not a bad idea since we can place it there during daylight. I am fairly certain this vampire doesn't venture out in the day," Aiden replied.

"Well, who knows what he is capable of, given that he is a close ally to Bathory. Maybe he can walk around in the sun," I said grimly.

Aiden nodded. "He is certainly faster and stronger than an average vampire."

"We never had issues catching or cleaning up vampires in the past. Most of them were minions though. Bathory was the first real threat we have encountered in the Divine Assassins. And while we love having you along with us, not being able to use our silver dust makes us slightly weaker," Ridley said as he stood up.

"What is our next step then?" I asked. I needed more blood, and made my way over to grab a glass.

"I need to check in with headquarters and report this to them. And you need to get your energy back, so you're staying put for tonight at least. I'll let you know what we decide once I talk to everyone." Ridley said his goodbyes, and I thanked him for all of his help.

Once he was gone though, I drank two more glasses and then sat down to talk about the situation with Aiden. "I don't think sitting it out tonight is a good idea. There is a strong chance he'll be back there again, and without us I fear they might not have any chance at all at catching him."

"I know you're anxious to help Skyy, but you do need to rest. An injury this major, while it does heal, takes a lot out of us. I was actually going to suggest seeing if Lucius could come out and help us. I think we can use all hands on deck for this, Divine Assassins or not."

I didn't like being told to sit in a time out, but I was going to have to learn to trust Aiden and listen to what he suggested. He knew better than I did, and I didn't' want to jeopardize the operation because I was still weak.

"Doesn't sound like a bad idea, especially with what we are up against. I can see if Christian can come out as well."

Aiden nodded as he reached in his back pocket to pull his phone out. "Alright, I shall call Lucius and you can give Christian a shout. But you should know where he goes, Mother goes too. You'll have to be subjected to more wedding planning," Aiden said with a grin.

I chuckled. "Whatever it takes to catch this asshole. I can put up with wedding planning, as long as it means they'll come and help us. I'm not sure if I should ask Ridley's permission or not, what do you think?"

Aiden shrugged. "I think if we want to invite some of our friends along to help that he wouldn't mind. Headquarters might, but they don't need to know. From what I know of Ridley, he is a lot like you – doesn't like to follow the rules. But he does it for the right reasons most of the time," he said as he winked at me.

I threw a small throw pillow off the couch at his head, which he grabbed with lightning reflexes. He stuck his tongue out at me, which made me laugh. "I'll call Christian. I'll go into the bedroom so you can call Lucius."

It wasn't a shock that both of them agreed to come with no hesitation. And as we thought, Fiona would be coming along as well. We didn't have much time until it got dark, so I called Ridley over to see if he'd mind grabbing them via portal since I was still recovering. He agreed that headquarters didn't need to know, and thought it was an awesome idea.

As an added bonus, I asked them if they could bring Cupcake from Lucius' villa for the night, since I'd be staying in by myself. I missed her something terrible, and being with her would cheer me up. The Divine Assassins went to fetch the vampires and Cupcake, and we were all assembled in the living room of my suite within the hour.

After greetings and hugs were exchanged, Ridley filled them in on the happenings so far. Just having Lucius here with us made me feel loads safer already. His giant form was comforting, and he and Aiden together were a force to be reckoned with. Fiona was no joke either, and I knew that Christian was doing a hell of a lot better with his transformation than I was.

Aiden ordered yet another delivery of blood for me, and I assured them all I was going to stay put and follow orders. Cupcake and I would relax in the room and watch some television. I visited with Fiona while the men talked, and around nine that night the crew got suited up to go. Kissing Aiden, I wished them all luck, and watched them filter out the door.

Cupcake jumped in my lap to settle in for a movie marathon. I did feel a lot weaker than usual, and still had some considerable pain where my throat was slit. I felt tired and lethargic. I had my phone with me in case they needed me for anything, but without realizing it I drifted off to sleep…

Chapter 10

Jackson Ripleigh stormed through the front door of his house, almost ripping it off its hinges as he entered. He was enraged beyond control. This was the second time he was interrupted. He wasn't having a good week. With news of Bathory coming to pay him a visit and now this, he was about to snap.

He had no idea who the people were that were on his trail. Two of them were vampires, of that he was certain. He rushed down into his basement, and began to trash it in anger. He was throwing things across the room, then flipped a table over and all of its contents flew in different directions. Picking up an old picture frame, he tossed it against the wall, watching the glass shatter into a million pieces. Nothing would quench his rage but killing. He had to kill, and it had to be soon.

Jackson pulled out the large hunting knife that he used to slit the throat of the female vampire. Her blood was all over it, not dried. He could use this to track her, using a simple sorcery spell that Bathory had shown him years ago. He'd find her, and then he'd find the rest of these pests. Once they were dealt with, he could finally get back to business as usual. Jack did not like his plans to be interrupted. He was a creature of habit, and of repetition. If he couldn't kill in that location, then bad...very bad things would happen.

Within the hour he had her location. She was residing at the Royal Horseguards hotel. All he had to do now was wait until the sun set. Judging by her blood, and what he saw, she was a fledgling...a new weak vampire who would be easy to capture. The hard part was waiting for the right time when she was separated from the bunch. The other vampire was much older and very powerful.

Later that night, he showered and put on one of his best suits. Combing his hair and making sure every piece was in place, he once again packed his bag of knives and was off into the night to pay a visit to the meddling vampire.

Chapter 11

I woke up to Cupcake barking. She had jumped off my lap and was at the door growling at something. Still groggy and weak, I got up to see what was going on. I wasn't prepared for the door to open suddenly.

I was once again knocked on my ass as a man shoved his way into my room. I instantly recognized him as the murdering vampire. And I was all alone. My phone was way across the room on the couch where I had been sleeping. However, by pure luck, my enchanted sword was laying on a small table right by the door.

Getting back up on my feet almost instantly, I barely had time to act before the vampire lunged on me. He was well dressed in a suit, which I hoped might limit his mobility. Cupcake was tearing into his leg, but he didn't even blink an eye at it, because he was fully focused on me.

His hazel eyes were reflecting and glowing, and there was nothing but hatred on his face. I pitied the poor women who he murdered, that this horrifying monster was the last thing they would ever see. "So, we meet again. But this time, on my terms," he said. His voice was smooth and deep, giving me chills up and down my spine.

I had to get my hands on my sword, a few small steps to my left and I'd be in range to grab it. "Who are you, and why are you following me?" he asked me. When he spoke I could see all his teeth perfectly, including his vampire incisors. He wouldn't be a bad looking man, if his face wasn't twisted with hate and rage.

Boldly defying him, I answered his question, refusing to show him that I was scared. I had been in a similar situation before, looking into the terrifying face of Elizabeth Bathory and if I could live to tell that story, I was sure I could stand strong in the face of this new enemy.

"We're the Divine Assassins. Hasn't Bathory told you about us?" We were facing off, head to head now in my suite. If he knew who we were, his face didn't give any hint of it.

"How do you know Bathory?" was his next question. He shook his leg to get Cupcake off of him, never breaking eye contact with me. She was right back on him in seconds.

"We're looking for her, and we ran into you instead. You know her, correct?"

His eyes narrowed down to slits. I could almost hear the wheels turning in his head. He wondered how the hell we knew about his relationship with Bathory. And he was probably wondering how we knew who he was.

"Who I associate with is none of your business. You won't be a problem after tonight." Jack wouldn't break. But he did give me the moment I was looking for to lunge for my sword. He bent down to pick up Cupcake, and in that instant I dashed for the sword unsheathing it in one quick movement.

The bad part was that he was holding my sweet dog up by her neck, about to crush her. This changed things a bit. "Please! Please don't hurt her. I'll answer your questions, or do anything you want. Just please put her down," I begged him.

Cupcake was dangling in the air, struggling against his large hand. He threw her across the room and she hit the wall, sliding down it yelping loudly. The very next moment, someone knocked on the door, and didn't wait for an answer before opening it. Now I had two vampires standing in my doorway.

The new one was a young man, very handsome. He didn't so much as look at me, but he addressed Jack. "You'll need to sit this one out, Ripleigh. Bathory has arrived, and you're being summoned."

I was beyond confused now. "Who the fuck are you?" I asked.

He looked at me, as if I were an insignificant piece of trash. "Who the fuck are you? Who I am is none of your business, slut." How dare he call me a slut! Did he think I was one of Jack's marks?

Before I could reply, Jack spoke up. "I don't answer to her beck and call, and I am sick of you and your men following me. Tell her to fuck off, and I'll see her when I see her."

The other vampire didn't like that answer. He tried to take Jack by the arm, but he shook him off. They struggled for a moment, and I took that as a cue to strike at him. They were moving so fast, that the slash with my sword that should have removed his arm only nicked his fingers, chopping off his pinky and ring finger.

Jack screamed out in rage, and I was certain that anyone on this floor, or on either of the floors above or below us would be alerted. The other vampire put something on his hand that covered his fingers, and grabbed Jack around the base of the back of his neck.

Moving him towards the door, he said, "Let's go. Now." Whatever it was that he put on his hand tamed Jack, and he stopped fighting. The vampire walked him out of the room, shutting the door behind him without as much as a glance back at me.

What in the fuck had just happened?! My heart was racing, and I didn't know what to do first. Not sure which of the vampires had done it, the door to my hotel room was still intact, but the knob on it was busted so it wouldn't lock.

Cupcake was whining on the floor in the same spot that she had landed in. I needed to get to her to make sure she was alright, but first I needed to call the guys and get them back here. Running to my phone I dialed Ridley with trembling hands.

Before he could even answer I was speaking. "Get back here, now! All of you! The murderer was just in my room!"

"Stand by," was his reply before he hung up. Within three minutes, the men started to portal into the suite. Ridley and Aiden came first, followed by Logan and Lucius, and Fiona and Keith. Logan went back for Christian after that.

I was sitting on the floor cradling Cupcake. Her neck seemed to be fine, and not broken because she was moving it around looking at everyone. She couldn't stand though, and I assumed she had at least one broken leg. Bless her little heart, she was wagging her tail excited to see everyone.

Aiden rushed over to us, and Ridley saw the blood and the two fingers lying on the floor. "What's this?" he asked, pointing to the fingers.

"Those are Jack the Rippers fingers. I cut them off with my sword. You guys won't believe what just happened here," I said.

Aiden made sure that I was alright, and before he let me relay the story he wanted to see to Cupcake. "First things first. We need to find a twenty-four hour vet and see to it that Cupcake is alright."

Fiona nodded her head, and without being told she started looking up numbers. "There is an emergency vet not too far from here that is open all hours. Christian and I can take her there if you're fine with that Skyy?"

As much as I wanted to be by her side, I nodded my head. Christian would take just as good care of her as I would. He loved Cupcake like she was his own. I needed to stay behind and tell the others what had just gone down.

I kissed Cupcake on top of her head, and gently passed her over into Christian's arms. "That's fine with me Fiona. Thank you for offering. Call me as soon as you know anything."

Christian gave me a sideways hug with his free arm. "I'll make sure that she is comfortable. I'm sure she'll be fine, we'll let you know what the doc says."

I watched the two of them leave with tears in my eyes. Wiping them away, I sat down to tell the men what had happened. Lucius went to the fridge to make me a cup of blood, sensing that I needed it.

He handed it to me, and pat me on the back. "Drink this, love. You need it." I smiled at him and thanked him. While I drank my blood, Logan went into the hallway to clean up the blood that had dripped out of Jack's hand. Moments after he shut the door, someone knocked on it. All the men were alert and ready in case it was one of the bad guys. Everyone hid behind the door except Lucius, who opened it casually, smiling as if nothing was amiss.

It was one of the front desk staff. "We had a complaint of yelling coming from the room. Just wanted to make sure that everything was fine in here."

Lucius assured the man that everything was fine. I knew he had mind whammied him as well, and he left without any issue. Once that was over I was finally able to tell them the crazy event that had occurred.

They all listened, in shock. When I was finished, Ridley spoke first. "So let me get this straight. Jack came here to murder you, or kidnap you? And then one of Bathory's vampires came to get him, because Bathory is in town?"

I nodded. "Yes, that is what I got out of it. It was totally weird. I think Bathory's vampire thought I was one of Jack's prostitutes that he was about to murder. It seemed like he was used to following him and cleaning up after him. And he called him by the name of Ripleigh."

Everyone sat in silence for a minute, mulling over the information. Ridley spoke again. "I have to get this to headquarters. This is huge, and if Bathory is here in London now, we need to get a larger team assembled immediately."

"I agree. And, I am not sure how much help it might be, but maybe we can run those fingers through the databases and see if we can find a match?" I offered.

"What has me uneasy, is how he located Skyy to begin with," Lucius said. "It's clear that we need to move locations as soon as we can, because she isn't safe here. None of us are if Bathory is back in town."

"I was thinking the same thing," Aiden replied.

"Let's start packing up, and we can move the whole team to my villa in Italy to come up with a plan. Mr. Huntington is welcome to portal over as well. We'll wait for Fiona and Christian to get back with Cupcake and then we'll all move out." Lucius wasn't asking for permission from anyone, he was telling them. And Ridley didn't challenge it at all.

"We'll go get our bags packed from our rooms then. Shouldn't take but a few minutes," he said as he, Logan, and Keith left.

Aiden started to pack up all of our things as well. Lucius came over to me, inspecting me. He saw the almost fully healed wound on my neck. Tracing it softly with his finger, he smiled at me. "We've got to keep you out of trouble, dear Skyy. You sure have a knack at getting into it though, I'll give you that."

I laughed, replying, "It sure didn't feel good. I guess trouble just follows me no matter where I go."

"Indeed. We need to do a better job of keeping you in one piece." With that, Lucius went over to the fingers that were still lying on the floor. He took a handkerchief out of his back pocket and picked them up. I guessed after watching him behead vampires without batting an eye that picking up some fingers was child's play.

Aiden had us packed up in record time, and Ridley and the others were back in the room shortly after that. Christian called about thirty minutes later.

"Hey Skyy. Good news, Cupcake is going to be just fine. No internal injuries just a broken front leg. The doc is getting her fixed up now, we should be back there within the hour."

Relief flooded me and I could breathe easier. "Thank God! It could have been much worse. Give her a kiss from mommy, and we'll see you guys soon."

"Will do," he said and we hung up.

Once Fiona and Christian returned with Cupcake, we sent Ridley down to the front desk with Lucius to check out. The rest of us got portaled over to the villa in Italy from the suite. It was still the middle of the night, and none of the humans who lived and worked on Lucius' grounds were awake thankfully.

I set Cupcake down on the floor. She was softly whining and I could tell she hated the cast they had put on her front leg. Christian instantly picked her back up, cuddling her close to him. "It's ok sweetheart, you don't have to walk if you don't want to baby girl," he said talking to her in his doggie voice. She licked the tip of his nose in thanks.

Lucius, Ridley and my grandpa all arrived shortly after we did. He brought two of his Divine Assassins with him. Lucius handed him the fingers after we filled them in on the story so far.

Grandpa was in his typical civilian attire – a Hawaiian shirt and some cargo shorts. We must have woken him up. "We'll run these fingers through the database back at the lab right away. I'll get a team assembled at once. Until then be on full alert, with the assumption that Bathory is in London somewhere."

There wasn't much we could do in the meantime. Grandpa and his men left shortly after they arrived, taking the fingers with them. We had to wait for the results, and hope that they put us on the right track.

Logan and Keith went with Grandpa, but Ridley stayed behind with us vampires. We stayed on alert even though we were now in another country. With Bathory, you never know what could happen.

It didn't look like our wedding in The Lucent was going to take place anytime soon either.

Chapter 12

Jackson was beyond pissed at the vampire using sorcery to control him yet again. For the millionth time, he wished he had never met Bathory. She was just too strong and powerful to defy. Her vampire led him back to his house, and he could do nothing buy comply.

Once they were inside, he noticed that she had several other vampires with her, guarding the doors and windows of the house, presumably from intruders, and to keep Jack inside. The vampire released his grip with the magical glove, and without a word gave him a look that told him he better behave. What other choice did he have really? He clenched his fists in a tight ball, a habit of his that gave away his level of anger.

Bathory was in his living room, sprawled out on one of the couches. There were five dark fae with her as well, which he wasn't happy about. He didn't like them at all, and certainly didn't like them being in his house. Something seemed different about Bathory, she didn't have her usual glow and air of confidence…it was subtle but he picked up on it.

Through gritted teeth he addressed her. "To what do I owe this pleasure?" The sarcasm was dripping off of every word.

Bathory barely even looked at him, as if she were bored out of her mind. "Hello to you too, Jack. Hope you don't mind me dropping in last minute."

Jack's temper rose to a boiling point. He picked up a crystal vase that was on an end table and threw it across the room to hit the wall just above Bathory's head. Glass shards rained down on her, but she didn't bat an eye. "Would you mind explaining to me what the fucking Divine Assassins are doing on my trail? What kind of shit have you wrapped me up in, Elizabeth? You promised me that my identity would be safe."

The dark fae guards that were with Bathory all moved towards him, but she gave a flick of her hand to dismiss them from grabbing Jack. One of the females was missing her left arm, he'd seen her before…she was usually Bathory's personal guard. Gracefully and deliberately slow, Bathory lowered her legs off of the couch and placed them on the floor, brushing off the glass from her body. She was dressed in a simple black ensemble of slacks and a turtleneck sweater, which blended right in with her silky jet black hair.

"It's ok Valentina, Jack here is just having another of his temper tantrums," she said as she stood up. The dark fae moved back to her previous position without a word. "I'll tell you what the fucking Divine Assassins are doing on your trail. They are after me. They destroyed my book, killed almost all of my vampires, and almost killed me." Jack could see the anger and impatience spreading across her face. And he could also see a hint of fear, which was something he had never seen on her beautiful face. Her eyes were beginning to change colors too, another sign that she was getting pissed.

Of all the reasons he could think of for Bathory paying him a visit, this was the last thing that he would have suspected. "They finally figured out the ritual then?" he asked, secretly smiling inside. Without her book, she had limited power…something he had been waiting years for.

She nodded once to answer his question. "I've been hiding in The Gloom.. I thought I would be safe here, but I see that isn't the case now. You've been fucking around again, getting yourself into trouble which has made it into the news. You never learn, do you Jack?"

"What I do is my business!" he shouted at the top of his lungs. His eyes were glowing on fire with rage, and he knew he needed to calm down before he did something stupid that could cost him his life. He'd find a way to challenge Bathory soon, but he couldn't take on her and all of her bodyguards at the same time. "I have told you to leave me the hell alone, you insist on meddling in my affairs!"

She moved closer to him, her face just inches from his. Her eyes were two black orbs now, and she narrowed them to slits of anger. "And I have told you that you need to be more careful, you dolt. You never learn, you have some sick obsession with being one step ahead of the law. They will catch you Jack. Things aren't like they were in the 1800s. Life has evolved, there is technology and cameras now. Everybody has a phone or device to film you or snap a photo of you, traffic lights have cameras, most stores and banks have cameras. You'll get caught. Police are much smarter, there are forensics. It's just a matter of time."

He knew she had a point, but reason was never something that Jack succumbed to. Killing for him was ritualistic, it had to be in the same locations because they meant something to him. He was obsessive compulsive about who he killed, and where it happened. And he craved the spotlight, he wanted his murders to be seen and admired. In his mind, getting caught just wasn't going to happen.

Bathory spoke again, "Do they know where you live?"

Jack was pacing the room in anger. "I don't know what they know, Elizabeth! I didn't know they even knew I existed until about an hour ago. How did they find out about me?" he asked again.

Bathory was in the hot seat now. She failed on so many different levels. How could she criticize Jack for his shortcomings, when she had been just as cocky as he was? She never thought that her book would be destroyed, and she left personal things all over her castle that they surely had raided. "I don't know Jack. They may have found our letters in my castle after I left. Though they were vague, I suppose they could have put two and two together. This is another reason I told you that lingering in the same location was a bad idea," she said, trying to place more blame on Jack.

Arguing with Bathory wouldn't get Jackson anywhere, he knew this from past encounters with her. He wanted her out of his house as soon as possible. "So what now? And how long will you be here?" he asked, not so subtly.

This just pissed her off even more. Jack thought it was funny to watch her act cool and collected because he knew just how easy it was to get her temper to rise. Like taking candy from a baby. "I suppose if they are on your trail now, neither of us should linger here."

"They won't find this house. There is no record of me in any database, no way for them to link it to me. I'm not going anywhere…as for you, please feel free to leave at any time," he said to her while waving his hand towards the door.

"What if they followed you? Or used a tracking spell? The Divine Assassins have plenty of ways to get things done." He could see the fear rising on her face again.

"I am sure they are long gone by now. They won't let whoever that girl is that they are protecting get into harm's way." Right after Jack made his statement, the vampire who had brought him back from the hotel chimed in that he was sure nobody had followed them.

But the look on Bathory's face was of shock. "What do you mean 'whoever that girl is that they are protecting'?"

Jack shrugged it off, not having any idea it was the same group of people who she faced off with. "I don't know who she is. Some redheaded fledgling vampire. Young, pretty, with a small army of vampires and Divine Assassins. They were on my trail, tried to catch me two times. I tracked her back to the hotel they were staying in. My little rumble with her resulted in this," Jack held his hand up, wiggling his fingers to emphasize the missing ones. "And I'd like to go feed before the sun comes up so I can heal, so how much longer is this conversation going to go on for?"

Bathory looked panicked though. "You're sure she was a vampire? Did she have long, red hair?"

Jack rolled his eyes. "Yes, I am sure she was a vampire. Brand new. And yes, she had very long hair. And a sword made of fire that burns like hell," he said as he cradled his injured hand.

Bathory began talking very quickly in another language to the dark fae leader she called Valentina. The one-armed fae nodded and gathered the others around her. "Jack, listen to me. If you've never listened to a damn thing I have ever said before, you need to take this seriously. These people are a serious threat to both of us. I have little to no power right now, though I am slowly working on getting it back, it will take several years to get back to my previous level of sorcery. I can be killed, and very easily right now. They know you're here, who you are.

Please come with me to The Gloom. We'll be much safer there," she begged.

Jack laughed, "I'd sooner die than go running into hiding like a chicken! And certainly not with those…abominations," he said as he glanced over at her dark fae body guards.

Bathory shook her head. "And that is where you and I differ dear Jack. I have come to realize that self-preservation is more important than anything else. I am not ready to die, or give up. Power can be rebuilt, it just takes time. I want to live until the end of time, powerful, beautiful, and strong. Come with us Jackson, don't be stupid."

Jack wouldn't budge. "No…where you and I differ Elizabeth, is that you care for me and I don't give a shit about you. Just leave me be. You brought all this trouble to my doorstep, take it with you on your way out."

His words stung her more than she realized. She knew that he never cared for her as she did for him, but hearing it out loud hurt her. Had she deluded herself into thinking it was something more than it really was?

With tears in her eyes, and rage rising to the surface, Bathory moved closer to Jack once more. She placed her delicate, porcelain colored hand onto his chest. "I don't want this to be goodbye forever Jack. Please don't do anything stupid. I'll still have my men watching over you, and if you change your mind they'll know where to find me."

Jack grabbed her hand in his intact hand, and squeezed it so hard he could hear bones crushing. "Get. Out. Of. My. House," he said to her, with nothing but hatred.

He watched as her dark fae opened a portal to The Gloom, and she stepped into it. All but two of her vampires went in with her, and they exited the house shortly after she left.

And so two of the world's most egotistical and insane serial killers parted ways for the time being. Little did Bathory know that she hadn't just left the home of her ally, but another one of her enemies. Jack would get started immediately on a plan to take her down. He was sick and tired of her, and the last thing he needed was Elizabeth gaining her powers back and being a slave to her once more.

Chapter 13

The fingers didn't lead us to any results. There were no records of the fingerprints in any database. Which made sense, if the killer was older than the fingerprint system we use today. The UK didn't open its fingerprint bureau until 1901, and if we were dealing with Jack the Ripper, he would have been able to avoid being printed. He was smart, and while he loved his crime scenes to be in the spotlight, he wasn't stupid enough to leave prints behind. Even if he had, with no record of them, he was still safe.

So now we were back to square one. Since he had found me before, we had to assume he could do so again, even if we were out of the country for the time being. While this was bad news for me, it was also bad news for the killer. I wasn't going to be alone until the situation was resolved, so if he showed up again things might not work out so well for him.

Ridley talked to my grandfather and the Divine Assassins in charge about keeping the vampires on the case with us. Normally they wouldn't want anything to do with it, but since they had proved to be valuable in the past, they agreed that they could work with them again. Which was fortunate that they came to this agreement, because with or without permission my vampire family wasn't letting me out of their sight.

Grandpa had decided that we would all go back to London as soon as possible. They were arranging to rent a large house for the time being, big enough to house all of us in, instead of going back to a hotel. They also made sure it was not in a busy area, in case shit went down. The less witnesses the better.

Though I was sad to leave my dog behind, I knew now it was for the best until we could get all of this straightened out. I felt terrible that she got injured, but I knew Miss Abby would take fantastic care of her. It also warmed my heart to watch Cupcake play with Lucius' dogs. She loved being around them, and they all got along great.

After a short stay at the villa in Italy, the rental house was ready, and the team along with the vampires portaled back over to England. It was a huge three story house, with plenty of room. Aiden and I shared a room, Lucius roomed up with Ridley, Fiona and Christian took a small room on the first floor, and all of the Divine Assassins with us boarded up two or three to a room. We didn't want anyone to be alone if it was possible.

Unfortunately all the extra humans on the property had me struggling almost nonstop to keep my bloodlust in check. I was going through blood like crazy, and Aiden had to stop me once from racing out of the room to attack Logan. Thankfully he got me before I even left the room, and Logan was none the wiser. I knew that none of the Divine Assassins, with the exception of Ridley, really wanted me around. And the fact I rarely wore my special contacts to hide my purple eyes around the house freaked them out even more.

After we were settled in the rental house for a few days, Aiden, the vampires, and I were sitting in the living room watching TV. We all kept a close watch on the news, hoping that we wouldn't see another murder…but lo and behold "Jack" struck again.

"Shit!" I exclaimed as I turned the volume up. "Ridley!" I yelled out for him to come join us. He came flying downstairs, with Logan and Keith hot on his heels. The news anchor was at the crime scene, and of course we knew exactly where it was.

"Another murder has struck in London. The victim is unidentified at this time, and police are still on a manhunt to find the killer. It appears this murder could be linked to the others. Witnesses didn't report any kind of disturbances, and the body was found in the early hours before dawn."

The reporter continued on with more of the same. We sat and listened to every word, and once it was over we called a meeting. Although my grandfather was present, Ridley took the lead since he had the most information on the case.

"That is the exact location we have been hunting the killer. I knew that arrogant bastard would go back and try it again! With all of the clues and evidence I think that we would be smart to assume that he will move on to his next location. We need to get the Ripper murder files out again and see where he will strike next. Try to set up some kind of trap to nail this guy," he said as he ran his hands through his neatly combed hair. I could visibly tell he was frustrated.

I nodded my head and agreed with him. "I think you're right too. We may have just gotten lucky but I am pretty sure we're on to something here with Jack the Ripper. I just feel terrible that we couldn't have saved this new victim by catching him sooner." Sighing loudly, I sat back down on the couch.

Aiden had left the room and retrieved his laptop, and pulled up the information about the murder scenes, both the new ones, and the ones from the 1800s. We all gathered around as close as we could to see the screen.

"Some of his kills have been in new locations, but a couple of them have been in the same exact location as they were back in the 1800s," Aiden said. He pulled up the address for Annie Chapman's murder. "29 Hanbury Street, Whitechapel...I think we should definitely look into that location. We have enough resources that we can put men on several locations at once though."

My grandfather was getting visibly upset at Aiden's suggestions. He cleared his throat and tried to take command of the ship. "You let us worry about who is going to be stationed where. I want one vampire with each team, at the four locations left for the original murder scenes. We'll scout these locations out, see if they are even viable still."

Aiden looked at me and rolled his eyes, cracking a small smile at my grandfather's behavior. I almost laughed out loud but kept it under control. Grandpa tried to assign Aiden to a different team, putting me alone with Ridley, Logan and Keith. But Aiden would have nothing to do with it.

"Sir, all due respect...I know this is your operation, but you did ask for our help. And I don't think Skyy should be left alone without one of us vampires with her, for more reasons than one. I'll be with her, no matter what, so make whatever adjustments you need to. This isn't open for discussion." Aiden was standing up, in a non-confrontational stance. He had said it in a nice tone, but of course Grandpa had to find an issue with being told what to do by a vampire. After a couple of words back and forth, Aiden told him he was either with my team, or all of the vampires were leaving. That shut Grandpa up, even though I knew he was livid about it, he knew that the Divine Assassins needed their help.

"Fine, lets split into our groups and head out as soon as possible," he said and dropped the subject.

Aiden and I went up to our room to change and gather up our arsenal. I wrapped my arms around him and embraced him in a huge hug. "Thank you for watching out for me. You really got Grandpa upset down there. I don't think he'll ever fully come to term with vampires, or maybe it's just being told what to do by his granddaughter's fiancé," I said as I kissed the tip of his nose.

He returned my hug and chuckled. "I don't care if he liked it or not, I am not leaving your side in your state of bloodlust, and certainly not when we have two serial-killing vampires out there who want you dead."

He walked over to the closet and took out a little knapsack cooler, packing it up with some blood for me for the evening from the mini-fridge we had bought and placed in the closet earlier. "Speaking of which…you should probably have something to drink before we head out," Aiden said as he warmed me up a mug of blood.

I sighed but graciously took it from him. He had made two mugs, one for each of us. Clinking his cup on mine, he smiled at me. "Cheers," he said as he put his to his lips. He took a long drink from the cup and when he removed it, his lips were tinted slightly from the blood, which turned me on.

I was on his lap in a heartbeat, lips pressed to his. He opened his mouth and greeted my tongue with just as much anticipation. I snaked my hands through his hair, pulling him even closer to me for a deeper kiss. The taste of the two blood types mingled together was heavenly. I nipped at Aiden's neck, drawing a small amount of his blood, lapping it up gently. I could feel him through his jeans beneath me, and knew he was just as aroused as I was. He returned the nip on my neck.

It wasn't long before I was trying to take his shirt off over his head. We were both breathing heavily, getting carried away in the moment. Aiden didn't hesitate to let me take his shirt off, and before long I was caressing his wonderfully sculpted abs with my hands. That is when Ridley knocked on the door.

"You two almost ready? We're about to head out," he called from the other side. Aiden and I locked eyes, his were green and reflecting brightly.

Sighing loudly as I continued to nip at his neck and drink his blood, he replied, "Yes, give us a moment Ridley, we'll be right down."

It was going to take me more than a moment to calm down out of my bloodlust. "Here, let me make you some more blood darling," he said as he gently moved me off of him. I could tell he was trying to gather himself back up as well.

I drank six mugs of blood before I was even remotely ready to face the others. Aiden assured me if I didn't think I was ready to go out, that I didn't have to. "I need to get used to this eventually, Aiden. If I keep hiding away inside I'll never control it. I might slip here and there, but I need to try," I assured him. He smiled at me and kissed me once more before we met Ridley downstairs.

We got assigned to the Hanbury Street location. Since we were outside of London itself, we had rented several cars to get us to and from the city. Ridley and Logan were with us, and I was glad it was Ridley instead of the others. At least he treated me with respect. We didn't know what to expect so all of us were armed properly. I had my enchanted fire sword attached to my belt, and Ridley and Logan had all the usual gizmos and gadgets with them.

Once we arrived at the location we quickly saw that it was a very busy area with a lot of shops. There was no back alley like the Argyle Square scene, and it was buzzing with people. We did a couple of loops around the block, scouting the area.

Finally we parallel parked on the tiny street. Ridley shut the car off. "This doesn't look very promising. I don't see how anyone could get away with a murder here," Logan said.

I pointed to the floors above the ground levels. "Unless he took them inside, like the murder scene we saw at the apartment complex. But even then, this area is so busy I don't know how that could go unnoticed. Strolling down the street with a hooker would probably get attention here."

"Well this is the location we were assigned to, there isn't any harm in staking the location out and see what comes from it," Ridley said. He was right, we wouldn't know what would happen until we tried.

"It doesn't look like it's the safest area in town though either, judging by all the graffiti on the walls. We won't know for sure what happens until it gets dark, that is when the freaks come out," I said laughing.

"And who knows who owns the top floors of these places. Perhaps our murderer owns one of the buildings. Anything is possible," Aiden chimed in.

Since it was still daylight, we decided to walk around and see if we could get a better feel for the buildings. There was a pub at the end of the street, and once we had walked around enough, we settled in there for a few hours. Looking like a group of friends out to have some fun for the night, we didn't feel that we looked too suspicious. It stayed open late so we at least didn't look like we were loitering on the streets.

It was well after eleven at night, and we took turns going out to the street in teams looking for anyone suspicious. To my complete and utter shock, our murderer walked right in the front door of the pub. His hate-filled eyes were locked with mine. He knew we were here, and he was taunting us, knowing there was nothing we could do in a crowded bar in public.

Aiden saw the look of horror on my face, and asked me what was wrong. "He's here. In the bar. The man with the light gray suit on and black scarf," I said as quietly as I could. I knew the vampire could hear me, and he smiled ever so slightly as I spoke, cocky and assured of himself.

Ridley and Logan were out on the street doing surveillance, and I reached in my pocket to call them. Before I could even dial the number, Ridley called me. "Skyy, Logan was attacked. The vampire flashed by us so fast I could barely see him. He didn't even stop…he flew by and slashed Logan's throat open."

"What!? Is he alive?" I exclaimed, trying to keep as quiet as I could. The bar was loud and there was music playing. I could hear Ridley just fine with my vampire hearing but I didn't want anyone near us to hear.

"He is barely alive. I don't think there is anything we can do for him. I teleported him back to the house off a side street when nobody was coming. I am sending Keith over to you guys to bring you back to the house, go back to the car he'll meet you there," he said.

"Ridley, he's here. In the bar, right now," I whispered into the phone. I glanced up and saw the smug look on the vampires face. "This could be a setup, I have no idea what is going on."

'Shit! Are you serious!? Ok, you two stay put, and I will bring back the others. I don't think Logan would want to be turned but do you think your vampires would agree to it, if he does?" he asked.

Aiden, hearing the question easily, nodded his head yes without me having to ask. "Yes, I am sure they would. If he wants to turn, they should have no problems with it."

"Keep your phone on you, I'll call back soon," Ridley said and hung up.

I glared at the murderer, and he didn't even bat an eye. He just sat there, staring and smiling at me. At least Aiden was able to get a good look at him as well. He took my hand into his to comfort me. I didn't want to talk out loud because I knew he would hear every word that we said, so I took my phone out and typed on it.

Do you think this is a setup, or do you think he is just taunting us?

Aiden read the text on the screen then took the phone from my hands to reply. Anything is possible. I'm fairly sure he works alone, but we shouldn't take that chance. Let's stay put and play it safe.

His reply made me wonder if he was indeed alone, or if Bathory could be lurking around here somewhere. The answer to our question was soon answered when we saw a young woman in her mid-twenties come in the door. He noticed her and stood up to greet her. She was a human, and it looked like they were meeting for a "first date"…in other words it was soon to be his next victim. Aiden took the phone and typed again.

I can't believe he'd be stupid enough to be seen in public with someone he was about to murder. This is probably him taunting us, to get a reaction.

He may have been right but either way, how could we sit there and let him walk out with her? We were caught between a rock and a hard place, not knowing what might be waiting for us outside the door of the pub. Aiden and I sat there trying as best as we could to blend into the crowd and not look too out of place. It was awful to watch him flirt with the poor woman. She was hanging on every word he said, smiling and giggling like a school girl. Though she wasn't dressed like a prostitute, we still weren't sure if she was a working woman, or just a random person he may have picked up on the Internet.

After about a half hour of watching him buttering her up and buying her drinks, he finally paid the bill, and stood up smiling at us. He was going to walk out of the bar with her. I called Ridley immediately.

"I know you are busy with Logan, but he just walked out of here with a woman Ridley. What should we do?" I asked, panicking knowing that every second we waste was a second she might not live.

His voice was monotone and bleak in his reply. "Logan didn't make it, Skyy. He didn't want to be turned, and we had to respect his wishes. I'll teleport in with a few others and meet you by your car. We'll be using the invisibility cloaking to avoid another incident like Logan again.

He hung up before I could even say anything. Aiden heard that Logan had passed away, though we didn't speak about it, I knew that he wasn't feeling any better about it than I was. He threw some money on the table to pay the tab, and we bolted out the door into the night after the killer.

I had my hand on the hilt of my sword the entire time. There were people lingering on the street in front of the pub, but the further we walked down the side street to our car, the less people we saw. We made it to the car with no issues, and no sighting of the vampire. Neither Aiden nor I heard anything weird or off in the area, no screaming or struggling like his last victims.

As soon as we got to the car, Ridley, Keith, and three other Divine Assassins let us know they were there. But before we even spoke Aiden was on high alert, pushing me behind him.

"We have an issue here," he said. The Divine Assassins stayed invisible for their own safety, but I saw Aiden looking into the window of the car.

Ridley cursed out loud when he realized what Aiden was looking at. "That cocky son of a bitch! He dumped a body in our car?!"

It didn't take long before I could smell all the blood. Before we could decide what to do with the situation, we noticed a cop car patrolling down the street slowly. "Shit! You two get in the car, drive it back to the house we'll figure out what to do from there!" Ridley said.

Having no choice, and not wanting to be framed for a murder we didn't commit, Aiden and I hopped into the car trying to be as inconspicuous as possible, which was the worst possible scenario for me.

The cop drove by us slowly, but didn't take much notice to us. He nodded in our direction and kept driving. I guess we looked like a decent young couple out on the town for the night. Aiden pulled out into the street as I struggled to control myself.

"Breathe Skyy, focus on my voice. Get the pack out and have some blood," he had his hand on my upper thigh trying to calm me down. I reached down between my legs to find the cooler, when I realized that the woman was not dead. I heard a faint heartbeat.

'She isn't dead Aiden! Fuck! Call Ridley right now! Get him to meet us somewhere around here to teleport her, she'll never make it back to the house!" I yelled as I climbed into the back seat.

He tried to grab me but it was too late. The mixture of emotions running through me was hectic to say the least. I wanted to help this poor girl, but her blood was pushing me into bloodlust. He had stabbed her several times, but I couldn't tell where or how bad it was because it was dark and she had clothing on.

Aiden made the call to Ridley, and didn't dare stop the car even though he knew having me in the backseat with her wasn't safe for the girl either. They would meet us a mile up the road, get her and teleport her back to the house where we could try to save her, or turn her.

"Skyy, honey. I know you're trying to help, but I think you should come back up in the front seat," he called gently as he tried to grab my arm again.

"She's going to die!" I said as I began CPR on her. I wanted to help her desperately but she was coughing up blood and it was all over her lips and mouth. She spit up blood into my mouth while I was performing mouth to mouth resuscitation, and that was all it took. I couldn't control my thoughts, my breathing, or my actions. I tried to focus on Aiden's voice but all I wanted was more blood. I began to lick up the blood off of her face and neck, and then felt the car jolt to a stop.

Aiden ripped me off of the girl before I could actually harm her. I was fighting him with everything in me. We were on a pitch black side road, and Ridley had picked the woman up and was gone with her so fast I didn't even have time to comprehend what had just happened.

I was pressed up against the car by Aiden. He grabbed my face and forced me to look him in the eyes. "Skyy! You need to snap out of it darling. Look into my eyes, breathe…calm yourself down. We have to get this car off the road and back to the house."

I was trembling and angry. At myself for almost attacking her, and at Aiden for holding me back. This was another test, and I had to get myself in check and fast. Everyone was in danger here if we got caught.

Suddenly my grandfather and Ridley teleported in right beside us. He barked out, "Ridley, get her back to the house now! Aiden you're riding back with me in the car." I was being taken from Aiden's arms and teleported before I could protest. Lucius was waiting for me on the other side and immediately took me into his arms and up the stairs to a private room.

I still couldn't talk and was having seizure-like convulsions. Her blood was all over my clothing and my skin, and more importantly I could taste her. Now I was under the same roof with her again and could still smell her blood. Lucius grabbed some towels out of the small guest bathroom and wet them, to clean me off.

He began to wipe my hands and face down. "It's hard, I know how hard it is Skyy. Stick with me though. You'll get through this," he said in a calm, fatherly-like voice. Christian came into the room moments later and made me a mug of blood.

I drank it reluctantly, but knew it was the only path to calming me down. It took about twenty minutes for Aiden and Grandpa to make it back to the house, and once he was back Lucius left me in his hands. Christian stayed to help.

"Thank you for the help Christian. How is the girl?" I heard Aiden ask as he made me some more blood.

"Lucius turned her almost immediately after they brought her in. She was conscious enough to answer if she wanted to live or die. She'll make the conversion and be fine," Christian replied.

"And I am sure she'll be in for one heck of a shock once she wakes up as a vampire," Aiden said grimly.

Christian nodded in agreement. "I am sure she will be, but it's better than the alternative. Or even worse, better that we were the ones to turn her, instead of the killer or Bathory."

Aiden was rubbing my arms up and down trying to comfort me as I settled down. I was feeling much better but I needed to get these clothes off. Every time I would start to feel like I was coming out of bloodlust I smelled her blood on me and I got fired up again.

"I need to get out of these clothes and into the bath," I said, barely able to get the words out through my chattering teeth.

"If you don't mind Christian, stay here in the room. I'll get her settled into a bath, but I'd like you here just in case." Christian nodded at Aiden, and I felt like the world's biggest burden. I needed two bodyguards to keep me in check.

Aiden drew me a hot bath, and I sank down into it feeling better by the moment. The house was older and didn't have shower heads in any of the bathrooms. So I had to clean myself off twice to get the blood off, drain the tub, fill it again, and repeat. Aiden sat quietly on the toilet with the lid down, giving me privacy. At some point he handed the bloodied clothing out the door to Christian to get it away from me.

Once I felt clean enough, he handed me a towel and I drained the tub and hopped out. He had a mug of blood waiting for me, and I drank it up quickly. "Feeling better now?" he asked.

I put my face into his chest, breathing in his comforting smell. He wrapped his arms around me. "Yes, and once again I am sorry. I really tried to help her though. It was just too much to handle. She was spitting up blood into my mouth when I tried to revive her Aiden."

"I know darling, it's ok. Once again you were put into a situation that normally would never happen, and you meant well by trying to save her. The point is though, that you didn't harm her any more than she already was, and your CPR probably bought her the extra minutes she needed to get back here for help," he said as he kissed the top of my wet hair.

Once I was all dried off and dressed, we went back into the bedroom. Christian was still there, smiling at me. "Lookin' better by the minute Skyy. I knew you'd be fine."

"Well I am glad all of you have so much confidence in me. That was not something I want to repeat again," I said as I flopped dramatically on my back onto the bed.

"I imagine not," Christian said.

"How do you do it Christian? You make it look so easy. Doesn't the blood make you nuts? It was all over me," I inquired.

He shrugged and smiled his big infectious smile at me. "I am not sure Skyy. Lucius keeps telling me that I am not normal...whatever that means. I guess in a good way? The blood just doesn't control me. Smelling the live blood from the girl downstairs didn't affect me at all. I'm weird, I know," he said and laughed.

"Pffft well if you're weird, I wish I was weird too. Trust me, being controlled by nothing but thoughts of blood from the vein sucks. You're really lucky."

"You'll get there Skyy, I know you will. You're tougher than anyone I know, you always have been. And we will be here to help you along the way," he said to reassure me.

"And I am thankful for that. I have the best people anyone could ask for in my corner, and I am so grateful for that," I said as I got up and gave Christian a hug. "Speaking of which, here comes another one now." Fiona had just knocked on the door to see how I was doing.

She walked into the room and embraced me. Her beautiful golden hair was up in a high ponytail and she had her pajamas on already but still managed to look gorgeous. "I'm sorry this happened again Skyy, you alright?" she asked as she held me at arm's length to look me in the eyes.

I nodded, and assured her I was feeling much better. The four of us hung out in our bedroom for quite some time, chatting and relaxing. They didn't bring up anything to do with Bathory, the murderer, or the night's events. Trying to get my mind off of

144

those things really helped me, and I was feeling like my old self again. I could hear the men downstairs talking though, and I was pleased to know that the girl we brought back was transitioning just fine and would make it after all.

I decided to let it go for now, but I was so mad inside about the balls on the vampire to attack that girl and dump her in our car. We had to find him, and put a stop to him once and for all.

Chapter 14

We all waited patiently for the victim to transition to vampire. It took almost two days, and we stuck by the television and news websites diligently looking for anything that might point to another murder. Our killer was staying in the shadows, and it was my guess that his latest stunt was just him playing with us for fun. We lost Logan over his little game, and almost lost the poor girl too. The only family Logan had was his brother, who was also a Divine Assassin, so arrangements for his body were quick and easy. It still didn't make any of us feel any better about the situation though.

We felt that Fiona and Lucius would be the two best choices out of the vampires to break the news to the girl when she finally woke up. It looked like we had another addition to our growing family. I was more than curious to see what she looked like now, to find out how she met the killer, and the events that led up to the attempted murder. But we needed to make sure she was comfortable first, and breaking the news to her that her life was changing forever would probably take a while to sink in.

Everyone in the house left Fiona and Lucius in privacy with her while she woke up. Though Aiden and I were upstairs, we could hear every word that was said. Christian joined us shortly after she woke up. We all felt like eavesdroppers but it was just too intriguing to not want to listen in.

Lucius was the first to speak to the girl. "Easy now, love. You've been through a lot. Do you remember me? I was here when they brought you in. You were injured very badly," he said in a soft, gentle voice.

There was a long period of silence before she finally spoke. "Where am I? And who are you?" she asked in a timid voice.

"I know you're probably really scared, and there is a lot to explain. This is Fiona, and my name is Lucius. We're still in the London area. You're safe here though, nobody will hurt you here," he replied.

"How long have I been here? I almost died, I remember a girl trying to give me CPR in the backseat of a car. I feel better than I ever have in my life, was I in a hospital?" she asked. The confusion and unsureness in her voice was hard to listen to.

Fiona spoke next, and I could picture her rubbing her hand on the girls back to comfort her as she did so. "Darling, we have some things to talk to you about, that might be shocking. Please believe me when I tell you that everyone here is on your side, we just want to keep you safe. What is your name?"

Another moment of silence before she finally answered quietly, "Arabella."

Fiona answered her, "Nice to meet you Arabella. To answer your question, no you weren't in a hospital. You were very badly injured, and yes you did almost die. This is going to sound unbelievable but please bear with me. We healed you, well Lucius is the one who healed you. And you feel better than you ever have in your life because we've turned you. Into one of us. We're vampires, Arabella." I heard her pause, waiting for the reaction from the girl.

A few seconds passed, then I heard the girl do a kind of snort-chuckle type of laugh, as if she didn't believe it. "Vampires?" was all she said.

"I know it sounds crazy. But look at yourself darling, and how do you feel? Better than ever, right? But craving something...you just can't put your finger on it? Blood?" It sounded like Fiona was offering the girl blood.

We heard what sounded like gulping noises, which could only mean the girl responded to the blood the way any new fledgling vampire would...eagerly. It was instinct and she knew exactly what to do. Seconds later, we heard her come up for air and ask, "What in the hell is going on? Why did I just drink a glass of blood? And why did it taste so good? I'm scared."

Lucius took over again. "Arabella, you're new body will require blood now. It will replace food, and water. You'll heal rapidly, your senses will all be tweaked. You'll acquire special abilities over time. It's actually not all that bad. And we'll be here to help you every step of the way. In fact, there are two others we'd like to introduce you to when you're ready that have also just recently made the transition."

Arabella blew out a long sigh. "What about the man I was with the night I was attacked? Is he still out there?"

She was getting right to the point. I liked that. Lucius replied, "Yes, and hopefully with your help we can come closer to finding him. He's been murdering young ladies for a very long time and it needs to stop. But one thing at a time, we don't have to talk about that until you're ready. First we need to get you comfortable in your new body."

"Alright. Well what is this place? Your secret vampire hideaway? Are we safe here?" she asked.

Fiona chuckled at how she worded it. "No this isn't a secret vampire hideaway. We're here working with another group of people, they aren't vampires but they know how to track down and kill the bad vampires. We've been trying to find and capture the man who attacked you, and an associate of his, for quite some time now. They are both vampires, and very dangerous ones at that. This is just a place for all of us to work together, protect one another, and stay out of the public eye while we do it."

"You do know how crazy this all sounds, right? But I can't explain how I feel, or why I just drank a full glass of blood and want more. So...where do we go from here?" the girl asked.

I heard someone pouring some more blood into a glass for her. Then Lucius spoke again. "Well, we'll get you some more blood first of all. And then we'll answer any other questions you might have. Then introduce you to the others. I think you'll like Skyy and Christian very much, they are around your age. And when you're ready, we can talk about the man who attacked you."

Christian was grinning like an idiot sitting in one of the chairs in our guest room. "What is so funny?" I asked him.

"Well, we are pretty likeable, if I do say so myself," he said as he blew on his nails and pretended to polish them on his shirt.

I threw a throw pillow at him from across the room, which he caught effortlessly. "Yeah, I am sure she'll be charmed off her feet by you and your cheesy jokes."

We piped down when Lucius spoke again. The touchy subject was coming up now. "Arabella, I have to ask. How close are you with your family? And friends? Your new lifestyle is going to require some serious changes."

She hesitated a bit, but answered. "Are they in any danger?"

"Not from us, no. And I doubt they are in any danger from the man who attacked you either, but the reason I ask is because you're only going to be able to go out at night from now on. You won't be eating normal food, and you're not going to be able to tolerate being around humans easily for quite some time. And, the biggest thing is, you won't age like a human does…so eventually people will notice. This makes things very hard for people who are close to their families, but it is for everyone's best interests to try to come up with a reasonable solution as soon as possible."

I could tell Arabella had started crying now. I knew exactly what she was going though. "My parents passed away when I was young, I have two brothers and a sister though, and we're very close. My sister lives local, my brothers live in France. I have some aunts, uncles, and cousins but we're not very close. I'm enrolled in university, and have quite a few close friends there."

Fiona chimed in again. "I know it's going to be difficult darling, but is there any way you can tell them you've gone out of town? Or some way to avoid contact with them for now? You can't be near humans without supervision from one of us, and eventually you'll have to let go of your old life."

"I can't just drop out of school! And anybody who knows me would know that I never go anywhere on holiday, and certainly not on a whim," she cried out.

"You can rest assured, that even if you leave your university now, you'll have every advantage and then some to continue your education. Our family has unlimited resources when it comes to money and education. The sky will be the limit. But, there is nothing that we can do about the family. You have to sever ties with them, sooner rather than later. The alternative is you attacking them out of bloodlust, or you staying in your twenties when you should be in your sixties. People will notice, Arabella." Fiona's voice was sad and sympathetic, but I knew that they would have to put their foot down if she continued to argue the matter.

"So that is it, then? Nothing can be done, I have no choice or say in the matter?" Arabella was still crying, but getting angry.

"We asked you while you were on your deathbed if you wanted to live or die, and you made it clear you wanted to live. Granted, you had no idea that this would be the outcome, but nevertheless, you've made the transition. Things will be hard, for a long time, but you won't be alone. There is no sense in dragging out the inevitable," Lucius said.

"Bloody hell," the girl whispered. "Well it looks as though I have no choice in it, so what do I do? Nobody will believe I just up and left town."

"We'll come up with some options for you, but for now just try to take it one step at a time. We've prepared a room for you, but you'll be sharing it with Fiona. Someone needs to be with you at all times for the first few days of transition. And as we mentioned, you can't go out in the sunlight. We may have a fix for that if our friends will cooperate, but for now just assume that you need to stay indoors during the day. There are other humans on the property as well, you'll be getting temptations left and right, when you feel the urge you tell one of us right away so we can get you some blood." Lucius was reading off all the do's and don'ts of being a new vampire to her.

They continued to talk to Arabella about her new life and what to expect. I felt sorry for her, but knew she was in good hands with us. "I just hope that she doesn't have to be put into any kind of situation like I have, and her transition can go smoothly," I said to Christian and Aiden.

Aiden pat me on the back, "Me too, and I hope you don't have to be put in anymore situations like that either."

"I have a feeling things are only going to get worse before they get better guys. It just sucks that we had to drag someone else into the mess. But I am glad we could save her." I put my head in my hands and took a deep breath in while sitting on the edge of the bed.

"Want me to make you some blood?" Christian asked kindly.

I nodded without saying anything, and moments later I had a mug in my hand. "Thanks, Christian."

"I'm sure Grandpa will be thrilled we have yet another vampire here," Christian said as he chuckled.

I rolled my eyes and sighed, "Ugh, don't remind me. I just hope we can convince them to get her protected from the sun. It'd be one less thing for her to try to get accustomed to."

"I am sure between you and Ridley you can talk some sense into him," Aiden said.

Before long Lucius and Fiona were knocking at our door, wanting to introduce us properly to Arabella. Aiden opened the door with a welcoming smile, and offered his hand to the girl. "Pleasure to meet you, Arabella. I'm Aiden Carrick. If there is anything you need from us just let me know."

She took his hand and smiled back at him. It was obvious she thought he was handsome, heck anyone with eyes in their head would appreciate Aiden's good looks. "Nice to meet you, sir," she replied.

He gestured behind him with his hand, and motioned for me to come up to his side. "This is my fiancé, Skyy Huntington. She is also a newly turned vampire, so you two will have a lot in common."

I shook her hand and smiled. "Nice to meet you," was about all I could think of to say. It would be like the blind leading the blind with the two of us. Up close, and in the light now, I could get a better look at her. She was actually quite pretty, with long wavy chestnut brown hair and light brown eyes.

Her teeth were very straight and white, and she had a slender build.

However she stood there in silence, with a slight look of shock on her face. It took me a moment to realize why. I wasn't wearing my contacts and I am sure my eyes scared her. I let go of her hand and immediately assured her it was alright. "Oh! My eyes…sorry about that. I usually wear contacts to cover them up. Don't worry, yours won't look like this."

She smiled sheepishly at me, "They look pretty neat actually. Sorry for staring. It's nice to meet you though, Skyy."

To keep things moving along I pointed over to Christian to introduce him to her. "That there is Christian Vane, he is also a new vampire. We've known each other for years, he is a pain in the ass most times, but he's my best friend. Let me know if he gives you any trouble and I'll straighten him out for you," I said and winked at her.

Christian gave me a playful shove out of the way and took her hand. "I'm not as bad as she makes me out to be. Nice to meet you, Arabella," he said as he flashed her his big smile.

Considering the situation this poor girl was thrown into, she was handling it better than I expected. She was not only in a room full of total strangers, but vampire strangers. Fiona wanted to show her where the bathroom was, and then show her to the room she'd be staying in, and invited me along for some "girl time".

We entered into the room that she was currently sharing with Christian. I noticed he hadn't moved any of his stuff to a different room yet. "So where is Christian moving to?" I asked.

Arabella had no idea that she was inconveniencing us with the living arrangement. "Oh, I didn't realize you and Christian were…together, Fiona. He doesn't have to leave the room just for me, I am sure I can find another room," she offered, feeling bad.

Fiona waved her hand to dismiss the statement. "We thought you'd be more comfortable rooming with a female, it's not a big deal at all darling. Skyy isn't ready to be left alone just yet either, so I am your only option. Don't worry though, we'll have plenty of fun together."

I could only imagine the fun she had in store for her. Makeovers, and trying on clothes, and styling each other's hair. Fiona meant well, and hopefully Arabella was more into fashion and makeup than I was.

Arabella was over at the window, looking out into the darkness now. I saw her put her arms around her body, then she spoke out quietly, "You're sure that we are safe here? From…him, I mean?"

It was obvious she was terrified of her attacker, and justifiably so. "We're as safe as we'll ever be here in this house. Try not to worry too much dear, we'll protect you. The humans here on the property have many ways to ward off harmful vampires like the man who attacked you. And we are five vampires against one on top of that," Fiona assured her.

I was dying to ask her how she met "Jack" but knew that now wasn't the time. Thinking back to the night we saw her in the pub with him, she was clearly attracted to him, and making a fool of herself. I would never tell her that of course. Meeting in a public place is one thing, but leaving with someone you don't know is pretty dumb on a first date.

My phone vibrated in my back pocket with a text message. It was Ridley, and he wanted to know if I had a minute to talk. I made sure Fiona was alright with me leaving for a while, and let him know I was on my way down to the first floor to meet him.

I found him in the living room sitting on the couch by himself. He had on his usual nerd outfit, a button up shirt tucked into his neatly pressed khaki pants that were hiked up way too high, and his hair split perfectly down the middle. He hadn't been acting like his normal self ever since Logan's death, and I knew he was taking it hard. They had known each other for twenty years, and I am sure watching it happen before his very eyes was not a walk in the park.

I smiled at him and sat down in the love seat across from him. "What's up Ridley? You doing alright?"

He nodded and gave me the best attempt at a smile that he could muster up. "Yes, I just wanted to see how the girl was doing, and also check in on things with our ghost friend back in Scotland. Have you heard any news from Alana since you were there?"

We had so many things on the burner that I had almost forgotten about that until he mentioned it. "Actually, I haven't, but we could pop over there and see if we can get in contact with her if you'd like?"

He gave a halfhearted nod, "Sure, we could take an hour or two to see if we can talk to her. We don't have anything going on this afternoon. But how is the girl doing? I heard she woke up."

Smiling at him, I told him about her progress. "Her name is Arabella, and she is transitioning just fine so far. She is taking it hard about having to sever ties with her family, but who wouldn't?"

"True. I know it is a delicate time, but we need to get her talking about what happened with the killer. The sooner we can pin him down, the sooner we can find Bathory and end all of this," Ridley said as he pulled his phone out of his pocket. "Your grandfather isn't as patient or as nice as I tend to be, if he gets his way he'll be pressing her for information by the end of the day. I'd try to get her talking before that, between you and Fiona I am sure you can make her feel comfortable enough. Let's try that, then we'll head over to Aiden's castle and see if we can get in touch with Alana."

We stood up, and I started for the stairs again, but decided to add in a few more words. "Ridley, I know what you're going through is hard, it's hard on all of us. If you ever need to talk to someone, I'm always here for you."

He smiled at me, "Thanks Skyy. I'll be fine, it's just been hard to process everything that has happened, and we keep getting more thrown at us. You've been through way more than me, and you're standing strong. I am just a computer nerd...I wasn't used to all of the fighting and action I guess."

154

I snorted at his comment, "I'm glad I appear to be strong to others, because I sure feel like a mess on the inside. But we have to take it one day at a time, and together we'll find a way to take both of those assholes down."

"You know, I've got to admit, as far as partners go I really lucked out getting you Skyy. I think Mr. Huntington put us together as sort of a punishment, or because he didn't know what else to do with us, but you're pretty darn awesome," Ridley said as he smiled at me. I guess my pep talk lifted his spirits, and I was glad it did.

"You're not so bad yourself Ridley. Keep your chin up," I winked at him. Then I made my way back upstairs to see if I could get Arabella to talk.

I found the two of them sitting in Fiona's room, and as expected Fiona was already bombarding her with fashion. They were on her bed, with the contents of one of her makeup totes spread out all over the top of the bedspread. Arabella was taking the top off of a tube of lipstick and looking at it, as Fi excitedly explained that it matched her skin tone perfectly.

I cleared my throat as I walked in the room and sat down in a chair. Both of the women smiled at me, and Fiona pat the bed beside her. "Skyy, come sit with us!" she said merrily. I obeyed, though reluctantly. I didn't mind so much when she played with my hair, but I was never one for excessive makeup. But I played along, and we sat there for over an hour while she tried colors on both of us until she was satisfied. Just what a newly turned vampire who was scared out of her mind needed – a makeover.

After our beauty consultation, I offered to make Arabella some blood. We drank it in relative silence as I wracked my brain trying to figure out how to bring up the subject. My dad always said clear words make for clear understanding…so getting right to the point would probably be best.

"I know that all of this is new and difficult to grasp all at once, Arabella. Believe me…I know. But we need to ask you some questions that might help us find the man who attacked you. We need to get him sooner rather than later, so that nobody

155

else has to suffer like you did. He's murdered dozens of women, maybe hundreds. Do you think you can talk to me about him?" I asked her as I made us both another mug of blood.

She nodded as she took a sip. Lifting her lips from the cup she replied, "Yes, of course. Believe me, I want to see him brought down more than anyone. What do you want to know?"

Good, she was at least level headed enough to know that we needed her help. We all had problems, but there wasn't much time to sit back and feel sorry for yourself. I had already wasted enough of everyone's time with my drama.

"How did you meet him? And how long did you know him before the other night?" I asked.

She didn't hesitate to jump right in. "We met online, a dating site. I talked to him on the Internet for a couple of days before we spoke on the phone. We talked once on the phone, and that is when he asked if I'd like to meet in person for a drink. I guess it was about two weeks ago that I first met him on the dating site."

"What name did he use on the dating site?" I was curious to see what the name would be, and if it would have any significance at all to him.

"Henry Holmes, he said he was a doctor as well." I asked her to spell out the name, and wrote it down so we could look into it. Then I handed her the pen and asked her to write down all the information for the dating site; her user name and login information, as well as his user name.

Once we had that settled, I moved on to the next round of questions. "The night you were attacked, we were in the pub that you met Holmes in. We were actually there looking into a lead in the area, staking out a possible location that we thought he might attack at. I saw you come in, and observed your entire meeting at the pub. He seemed pleasant and the conversation was kept light. What made you decide to leave with him? Was that the plan all along, drinks first then a night out?"

To this question she looked down at the mug in her hands and became silent for a few moments. She finally shook her head no, and looked back up at me. "No, that wasn't the plan

156

all along. I wasn't thinking clearly. It was as if I had no control over my own thoughts almost. I had a burning desire to be closer to him. It wasn't like anything I would have done, I am usually very cautious. I remember thinking how handsome he was, and how I wanted to run my fingers through his hair."

"He is a good deal older than you, do you usually date older men?"

She shrugged, "Sometimes. I have dated men much older than me before. They are more mature than men my age. I thought he was handsome from the photo I saw on his dating profile, and he was a doctor to boot. I didn't think meeting for a drink would end up with me almost dying."

"Well don't be too hard on yourself. While it wasn't the best idea ever, you did meet in a public place and that seems safe enough for a first date. He more than likely used mind manipulation on you, older vampires can control your mind, or even erase certain things from it. That would be the reason you felt the need to leave with him," I explained.

"Great, more weird stuff to get used to," she said sarcastically.

I laughed but reassured her she wouldn't have to worry about being mind whammied now that she was a vampire. "Vampires can only manipulate humans, so you don't ever have to worry about him trying it again on you. Chances are he thinks you're dead, and you're safe anyway. Now, is there anything else you can remember, did he talk about himself much? Even the smallest thing could help," I probed her for more information.

"Well, he didn't talk much about himself now that I think about it. He said he was a doctor, but didn't state what kind or where, said he loves animal...dogs in particular. I suggested that we meet for lunch, but he said he was more of a night person so that is why we met at the pub after dark...looking back on that comment, I get it now. I asked if he was ever married, he said no but that he has a pest of an ex who won't leave him alone. Really that is about it."

I glanced over at Fiona when she mentioned the pest of an ex. Could that be Bathory? And who knew how much, if any of it, was true. He could have made all of it up. Our killer wasn't stupid, and wasn't going to get caught over something like this. I needed to get Aiden and let him know Ridley wanted to head over to the castle still, so I stood up and excused myself.

"I have some other stuff I need to do, so I am going to look into this information you gave us Arabella, and we'll let you know what we find out. Just try to relax, and listen to Fiona... she is smart and kind, and she'll get you through this tough time. I'll come check in on you later tonight," I said as I excused myself.

They both stood up to see me to the door. I gave Fi a hug and thanked her for all her help and kindness. Arabella thanked me, for what I don't know, but she seemed like a nice girl. I went to my guest room to talk to Aiden, and he was in there laying on the bed on his stomach with his laptop in front of him as usual. He smiled when he saw me walk in.

"Work, or pleasure?" I asked as I pointed to the laptop.

"Work. There hardly seems like time for pleasure of any kind these days. How did the chat with the new girl go? I heard bits and pieces of it," he asked as he stood up, stretched, and came over to kiss my cheek.

"I hate to tell you this then, but Ridley asked if we wouldn't mind going over to the castle to see if we can get in touch with Alana about finding any of Bathory's other locations."

He gave me a weak smile, it seemed like everyone was just running out of steam lately, but nodded his head anyway. "Sure, just let me wrap a couple of things up, and we can head over there. You should have some blood before we go."

Once Aiden was ready, we found Ridley and let him know we were good to go. He let Aiden and I portal over to Scotland first, then came in shortly after us. We spent about two hours there in the castle with no appearance of Alana, so I figured I'd try the spot she seemed most comfortable to appear in – my old guest room there.

158

Sure enough, her ghostly apparition appeared about fifteen minutes after I entered the room. Since Alana wasn't a big talker, and half the time she wasn't there mentally anyway, the conversation was short and sweet. She and the other ghosts were able to come up with four locations for us to look at. Two more in Hungary, one in Russia, and one in New Orleans. How totally cliché. Alana disappeared as soon as she was done, and we had no reason to stay there in the castle so we ported out of there and back to the house in London.

We had to wait for Grandpa to portal in, but once he did we called a small meeting in the living room of the house. I had a lot of information to give them now, and I hoped that something would come out of it.

I relayed all the information that Arabella gave us, and also the locations that Alana told us about. They wanted Ridley to get on a computer and look into the dating website and the name right away. We were to stay here in London, and other teams would go to the locations to hunt for Bathory and search for her phylacteries. I wasn't sure what I thought about that, I didn't think it was safe for them to possibly engage Bathory alone without the help from us vampires, but Grandpa made the call and I kept my mouth shut.

After everyone had left the meeting, I asked Grandpa if I could speak to him about Arabella. "Do you have a minute Grandpa? It's about the girl we brought here."

"You mean the vampire? What about her," he said impatiently as if he had somewhere else to be. I was getting used to it by now, realizing that the sweet, fun, playful grandfather I knew growing up in my human life was a totally different man as one of the leaders of the Divine Assassins.

"Well I was wondering if we might be able to get her some protection from the sun as well, she is going to have a hard enough time getting used to everything else, it might help her," I said in the most convincing voice I could muster up.

"Skyy, that isn't a priority right now for us. We don't know anything about this girl. Hell, for all we know she could be a plant for the killer. We can't rule anything out. And until we get to know her better, I'll have to decline on that. She won't be going anywhere as it is, day or night, for quite some time. I won't say no for good, but for now….I have to decline your request," he said.

I could understand his point of view, and had not even considered his viewpoint on her being a plant. I'd find it really hard to believe, given how frightened she was, and that she was nearly dead when we found her. But I wasn't going to argue with him. "Ok, I understand the reasons why. Just thought I'd ask, but you're probably right."

We parted ways and I went to find Ridley to see if he was finding anything out about our killer. It was a good thing vampires didn't need to sleep often, because the way things were going, it didn't look like any of us were getting a break anytime soon.

Chapter 15

I found Ridley clicking away on a laptop in the living room. Sitting down on the love seat, I asked about his progress.

"Well, it won't come as a surprise that the dating website is a dead end. We can't trace it because he used the website from a busy internet café, and everything on the profile is bogus. But, interestingly enough, a quick search for the name Henry Holmes led me to some information about a man that looks like a very good fit for the Jack the Ripper case. Of course this was back in the 1800s and he is long gone by now, but I think it is fitting that our killer would use this name as his cover up," he said as he slid the laptop over the coffee table towards me.

I picked it up and glazed over the information on the screen. It seems like this Henry Holmes was a serial killer that got caught and tried for his crimes. He was hung on May 7th, 1896. He was a very popular pick for the identity of Jack the Ripper, and the timeline fit the murders as well. After Holmes' death, no more Ripper cases were reported. And just before he was hung he supposedly cried out "I am Jack the…"

I shook my head in frustration, and slid the laptop back over to Ridley. "He wouldn't be stupid enough to use his real name. And Henry Holmes died in front of witnesses. He is just toying with us. Random women on the internet would never put two and two together, and it is a very common sounding name. The fact he chose another serial killers name as his alter ego though shows just how sick he is."

"We could try to reach out to him on the dating site, with a fake profile. See if we can get him to come out," Ridley suggested.

"It's worth a shot. I don't have any idea how our killer is picking his victims. Most of the other recent murders were prostitutes, but Arabella is a college student. I'd think it would be a lot more effort to try to lure a girl with decent morals out, than to just pay a random call girl who won't question your motives. But, we should explore every option," I replied.

I turned the television on while Ridley designed a fake profile on the dating site. I was sick of British television, and was homesick. The whole city of London was depressing in fact. It rained way more than I cared for, and it was foggy a lot. I started to daydream as I sat there pretending to watch a sitcom, wondering where Aiden and I would eventually settle down once all of this mess was sorted out. I missed the States and hoped that we could find a place we could both agree on there.

I was broken out of my daydream by Ridley, who had been trying to get my attention. "Hello? Earth to Skyy? Anyone home?" he said as he waved his hands in the air.

"Sorry, was lost in thought," I said as I laughed.

"I could tell," he replied and shoved the laptop my way again. "How's that look?" he asked as I glanced at the fake profile he had whipped up.

The girl looked wild, like a party animal. He filled in the details the same way…making her look like she liked to have a good time. Perhaps it might work. "It looks good. It's a longshot but we'll see what happens."

"I'm going to reach out to him, and see if we get anything back," Ridley said as he took the laptop back and started clicking away on it again.

After that we took a few moments to just relax. We checked all the news stations for more murders on the television, and then settled on another sitcom. Ridley looked a little more relaxed at least. After about an hour, I could hear his heartbeat getting louder and louder, which was a sign that I needed blood as soon as possible. I tried to tune out the pulses and heartbeats of the humans that were staying in our house as much as possible, but this was always the first sign that I needed blood.

I excused myself and went up to my guest room to heat up a mug full. I thought that it might be a good idea for Aiden to look into owning and operating a blood bank, with as much blood as I was going though. And now that we had Arabella with us, our consumption was sure to get worse.

As I was cleaning up and getting ready to head back downstairs, I heard someone ring the doorbell of the house.

Finding it odd, especially since we were in the middle of nowhere, and anyone who knew we were here wouldn't ring the bell...I tuned into what was happening down there. As it turns out, it was Dreamer. I rushed down the stairs to greet her.

She was very excited, but not in a happy way. No happy hugs or greetings when she saw me enter the foyer, she dashed over to me and got right to the point. "Skyy! We have news of Bathory! A scouting team we sent into The Gloom found her. She is heavily guarded but we know for certain that she is there!" She was wringing her tiny little hands in distress as she spoke.

"Let me get my grandfather and his men here and we'll come up with a plan," I said, trying to calm her down.

After a quick phone call, Grandpa and two others ported in with him. We wasted no time getting down to business. All of the vampires, with the exception of Arabella, were also present.

Grandpa took the helm, and began laying out our plan. "We can gather up fifty men, possibly more within a couple of hours that will be ready to move out. They'll need to get their supplies and weapons ready. We'll need about an hour to produce some of the iron powder that we used in the last fight. We know that the dark fae are affected by it, and it will be a huge help. We'll also assume Bathory is susceptible to light, and I want to get the vampires equipped with their UV lights and suits once more. Each of you will also need to carry the enchanted silver powder. I know that it can also harm our vampires, but it is a risk I am willing to take if we can stun Bathory or immobilize her long enough to get a shot, we're taking it," he said with authority.

Aiden glanced at me, and I could tell without him even saying a word what he was thinking: that it was too dangerous for me and he wanted me to sit it out. I silently shook my head no, letting him know it wasn't an option and to drop it.

Grandpa continued, "We have fought her dark fae before and they did not prove to be that much more of a challenge for us, but I have no idea what to expect as we fight them in The Gloom. Dreamer, will they have any advantages over us there?"

She nodded and stood up to speak. "Yes, much like us in The Lucent, the dark fae's magical abilities will be amplified. Without the sunlight there, they use the twilight and darkness to feed them energy. They will be much stronger than when you fought them in Scotland. And of course, don't forget they can fly which is a huge advantage over your humans on the ground."

"How many Radiant fae can your people bring to the fight?" he asked again directly.

"This is every bit as much our fight as it is yours. The dark fae are our biggest enemy, and let's not forget all the things Bathory has done to my race. We will be sending a small army in with or without you, several hundred fae," Dreamer said firmly.

Grandpa didn't argue with her, there was really no point anyway. We had no dictation over what the Radiant fae did, and their help and knowledge of the dark fae would prove invaluable for us. Instead he just asked that we could meet with whoever was leading their army before we actually went inside The Gloom so that everyone was on the same page.

Dreamer agreed to that, and took her leave shortly afterwards to inform her people that the humans and vampires were onboard. All of the Divine Assassins that were under our roof left for their rooms to begin gearing up and strapping their weapons on. Ridley left with Keith to our headquarters to pick up some supplies and wait for the enchanted powders to be finished. Grandpa ported back to headquarters to get the UV lights and suits for us to equip, and was back at our house in London pretty fast.

I went to our bedroom and changed while everyone was getting ready. I put on some simple comfortable jeans, and a long sleeve top. I took my leather jacket with me just in case…it could help protect my arms in a fight. A pair of combat boots I swiped from the Divine Assassins headquarters rounded out my battle garb, and I attached my trusty enchanted fire sword to my belt.

I met up with Lucius in the hallway before I hit the top of the stairs. He had on the black suit with the UV lights on it, with his long hair pulled back into a ponytail. His huge muscles bulged under the tight fabric of the suit and he reached out to pat me on the back. "Don't get into any trouble this time Skyy. You just stay back and follow orders please. Can't have any more scares from you, love," he said with a father-like sincerity.

I grinned at him, "But getting in trouble is what I do best!" He started to frown at me but before he could reply, I assured him I would play it safe. "Don't worry Lucius, I have no desire to get myself hurt or in any trouble. Let's just hope this is it, and we get Bathory this time. You better be careful yourself, the dark fae will be stronger in The Gloom."

He gave me a nod, and we headed downstairs. Aiden had already changed as well and was wearing black combat fatigues, however Grandpa caught us both when he saw us, and handed us each a suit with lights on it as well. Apparently they made some extras in preparation for another fight, which was a good idea. We had one for each vampire now, so I headed back upstairs with Aiden to change into the suit. It was tight but flexible, sort of like a diver's wetsuit. I slipped my combat boots back on and tied my hair up into a bun.

Aiden went into the bathroom to change once I came out and was back out in no time. I had to admit, he looked pretty hot in the black suit. It accented each and every perfectly defined muscle on his body. He wasn't the huge beast Lucius was, but toned and fit and delicious to look at just the same. However, it was obvious that sexual fantasies weren't what was on Aiden's mind. He had that worried look on his face again.

"What's wrong Aiden?" I asked, as if I didn't know. I crossed the room and wrapped my arms around his waist.

He did the same to me in return, and rested his chin on the top of my head. "You know what's wrong Skyy. I hate that you have to be involved in something this dangerous. And I know that the Divine Assassins are part of your life now, but I hate that all of this puts you in so much danger on a daily basis."

"I know sweetie, but there isn't much that we can do about it. I don't want you getting in harm's way either, but at least we'll be doing it together. We need to put an end to Bathory, and whoever this killer is here in London. Not just for us, but for anyone out there in the world who they could harm in the future," I said as I rubbed my hands up and down his back.

"Just stay with me the entire time Skyy. No heroics, just stay with me, or at least Lucius please. I know things might get crazy but please promise me that?" he asked gently.

"I promise Aiden. I won't leave your side unless I have to, I won't make you worry like that again," I assured him. The two previous times I had gone against what he told me had worried him sick and upset him a lot.

"You know I am not happy about this, but I know there is no talking you out of it, so just stay alert and remember that I love you," he said and kissed me softly on my lips. My hands wandered down to his rear end, but before I could get too sidetracked he pulled away, took my hand, and led me to the door.

Back in the living room, most of the residents that were living in the house were ready for action. We were only waiting on Ridley and Keith to get back with the enchanted powders. Seeing Fiona and Christian come down the stairs in their light suits got me thinking – what were we going to do with Arabella? She couldn't be left alone, and she sure as heck couldn't come with us being barely a day old.

I walked over to Fiona and expressed my concerns to her. She had been thinking the same thing. "I am only following orders. What we do with her isn't up to me. I doubt your grandfather even took her into account with all the chaos going on around him."

"I'll talk to him, stay here," I said to her and took my grandpa aside to mention it.

I pulled him into the kitchen and brought it to his attention. "So what exactly are we going to do with the new vampire we have upstairs? She can't stay here alone, unsupervised."

He looked irritated at the thought of one more thing to worry about. A vampire on top of that…his favorite subject. "I will put one of our men on guard duty then," he said as he pulled his phone out of his pocket to make the call.

"She is dangerous to humans right now, she is still transitioning," I reminded him.

"If she tries anything on my man, she'll be dead before she knows it. We have been fighting vampires for a long time Skyy, remember? And if she wants to make a stink about it, we can chain her with silver. So make sure she understands to play nice," he replied.

I sighed, but agreed…knowing full well that Arabella probably heard all of that even though she was upstairs. At least she'd know that we weren't kidding when we relay the information.

I found Fiona, and the two of us went back upstairs to tell Arabella that she'd be staying here alone for a while. She didn't take it well, and looked scared. "What if the man tries to come back while you're all gone? With only one person here with me, he'd get in easily."

Fiona shook her head no, "The house is protected with wards, and he wouldn't be able to enter the house. It's complicated and I can explain more later, but as long as you stay inside he won't harm you. But you need to understand that the person who will be here with you is under orders to restrain you by any means necessary if you get out of control. Not all of the humans we work with are fans of us vampires, so keep your head down, make sure you drink plenty of blood even if you don't feel the urge to, and everything should be just fine."

"How long will you be gone?" Arabella asked.

"Hopefully not long, but we can't say for sure. Maybe a day or two, maybe longer. I know this is all very scary for you, but trust me this person we are going after is a massive threat and needs to be dealt with," I replied.

She nodded and sat on the edge of her bed. What else could she do? With nowhere to go, and the risk of being killed if she tried to leave, she had to cope. I felt bad for her, but we had other things to worry about. Fiona and I each gave her a reassuring hug and we joined the others back downstairs.

Déjà vu hit as I thought back to the last time we all gathered together and geared up for battle. Once again we were each handed small vials of enchanted powder. One was silver, for Bathory, and the other was iron, for the dark fae. I slipped them into the tactical belt that was attached to my suit and double checked that my sword was secure on there as well.

Once the Divine Assassins had checked, and double checked all of our supplies, they had me send word out to Dreamer. I used my pink crystal that she gave me to call her to us, and she let us know that we'd all need to portal over to Canada. Since The Gloom (and all the other dimensions that existed alongside earth) mirrored our landscape we'd need to travel as close as we could to the location that they were at in The Gloom so we could avoid having to spend any extra and unnecessary time there.

She gave us the location, and we did as we were told. When we landed on the other side, I had no idea where we were. It was in the middle of nowhere in a huge forest. Even with the sun brightly shining, it looked dark and dim. If it was this depressing here on earth's dimension, I couldn't imagine what The Gloom would look like.

Dreamer and Solara were already there, and as promised they had gathered a decent sized army. Most of them were in their tiny light forms, huddling together in what looked like formations. Though there was some organization to it, they still looked like floating balls of Christmas lights glowing different colors.

My grandfather and his men met up with Solara and her leaders. Though I wasn't included in the conversation, I could hear it just fine. The Radiant fae would take care of any airborne dark fae. Our goal was to fight on the ground and keep moving towards the location they kept Bathory in.

"Once we open up the tear to The Gloom we will need to act fast and get all of your men inside quickly. Any dark fae within the area will be alerted of the disturbance and will move on us. Remember, the iron magic you wield also affects us, so use it wisely. There are no buildings here, it will look much like this forest in there…and the dark fae have a large encampment where they are protecting Bathory. Follow our lead once inside," Solara said.

Aiden took my hand in his and gave it a squeeze. Ridley was to my left, and promised me that he'd stick with us as well. I glanced over at Christian and Fiona, who were adequately decked out. Fiona was once again donning her knife and dagger collection, and Christian had two swords strapped to his back, and a bow and quiver on top of them. Christian gave me a smile and the thumbs up sign, which I returned to him.

Looking back behind me, I had to admit I was impressed. We had managed to get more Divine Assassins here and ready in time than previously thought, probably close to ninety or so. And with the colored lights of the Radiant fae illuminating the forest, I felt like we were as well prepared as we could be.

Grandpa shouted out, "Any last questions before we enter?" to which he got no reply. He nodded over at Solara, and I watched her and three other Radiant fae literally rip a hole into thin air. You could hear it, as well as see it. Glancing through the ever growing giant hole, I saw similar landscape – trees, trees, and more trees, but it was all cast in dark purples and blues.

Squeezing Aiden's hand even tighter, unsure of what was to come, we began to move forward quickly into The Gloom.

Chapter 16

I immediately hated The Gloom. It was freakishly cold, and eerie. Unlike The Umbra, which was just all-around dark, quiet, and creepy, The Gloom looked very much like our normal dimension on earth except the colors were totally off. It wasn't quite fully dark, more like twilight, and everything was softly illuminated in shades of dark blue, purple, gray, and deep red. The trees were all the same height as back on our earth dimension, but the trunks were twisted and gnarled in unnatural ways, and the needles were illuminated in dark blues instead of green. The needles glowed, giving off pale light that was hard on the eyes, making my vision seem blurry.

Something was chirping in a high-pitched, ear shattering way. It sounded like a bird, just amplified way louder than any bird should ever be. When we began to walk, I looked up and saw several dark winged creatures take off out of the treetops, and assumed that was what we were hearing. They looked like a mix between a bat and a bird, and about the size of an eagle. Whatever they were, I was glad they were taking off, and not swooping down and descending on us.

The Radiant fae stood out in the dim lighting of The Gloom brilliantly. Their rainbow of colors lit up the forest in a myriad of color. They stayed in their tiny light forms until everyone was through the tear, and then I watched them seal it up. We were officially in now. Our team moved silently through the forest. I hadn't even noticed the UV lights on our suits buzz to life, but I guess they did at some point before we entered the tear.

Solara informed us that we'd have about a mile to trek before we got to their camp, but we came across a small scouting party almost immediately. My guess is the flock of creatures that flew out of the treetops tipped them off to our presence. They were dealt with very quickly, as we outnumbered them greatly. However, we didn't see the ones perched in the treetops. Arrows that were coated in poison were being shot into our formation, and the people getting hit were being paralyzed almost immediately. Our Radiant fae allies took to their humanoid form and spread their beautiful wings to fly up and take care of the situation.

The whole encounter made way more noise than I was comfortable with. Aiden and Ridley stood at my sides flanking me at all times to protect me. We had to stop moving to see what we could do about the people who had been hit with the arrows. Once the arrow tips were removed, they slowly regained feeling in their body, but they still couldn't stand or walk. There wasn't much time to spare, and the men who were shot actually made the call to be left behind. It was seven men, and the Divine Assassins helped drag them together in a huddle, leaving them with their weapons. Hopefully they'd be alright.

From this point on, the Radiant fae took to their humanoid form so that their light wouldn't give them away before we wanted to be seen. At this point, we had no idea if somehow the scouting party was able to relay that there were intruders or not. Up in the distance I saw what looked like campfires, but the flames coming out of them were a deep purple and midnight blue. The trees were cleared out, and it was a decent sized encampment. A few small simple huts were erected out of what looked like wood, straw, and mud.

Several dark fae were armed with spears and weapons, patrolling the perimeter of the campsite. We weren't sure if Bathory was being held here, or deeper in, but we had to get past these guards somehow. I put my hand on the hilt of my fire sword, ready for action. The Radiant fae charged in head first, without waiting for a go signal, which caught all of us off guard. If there was a plan, it just got shot out of the water.

We heard one of the dark fae scream out something in another language which resulted in all of those little huts emptying out with more angry, battle-ready dark fae. Even from a short distance I could see their eyes filled with hatred, softly glowing in the odd firelight. Metal collided with metal as the Divine Assassins attacked. Aiden was already in action next to me, cutting off the arm of a dark fae who got too close to us. My fire sword was drawn and ready, lighting up the area around us with its bright flaming blade.

171

I was grabbed from behind by my hair and yanked to my knees as we were swarmed from above with dark fae that were descending around us. The Radiant fae were already in the air battling them, and bursts of rainbow colored magic collided with the deeper shades of magic from the dark fae. It was illuminating the ground like a fireworks show. Ridley was quick to take out the dark fae who had me by my hair before he could take my head off, and I swung around to slice the throat of one who was about to do the same to him from behind.

Aiden and Ridley then quickly shoved me between the two of them, with their backs facing out towards our enemies. Fae from both sides were falling out of the sky from battle, and one hit the ground with a huge thud right beside us. It was a dark fae, and I wasted no time in taking its head off so that it wouldn't be getting up.

Then we noticed the ground starting to slither and move. Whether it was magical illusion, or really happening, somehow they were controlling tree roots to grab the feet of the people who were still in the outskirts of the tree line. Radiant fae quickly flew over to the humans and lifted them up in the air, dropping them off in the campsite. We spotted a small circle of female dark fae chanting by one of the huts, and I pointed it out to Aiden, who teleported and took off the heads of all four of them faster than the blink of an eye. The tree roots stopped immediately after that.

Now that everyone was out of the trees however, we were in a different sort of danger. The odd campfires that were burning that deep purple and midnight blue started to rise higher and higher, and strange beings made of the odd flame began to step out of them. They took on the rough shape of the dark fae, wings included. Every step they took they dropped flame off their bodies, which was setting the ground beneath them on fire as well. The flame-beings began to attack our army, both in the sky and on the ground, surrounding anyone they touched with fire. Screams were echoing all around me as I watched bodies get engulfed with the unnatural firelight.

It appeared that the fire beings were also being conjured by the dark fae, as Lucius spotted another grouping of them chanting together on the edge of the clearing. He tried to teleport into the circle to take them out but hit a barrier that stopped him. They had erected a magical dome, which was glowing like a black light over the top of them to protect them. I saw smoke coming off of Lucius where his body had collided with the barrier. He teleported over to us immediately, still smoking.

"We have to shut that down, or there is going to be big trouble," he said, showing no sign of any pain.

"I think we should use the iron dust. It will be effective and shut all of them down, even at the risk of also paralyzing the Radiant fae," Ridley said. He was right, this all could have been avoided and probably with a lot less death, had we just neutralized them with the magical iron powder. The dark fae were way stronger on their home turf than the last time we fought them.

We fought our way over to my grandpa, who had blood splattered all over him, but didn't look like he was even breaking a sweat. Ridley told him his thoughts, and he didn't even need time to contemplate it because he was thinking the same thing. He began to bark out the orders for our Divine Assassins to move back into formation and fall back, so that they could cover the area in iron powder.

I yelled out to the first Radiant fae I could see, who flew down to me after ripping the wings off of a dark fae she was battling in the air above us. "Get your people out of the air, fall back! We're going to use iron, you need to get as far out of here as you can!" I shouted. She wasted no time in taking off to relay the message, and I saw the Radiant fae begin to fall back to our people as we all moved back towards the tree line.

A handful of Divine Assassins pulled grenade launchers off their backs, and loaded them with what looked like grenades. They began shooting the grenades into the campsite, even though some of the Radiant fae and Divine Assassins were still engaged in fighting. The iron wouldn't harm our men, but it would paralyze the Radiant fae. They exploded loudly, and fine black dust covered the air. We continued to back away from the fight to the tree line, but noticed that a huge magical barrier like the one the dark fae had covered themselves with was growing over the area like a dome closing. We were going to be trapped if we didn't move quickly.

Our team began to run, and the Radiant fae with us transformed into their light forms, buzzing ahead of us without having to be told twice. The magical iron spread across the campsite, freezing any fae it touched, but the dark fae who were chanting inside their magical barrier were unharmed, meaning the flame-beings were still on the loose. The majority of us made it into the trees and kept running full speed ahead. I glanced back and saw the magical dome they were erecting touch down on all side of the campsite now, locking in the remaining Radiant fae and the few Divine Assassins that didn't make it out in time.

As our men ran to get out, I saw them scream out as their bodies hit the dome. The skin melted off their hands where they touched it, and smoke was rising off of their clothing. The flame-beings swarmed on them, engulfing them with their purple and blue fire. Their screams were fading one by one as the fire choked the life out of them. Then they moved on to the Radiant fae who were paralyzed, taking them out efficiently. It was too much to watch, and I turned my head back to the front and kept up with the others.

"We have to get out of here, regroup on the outside! They are too strong to fight here! Open the tear up and get us out of here!" I heard my grandpa shout out. Solara was already on top of it...zooming ahead of our group with her fae to start opening the tear. None of the dark fae were following us, but the flame-beings were probably going to be coming at any moment.

We were passing by the men that had been hit with the arrows earlier, they were still huddled up together and alive. People helped grab them and hauled them along with us as we continued running forward.

The tear to get back to our own dimension was being ripped open, and I couldn't have been more relieved. I knew that this mission would have some dangers, but had no idea it would go downhill so quickly. We didn't even lay eyes on Bathory, and I had no idea if we even got close to her. Everyone was hustling to get through the tear once it was big enough. Looking behind me, I saw the flame-beings were indeed on their way, lighting the forest up on fire as they glided over the ground effortlessly. They were mesmerizing to watch, graceful like ballerinas but extremely deadly.

Aiden shoved me in front of him, and Ridley followed as he and Lucius brought up the rear. My grandfather and Solara, along with the fae helping her with the tear came last and began to stitch it up the second we were all through. Not wanting to risk them following us, the Divine Assassins immediately began portaling out of the remote Canadian forest and back to their headquarters. The Radiant fae were leaving for The Lucent, and things cleared out in a matter of minutes. I grabbed Aiden, and we were sailing through a portal back to our house in London.

The other vampires were brought back to the house as well, and after we made sure that everyone was alright, my grandfather insisted that we leave right away for Divine Assassin headquarters. Since I was the only vampire who would get through their security, the others would have to stay behind. There was no time to debate it, and I said a quick goodbye to Aiden as Ridley and I took off yet again through another portal, which left me wondering if vampires could get jet lag.

The Divine Assassins were clearly shaken up. We lost about twelve men total in The Gloom. None of them died a pretty death, but at least we were able to get the ones injured with the arrows out alive with us. Hopefully whatever kind of poison they were hit with would fade soon, they were already feeling much better, some of them being able to stand up now.

Grandpa was wiping his face down with a damp towel, trying to get the blood off of him. "We'll need to regroup and assess if going back in for another attempt will be worth it or not. And we'll need more men, more weapons if we do go back in. Skyy, I need you to contact the Radiant fae, apologize for having to use the iron, make sure they know we didn't have any other choice. The last thing we need is a war with them on top of it. Anyone who needs medical attention should head to the medical wing," he said. I could tell he was trying to stand strong but he was very frustrated.

We had a brief meeting before people started dispersing. and Grandpa pulled Ridley and I aside before we headed out.

"Stick to the plan in London until we can figure out what to do next with Bathory. Perhaps if we can nail the murderer there he can lead us to her. Either way, he needs to be stopped. Two crazy vampires on the loose is two too many. And please make sure relations with the Radiant fae stay intact. Keep your guard up, who knows what to expect after that escapade in The Gloom. You two stay safe," he said as he pat me on my arm.

I nodded, and we said our goodbyes. Ridley wanted to swing by his office to grab a few things he needed before we opened a portal back to the house in London. I couldn't wait to get into a hot bath and have some blood.

Once I had bathed and changed, I needed to get in touch with Dreamer and make sure everything was alright there. I used my pink crystal to contact her, and she appeared at the front door of the house a few minutes later. She wasn't smiling like she usually did, and walked inside as I opened the door for her without saying a word.

"I'm really sorry for everything that has happened, Dreamer. Nobody expected it to go down like that," I started cautiously.

I could tell she had been crying, her delicate face was streaked with tear stains. "We warned you that it would be hard to fight them in The Gloom. If we had known they had their Callers there with them we would have been better prepared. We had no way to neutralize their barriers," she said in a soft whisper.

"We all lost a lot today, Dreamer. I know it's hard, but I hope that you understand why we made the call to use our weapons against them?" I didn't know how to approach the subject, and had my grandfather not asked me to, I probably wouldn't have even brought it up.

She nodded her head, "I know, nobody blames you. It was good that we had a way to escape before we lost even more. At least most of us were able to get out."

That was all I needed to know, and I wasn't going to push it any farther. My grandpa wanted me to apologize, but it looked like they understood what happened and why. "I just wanted to update you from our end. We're just standing by to see what happens next. I don't think we're going to be sending more people in without a much more solid plan. But please keep us in the loop, if you do decide to retaliate. I realize that you've been fighting a war with the dark fae for a long, long time, but Bathory is a huge priority. We'd like to help, and be involved in any way we can," I replied.

We spent some time just talking and visiting after I got the important stuff out of the way. I saw some of her bubbly personality creeping back in by the time it was over. After she left, I almost didn't know what to do with myself. It was quiet and calm for once. So I took the opportunity to find Aiden and spend some quality alone time with him before the next shit storm hit.

Chapter 17

Jackson sat at his computer, about to delete the dating profile he had created to stalk women. He thought that he'd try something new, and it didn't work for him. The only women he liked to hunt and kill were prostitutes. There were too many complications with other women...the prostitutes never asked questions, they just took the money or drugs that Jack threw at them. He didn't enjoy the conversations he had to endure in order to get the girl Arabella out on a first date. The only part he did enjoy was taunting the other vampires with her in public, and then ripping into her throat leaving her on death's doorstep. He knew that they'd try to save her...and they did. He saved some of her blood, to use for tracking her. Although he didn't plan any of it, things worked out better than he expected. Now he had a way to find where they were hiding at again.

He absently rubbed his missing fingers that the redheaded vampire had cut off with her burning fire sword, cursing under his breath. They didn't hurt anymore, but all he was left with were two nubs where his fingers used to be. They'd grow back in time, but it would take at least a few years. Regenerating blood and tissue from wounds was a lot easier to recover from than missing limbs, appendages, or bones.

There was a message in his inbox, and curiosity got the best of Jack. He clicked it open and viewed the message. The girl was young, probably in her early twenties. Age didn't matter to Jack though...he wasn't picky when it came to that. What piqued his interest was that she looked like she had little to no inhibitions. And that interested him. After his last encounter with the chatty Arabella, he would look forward to someone who didn't ask a lot of questions as long as he kept the booze flowing or the drugs coming. Someone who wouldn't mind going for a walk in the dark alley behind a bar.

Jack usually picked his victims up off the street. He knew the areas that the working girls frequented, and it was always easy with no questions asked. The online dating profile wasn't his style really, it left too much of a trail to look into if the wrong person disappeared. But...the killer in him was just too tempted to reply to the girl.

He sat there pondering the situation for a moment, before he came to his senses and deleted the message, and then proceeded to delete the entire dating profile. He didn't have time for this. He needed to focus on tracking the newly made vampire, and coming up with a plan to get rid of Elizabeth Bathory once and for all. It'd be a lot less complicated to just go down to King's Cross and pick up a prostitute, than fiddle around on the computer for a week trying to convince the girl to meet up. And Jack liked to keep things simple... "if it ain't broke don't fix it" was a motto for a good reason.

One of the few useful things Bathory was good for was that she taught Jack some simple black magic spells. The tracking spell he had used to find the redheaded vampire the first time was going to come in use again. You had to have the person's blood that you wanted to find, and you could only use that blood sample once. You'd need another blood sample to perform the spell again, and unfortunately he didn't have any more of Skyy's blood. He did have plenty of Arabella's blood though, and he'd saved enough to be able to track her more than once.

Later that night after he had performed the spell, a plan was set into motion in Jack's head that even he could never have imagined could work out so perfectly....he was about to kill two birds with one stone.

Chapter 18

"Well, the dating website is officially a bust," Ridley stated as he walked into the living room where Skyy, Aiden, and Fiona were gathered.

"No reply?" I asked as I moved over on the couch so Ridley could fit.

"No reply, and the whole damn profile is gone now. I guess he deleted it," he said in frustration.

"It was a long shot anyway honestly. At least we tried," I said to reassure him. Everyone's morale was low after the disaster in The Gloom. "It's just too bad that those fingers I cut off of Jack the Ripper didn't lead us anywhere," I added.

Ridley got an odd look on his face when I said that. It got my attention, and I had to ask, "What is that look for Ridley?"

"Wellll...there is a way we could use those fingers to find him, but it's against Divine Assassin's rules," he replied.

I took my feet off the coffee table and sat up, even more interested than before. "Don't just keep us hanging! Spill the beans Ridley, what are you talking about?"

"I don't know the spell, but I know there is a way to track someone using their blood. It's black magic though, and if anyone knew we were even thinking about it, we'd be in serious shit," he said.

I cringed at the thought of using black magic. I didn't want any part of it, and I certainly didn't want to get Ridley in any more trouble with the Divine Assassins than I already got him into. I shook my head no, "Forget about it. We don't need to be messing with black magic. A little here, and a little there, and before you know it we're on the wrong path. I don't know much about it, but I know I certainly don't want to become anything even remotely close to Bathory, the Queen of Black Magic."

Aiden agreed with me, "You're right Skyy. None of us need to be messing with that kind of stuff. We'll find Jack sooner or later, or he'll find us. Either way, we'll get him," he said as he pat my leg for reassurance.

"And hopefully before he manages to kill again," I added glumly. He could be out there right now trying to kill again. The thought pissed me off beyond belief.

Ridley, who was pretty much as square as they come, wouldn't drop it though, "If I thought it would help though, I could try to figure out the spell myself, and perform it. You wouldn't have to be involved at all, and I would take full responsibility for it if I was caught," he offered.

I knew he was just trying to be helpful and nice, we were all at our wits end trying to find both of the serial killer vampires. "Ridley, I know you're just trying to help, but there has to be another way. I don't want you to even risk it," I said to him.

He nodded, and I knew that would be the end of it. Arabella came downstairs to join us and I was happy that she was venturing out of her room for once. I think we scared her when we told her that though the Divine Assassins on the property were human, they could still kill her very easily. Once we left for The Gloom, she didn't leave her room at all. Her bloodlust and cravings were starting to calm down to the point she could probably tolerate being in the same room with Ridley though. She gave a shy smile and a wave as she entered the room.

I waved back to her and smiled warmly. "Glad to see you downstairs, Arabella. Pull up a chair and join us," I said in a cheerful voice. I knew she had heard everything that we had said about her previously, including when Grandpa said she could possibly be a plant. And I also felt bad that none of us really had the time to focus on being there for her more to help her transition. Fiona spent a decent amount of time with her once we were back, but she was also alone for way longer than I would have liked if I were in her shoes.

"Hello everyone," she replied as she moved some books and papers off a chair so she could sit. We made some small talk with her, but since I had Ridley there in the room with me I took the opportunity to try to hammer out our next plan of attack.

"So when do you want to hit the bricks again after Jack the Ripper?" I asked. Our only option was to hope we ran into him again at this point.

"No time like the now," he replied and gave me a wink. "The sooner the better, in my opinion. We have some other locations we can still stake out, or we can try the ones we have already spotted him in.

I thought on it for a moment. Could he possibly be dumb enough to go back to that same alley we encountered him in twice now? Probably. "I say we try our luck with the Argyle Square alley again honestly. Even if we have to sit there every night for a month, I'll put money on him showing up there again." I really wished that Arabella knew more.

"Ok then, I'll go back to headquarters until it is dark out and get some work done, then we can head out there tonight," Ridley said as he stood up and fixed his pants, making sure his nerdy shirt was tucked into them sufficiently.

Everyone said goodbye to him, and I noticed a little smile from Arabella when she said her goodbye to him. I might have been mistaken, but it looked to me like she may have a spark of interest in Ridley. I didn't stare at her very long trying to figure it out, instead I just blew out a long breath. It'd be interesting to see how that would work out in the long run.

I entwined my fingers through Aiden's and took the remote off the arm of the couch with my other hand. We had some time to kill, and I figured we could surf for yet another horrible British television show to watch.

Christian eventually came down to join us, and not long after that Lucius. He didn't bother to sit down, but instead made everyone uncomfortable with his presence by standing up with his legs slightly spread and his arms crossed while he watched television. Lucius the Lurking Shadow was large and in charge. I kept glancing at him the whole time, hoping he would take a seat. After thirty minutes of him standing there silent and motionless, I couldn't take it anymore.

"For cryin' out loud, Lucius! Sit down already, you're making us all nervous!" I said as I laughed. I was half kidding, but half serious.

He glanced over at me and returned my smile. "Sorry, I got caught up in the show. I love British television," he said as he moved over to the only empty chair left in the room.

I moaned in disapproval, "You love British television?" I exclaimed. "It's terrible!"

He rolled his eyes dramatically in response, "I suppose you can't wait to get back to America and you're reality television and court room dramas? You know most of the best programs on back home are spinoffs of British programs?"

He actually had a point, and I knew it. Some of my favorite shows were on BBC first. "Yeah, yeah," I said dismissing his remarks. Try as I might, I couldn't get into the British versions of those shows.

We killed the rest of the afternoon chatting and watching bad television. Ridley portaled back in just before nightfall. I headed up to my room to change into my "field gear" tucking vials of the silver dust into hidden pockets, and strapping on knives, and finally my fire sword which would be concealed under my long coat. I tied my hair back into a tight bun, and put on a pair of running shoes.

My whole vampire family, with the exception of Arabella, would be joining me tonight as well. We met downstairs, and although we looked like a normal bunch of folks out for a night on the town, underneath we were armed to the teeth.

Once we were ready we piled into a minivan that Lucius had gone to rent earlier that afternoon. I wasn't upset at the fact that I didn't have to ride on the Underground again. The smells and temptations were just too much for me in such a small confined area. Being out around humans was bad enough, but I didn't like that I could possibly hurt people on a subway.

Aiden and I sat in the very back of the van, Fiona and Christian were in the middle seat, and Ridley and Lucius were up front. Not only did Lucius have bad taste in television, but he also had bad taste in music. He was listening to opera, and I don't think any person in the van besides him liked it. I know Aiden and I were ready to get out of the car as soon as possible.

We parked the van once we got to our spot, one we were getting more and more familiar with at this point. Lucius turned around in the driver's seat and looked at me as I was unbuckling my seatbelt. "I know I don't have to elaborate, Skyy...." he said as he gave me the "look" and I knew what he was about to say.

"I won't do anything silly, Lucius. I promise," I said as I smiled at him. It was nice having so many people who cared so much about me.

We walked down the street towards the entrance that we could easily get into the alleyway from. Aiden had his hand placed on the low of my back gently, but I knew he was also trying to protect me if things got crazy in an instant. And crazy would be a good word for what happened in the moments to come.

As we got closer to the alley we first encountered Jack the Ripper in, all of us vampires went on high alert. We smelled blood, and more importantly I smelled fresh blood, and that wasn't good for me...and certainly not good for whoever's blood it was that I was smelling.

Lucius and Fiona teleported out of eyesight in an instant, to access the situation. Christian followed in the blink of an eye. Ridley started running to catch up, and Aiden and I tried our best to keep pace with him so he wouldn't be left alone. We got to the same exact spot that we had interrupted Jack the Ripper in before, and were shocked at what we saw.

There was a brutally murdered woman spread out on her back on the ground. The blood was still very fresh, some of it hadn't even coagulated yet. Her clothing was in shambles and covered in blood. She had been cut wide open and her intestines were draped over her right shoulder. Her neck was cut straight down to the bone. The mouth had been slit open at the sides, from ear to ear, making it look as though she had a gruesome smile. Her nose was cut off completely. The smell of blood was overwhelming me.

But there was a note laying just to the side of her, carefully placed with a small rock on top of it so that it wouldn't blow away, and so it wouldn't get soaked with blood:

Sorry I couldt be here to meet you and see how our mutual frind Arabella is doing, I have anothr date I am off to tonight. Better luck next time – Jack

Lucius had been the one to pick it up and read it first before passing it around to us. I was pretty certain that Jack was long gone by now, but we were all on high alert.

Lucius spoke before any of us could really even think about our next step. "There is nothing else for us to do here, she is gone, and we need to get gone before someone comes along and sees us at this murder scene."

He had a point, and we hotfooted it back to our minivan, carefully keeping an eye out all around us for any sign of Jack. Once we were all inside and on the road, we figured it was safe enough to talk, in case Jack had still been around the area we didn't want him hearing us.

Aiden had dug inside our little cooler to get me some blood, since I was on the verge of bloodlusting again, and I thanked him as I sipped it to calm myself down. Fiona was very angry though.

"How the hell did he know we would come there tonight? That was a deliberate taunt," she said in a raised voice.

Lucius was calmer about the situation but I knew he wasn't happy about it either. "I'm hoping he hasn't found us again, I don't see how it would be possible. There would be no way of him knowing we were heading out to that exact spot again tonight. Other than…"

He didn't want to say it, but we were all thinking it: Arabella.

Fiona shook her head, as if to discard the idea he was putting out there. "Arabella? I don't see how she could have been in contact with him. We took her phone away from her, she has no access to any phones or computers. We've kept her on a tight leash since she's been with us, and she has barely even left her room."

Christian chimed in, "With the exception of when we were all in The Gloom, I think one of us would have been made alert if she were talking to someone on the phone. And as Fi said, she has no other means of communication."

Ridley turned to face the back of the van from the passenger seat, "Yeah, but she was the only one there who we aren't sure we can trust. And she heard us talking about our plans tonight, she came downstairs as we were talking about them."

"It's the most logical possibility. One thing is for certain, Jack knew we were coming to that spot tonight. And…his bad grammar aside…I hope that he was just bluffing about having another date tonight," Lucius said grimly as he glanced in the rear view mirror at all of us.

"Well there wouldn't be much we could do about it anyway, he is one step ahead of us. I say we get back to the house and see what Arabella has to say about all of this," Aiden suggested.

I didn't say anything at all about the situation, because I was busy sipping my bagged blood and trying to get myself back to "normal" but I wondered what the vampires would do if they found out that Arabella was somehow involved with Jack the Ripper.

We made it back to the house in London about a half hour later. I figured that we should have come up with a plan before we approached her about it, but nobody said anything. Instead Lucius barged in the front door and boomed out for her to get downstairs immediately. She came down the stairs cautiously, sensing the irritability in his voice. We were all in the living room by now, and Arabella gave us a shy smile as she walked in the room. I averted my eyes from her, because I knew we were about to grill the poor girl, and Lucius was pretty damn scary as it was, even without the yelling.

And boy did he yell. "You better tell me right now what is going on with you! Because right now I am regretting saving your life! Did he send you here to spy on us? Was it your plan all along for us to find you, half dead, and turn you?!" he screamed out at her. His voice was deafening.

Arabella looked genuinely shocked and confused. Her brow furrowed and she looked like she was about to cry. "W-w-what are you talking about, Lucius?" she stuttered out. Either she was a really good actress, or she was totally blindsided by this.

I didn't expect what happened next. Lucius grabbed Arabella by her throat and picked her up off the floor by it, slamming her into the nearest wall. I jumped up out of my seat and gasped, but Aiden grabbed my hand to stop me from helping her.

Lucius had pulled out a long silver dagger and held it to her throat. She was panicking now, and tears were flowing out of her eyes. "I'll ask you again, are you in contact with the man who attacked you?! Is this all a setup?! Have you been sneaking about, giving him information about us?! This sword is made of silver, Arabella...did we tell you what happens when vampires are cut with silver?" he threatened. He left the rest to her imagination.

I was not ok with how this was being handled at all, but I suppose in the long run it was better to catch her off guard and scare the shit out of her, than to beat around the bush. At least we'd get an honest reaction out of her.

She was gasping for the words to reply to him, and he loosened his grip on her throat so she could. "I swear to God, I don't know what you're talking about! Why would I be in touch with him?! He tried to kill me! I am terrified he'll come back to finish the job! Please, Lucius, you're scaring me!" she said as she convulsed with sobs.

Lucius and Aiden exchanged some sort of glance with each other, and I guess it was their silent way of saying they believed her, because Lucius let go of his death grip on her and lowered his knife. He pointed to the couch, and barked out, "Sit down," loudly to her. She obeyed, still terrified and sobbing.

He stood looming over her with his arms crossed. His violet eyes were reflecting and glowing. I knew he was pissed off and meant business. Everyone else in the room kept quiet. "Explain to me, how the murderer knew exactly where we would be tonight, and the exact time as well then?"

Her mouth fell open but no words came out. She looked confused, and of course she was scared. "L-lucius, I don't know what you're even talking about. I knew you were all going out tonight to look for him, I want you to catch him! I was scared to be here in the house alone without all of the vampires again, even though we have Divine Assassins here, I am terrified he will get to me again. What could I possibly gain by working with a psychopath!?"

By now I was pretty much believing her story was true. Aside from making a bad decision on a dating website, I didn't think she was hiding anything. Her fear was just too real to fake.

"I don't know what you could gain from it, Arabella. Why do people do crazy things, why do people kill and hurt others? I don't want to point the finger at you, but you showed up out of nowhere, and now the killer knows our plans. Seems fishy to me," Lucius said as he glared at her.

"I swear I would never betray any of you! You saved my life, I am forever grateful. You can keep someone with me twenty-four seven if you need to, I have nothing to hide, I promise. Please believe me!" she begged.

He bent down to look her in the eyes, with a menacing look on his face. "And that is exactly what we're going to do. If we find out that you're lying, don't think even for a second that I won't end your life. I don't take kindly to people betraying me, especially my family."

Arabella nodded at him, fully understanding his threat. If she was innocent I was sure that she was questioning how "friendly" we were now. She was brand new to this world, and didn't choose to be turned into a vampire like I had. It was a lot to soak in even if you did choose to be. I didn't want her to be afraid of us like she clearly was of Jack the Ripper, but until we knew we could trust her we couldn't take any chances. Lucius' method might not have been nice, but it was effective.

"Christian, come with me upstairs. We're going to do a full sweep of Arabella's room. In fact we're going to do a full sweep of the entire house to look for anything hidden she may have used to contact the murderer with," Lucius said. He was catching Arabella off guard, so if there was anything hidden now would be the time to find it for sure.

Christian nodded at him and stood up from the couch, "You got it boss," he said as he gave Fiona a quick peck on her cheek, then walked upstairs.

"Aiden, you are in charge of Arabella until we're done. She doesn't move off that couch until then. If she does…" he made a knife over the throat motion with his hand. Dramatic much? I didn't think it was possible for more fear to creep into Arabella's face, but apparently there was room for more. She folded her hands in her lap, still crying, and looked down at the floor.

Aiden nodded at Lucius, understanding his orders. Nobody knew what to say, so nobody said anything at all. It was an uncomfortable silence, with the exception of Arabella's crying. None of us wanted to make eye contact with her either. Ridley was fidgeting with his phone, playing a game on it. Fiona rest her head on the back of the couch, pretending to close her eyes and sleep but I knew better.

Once the men were done upstairs, they searched all the closets, nooks, and crannies of the downstairs area. There were no phones, or devices she could have used for outside communication that were unaccounted for. It turned out she was telling the truth…at least about that part of it.

Lucius told her that they didn't find anything, and that for now her story panned out. He sent her off upstairs, telling her he hoped that he could trust her, and Fiona went with her. For the foreseeable future she was going to be with one of us at all times.

Lucius then pointed to the remainder of us in the room, "You four, get in the van. We're going for a ride." He walked out the front door after that, and we all followed.

Once we were in the van, he drove a good distance away from the house and then pulled over to the side of the road. "I think the girl is telling the truth," he said.

Aiden nodded in agreement, "I think so as well. She was genuinely afraid and looked as though she was clueless about your accusations."

Lucius nodded with him. "Well there will be no more chances for her to communicate with him if that was what was going on for some reason. But it still leaves us with the question of how Jack knew we'd show up there tonight."

"Maybe he has figured out where we are again. He found me once. Ridley had mentioned that there was some sort of spell you can perform to find people. It might be a long shot but maybe he could do something like that?" I offered.

Ridley spoke up from the front seat, "Yes, those kinds of spells do exist but they are black magic spells. I have no idea how they even work either. It is possibly Bathory may have taught him some spells though."

Lucius pondered what we said for a moment. I wondered if he'd feel guilty for being so hard on Arabella if it turned out she was truly innocent after all. "Is it possible for your Divine Assassins to send some more men out here, to patrol the area at night? If he is lurking around here, that could explain it. And moving to a new location would be pointless too I suppose. We're as safe and well protected as we can be from him where we are now."

Ridley nodded to his question. "I'm sure of it. I can make the call right now and get some men here if you'd like." Lucius gave him the green light, and a two minute call to our headquarters was all it took. We'd have men here within the hour.

Lucius put the van back in drive and we headed back to the house. The night was still young, but we decided to stay in for the remainder of it. Lucius and Christian also went outside the house and patrolled the area with the Divine Assassins, looking for any sign that Jack might be hiding in the shadows out there. Nobody saw anything suspicious. Aiden and I kept checking the news stations and websites for any information on the murdered woman we came across tonight. There wasn't anything about the murder anywhere, so we assumed that the body hadn't been found yet. It was in a dark alley and it was still nighttime. Once morning came it was likely to be found.

We were fairly certain that Jack the Ripper couldn't go out in the daylight like we could. Once the sun was up, we came up with a simple plan: head back to the same spot again and see if we'd find another murder, or catch him in the act. Either way it was all we had for now, and something fishy was going on for sure.

Chapter 19

Jack had finally come up with a solid plan, one that he hoped would work. All he needed to do now was contact one of the vampires that Elizabeth had here to keep an eye on him. She told him if he changed his mind, and wanted to come to The Gloom to get in touch with one of them, and they could get to her. The pests had already cleaned up the body from the night before, yet another masterpiece that would go unnoticed to the public. He knew they wouldn't be too far away, all he had to do was walk outside into his backyard.

Dressed in a crisply pressed suit, which he always did himself, he stepped out into his backyard. "I need to get in touch with Elizabeth," he said out loud.

Within moments, two male vampires appeared. He was familiar with both of them, as they had been "assigned" to him for several years now. 'What a boring life they must have, to sit around and wait for me to kill again,' he thought to himself.

They didn't speak a word once they appeared, and Jack was going to keep it quick. "Please tell Elizabeth that I'd like to speak with her more about joining her in The Gloom. As you can see, things are getting rather dicey around here, with the other vampires following my trail. If she'll agree, have her meet me here, at this address at the time of her choosing," he said as he handed them a small piece of paper with the address on it.

One of the vampires nodded, "I'll contact her dark fae and have them enter The Gloom to relay the message. We will bring you a reply soon." That was all there was to it. The vampires were gone in an instant and a sinister smile crept across Jack's face as he stood in his dark backyard.

...

Valentina came before Elizabeth, who was holed up nearly all day and night in a small hut in the middle of one of the bigger dark fae settlements they had in The Gloom. There were guards both inside and outside the hut around the clock. She wasn't taking any chances. She was sick and tired of being in The Gloom, and living like a cavewoman in the stupid huts they called home. The dark fae still lived mostly off the land, and

192

much like The Lucent where the Radiant fae lived, there was no modern technology there. Not that Elizabeth really minded that, she had been around long before electricity, but she had always lived in luxury and wealth.

Her dark fae captain bowed down before her briefly, crossing her one arm over her chest as she did so, to show her allegiance. "Countess, we have received word from your vampires that your ally Jackson Ripleigh would like to meet with you to discuss coming here to The Gloom," she said.

Elizabeth's head snapped up from the spell book she was reading from. "Go on," she said, intrigued. Her odd eyes glittered in the flames from the candles that were lit in the hut.

Valentina handed her a small piece of paper, which she took out of her hand and read. It had an address on it in London. "What is the meaning of this?" she inquired.

"He said if you wish to meet with him, to go to this address at the time of your choosing," Valentina replied.

"Why doesn't he want to meet at his house, as usual?" Elizabeth pondered.

"I believe he thinks they are watching him, and does not want them to know where he resides." Valentina offered.

Elizabeth nodded, "Will your people allow him to take safety here, without issue?" She needed to make sure the dark fae would let another vampire come into their realm. They weren't thrilled about Bathory being here, but she had taught them so much about magic and the dark arts that they tolerated her and allied with her for the benefit of both sides. Elizabeth got her army, and the dark fae learned new magic...even if it did cost them a few hundred of their own kind to her experiments and temper.

"He won't be allowed to kill freely here. They barely tolerate your... 'activities'. They won't allow it from him," Valentina said, trying to put it nicely.

"Very well. Tell him I will meet him there tomorrow night, at eleven. I will need a few dark fae to accompany me through the tear," she said as she dismissed Valentina and went back to reading her book. It didn't hold her interest long before she drifted off thinking about Jackson. She was happy that he was finally seeing the light, and taking her advice to get out of London before things went south. Their relationship wasn't always great, but she had an odd attachment to him nonetheless.

…

Back in London, the vampire met with Jack again to inform him that Elizabeth agreed to meet him. They parted ways and Jack smiled again to himself. The hard part was done – getting her to agree to meet him. Now all he had to do was wait.

Chapter 20

Aiden and I decided to go for a walk during the day since it was so nice outside for once. It had been raining on and off for days, and the sun was finally shining. We were several miles from the house in London, and easily out of earshot of the other vampires. I wanted to talk to him about going into The Lucent and having a quick wedding ceremony. I held his hand, and smiled as I looked up at Aiden. He was still thrilled each time we walked in the sunlight, after being away from it for centuries.

"You always look so happy when we're in the sun," I said smiling at him.

He smiled back at me and kissed the back of my hand as he held it. "It's so beautiful, I'll never take it for granted. You don't realize how much you miss certain things until they are gone, or you no longer have the luxury of indulging in them any longer."

We walked long enough until we hit civilization again. There was a scattering of small shops and cafes, and a lot of people had the same idea we did about getting out and enjoying the sunshine. I was sure to not only drink a decent amount of blood before we left, but also had some packed in a small portable fabric cooler that Aiden was carrying over his shoulder. By the time we got to town I felt comfortable enough around all the humans, and not having any cravings.

We found a wooden bench under a nice shade tree in a park to sit down on. People were out walking their dogs, biking, and doing normal human things. Although Aiden and I were certainly enjoying each other's company and the nice weather, we had a lot more weighing on us than all the people who passed us by. It was nice to take a few hours to get away from the house and the others to just relax. We didn't know what tonight would bring, and I know that Aiden was constantly worried about me getting hurt or into trouble, no matter how much I assured him that I would be careful.

He told me more than once how proud of me that he was for not losing it last night when we came across the woman who

Jack murdered. The blood was fresh, and it was most definitely a temptation that set me back for at least an hour, but I did hold it together. I guess things were getting easier for me, and I hoped that it would continue to get easier.

Aiden sat close to me, running his fingers through my hair on the back of my head. It felt nice and comforting. "Now that we're away from prying eyes, I wanted to get your thoughts on getting into The Lucent for a ceremony?" I asked him.

He grinned at me with his perfect teeth. "Absolutely. I'd love to call you Mrs. Carrick as soon as possible. If we are able to, let's head there tomorrow," he said with enthusiasm.

I raised my eyebrows at him but returned his smile. "Tomorrow it is then. We should get in touch with Dreamer sometime today to let them know."

"So is this ceremony going to satisfy your legalities for me being your wife? Or will we still need to file for a wedding certificate and have a ceremony in front of family and friends before I can ravish you?" I said as I smiled slyly at him.

"You naughty girl. Your mind is always in the gutter," Aiden said as he pinched my cheek. "The Lucent ceremony will suffice. So long as we are joined together, and with witnesses I am satisfied. We'll just keep it our little secret until we have the big wedding for the masses."

I bounced up and down a little on the bench in excitement before throwing my arms around Aiden's neck and kissing his cheek. "Yay! We'll finally be married! Tomorrow no less!"

He smiled at me as our lips met softly. The kiss deepened and it was easy to forget we were in public. Before long I was lost in nothing but his embrace and I climbed up onto his lap with my arms entwined behind his neck. We were probably making out for a good five minutes, and it was getting hotter by the moment. I was seriously aroused, and because I was sitting on Aiden's lap I knew he was too. I broke away from his lips and our eyes met. I already knew mine were glowing by now, and his met mine with that beautiful bright green that I loved. "I love you," he whispered as he gently pressed his forehead up against mine.

I softly whispered it back as our lips touched again. I was going to need blood if we kept this up much longer. Had we not been in public I would have already nipped at him to taste his salty, wonderful blood. A few minutes later, as we sat there necking like two horny teenagers in the park, I heard someone say "Get a bloody room, there are kids here."

Aiden chuckled at the man and shrugged it off. But it ticked me off, probably because I was so horny and starting to bloodlust for Aiden. "Piss off, you old fart," I called out back to him.

He shot me the bird after he had passed us by and was a short distance away. "Fucking Americans," he said though he thought we couldn't hear him. I was up off Aiden's lap in a shot after him, moving way faster than a human would have. I was still trying to get used to moving like "normal" in public. Aiden grabbed my arm quickly as we heard a couple gasp out in horror at us. They were terrified.

Aiden told me to sit on the bench, and told me to drink from the Thermos of blood we had stored in there as he quickly moved over to the couple. He was smiling, looking friendly. I knew he was mind whammying them to forget about seeing us. I felt bad for letting my temper go like that in a public place.

The couple walked away from Aiden and went on their way as if nothing had happened. Nobody else had seen it, thankfully. Aiden came back over to me, with a smile on his face as usual. He never really got mad at me, no matter how bad I messed up. I took a sip of my blood, wiped my mouth and returned his smile.

He took my hand back in his as he sat down. "Finish up your drink, and then I think we should be heading back to the house," he said without a hint of irritation in his voice.

I looked over at him sheepishly. "You're not mad at me?"

He shook his head no, "It wasn't ideal, but it happens. You seem to keep forgetting how new you are to all of this.

You're very hard on yourself, but in reality this is all normal for a new vampire. It is also why the idea of you being out in the field alone with just the Divine Assassins doesn't thrill me. They can't neutralize a situation like that."

"Maybe they can," I said as I shrugged my shoulders. "Who knows what all they can do yet, I have barely scratched the surface of my duties there. They are all still unsure of me doing anything on my own. And clearly all of you think the same thing, for good reason."

I finished up my blood, and placed the empty Thermos back in the little cooler. We took our time heading back to the house, enjoying the last few minutes of our time alone together. As we walked up to the front door, it flew open and Lucius stormed out of it, almost mowing us down in the process.

"Whoa there. What's the hurry?" Aiden asked him.

Lucius just kept going though, and hopped into the rental van and drove away. "Ohhhh-kay," I said in wonder, watching the van disappear down the road. "I wonder what that was all about."

Aiden just shrugged as we walked inside. Fiona was making her way down the stairs as we shut the door. "He is sick of hearing Arabella crying non-stop. She hasn't really stopped since yesterday," she said as she rolled her eyes, clearly agreeing with Lucius but taking a much more mature approach to it.

"Well I hope he comes back with our ride before we need it tonight," I said and laughed. She nodded at me and went to the kitchen to heat some blood for herself. Christian was watching Arabella so she could get a break. I felt semi-bad for not wanting to get too involved with her, or try to comfort her. If it turned out she was guilty of betraying us, I really didn't know if I could be around when they dealt with her.

Aiden and I went to our room and shut the door. I needed to get in touch with Dreamer this afternoon, but didn't need anyone else in the house listening to our conversation. I hoped she could keep quiet about it. I took my pink crystal out and rubbed it, and before long she was flying outside our window in her tiny light form. I opened the window as she flew inside our room and appeared in her humanoid form, tucking her magnificent wings behind her.

She was all smiles, as usual. We met up with a small hug, and she ran over to Aiden to do the same. It was hard to not like her, she was just so adorable and friendly. "How are you guys?!" she squealed quickly and excitedly.

I chuckled at her enthusiasm, "We're doing well, Dreamer. We want to talk to you about that 'situation' we talked about last time we met?" I said as I emphasized the word situation, and then put my finger over my mouth to hopefully relay to keep quiet about it. I pointed to my ear, and then out towards the house, to let her know people were listening.

She winked at me and laughed, her pink eyes glittering like tiny gemstones. "Gotcha!" she said as she notified me that she understood.

"Would you be free tomorrow?" I asked her.

"Sure! No problem on our end, Skyy! How exciting!" she said as she clapped her hands together in glee.

We had a short visit with her, before confirming plans for me to contact her in the early afternoon tomorrow. I was really excited about the wedding, and also about going back into The Lucent again. It was breathtaking there.

Once we were alone again, I walked over to Aiden and he wrapped his muscular arms around me. I kissed and suckled on his neck softly and then asked, "So, you feel like finishing up what we started earlier?" as I wiggled my eyebrows up and down at him suggestively. If we were lucky, at this same time tomorrow we'd be able to consummate our marriage completely, but until then Aiden wouldn't let me have anything but some hot and heavy foreplay.

He didn't answer me with words, but instead he just took me over to the bed and began kissing my neck in return. My hands immediately slid under his shirt to take it off, taking the time to slowly run my hands over his luscious abs. He broke away from my skin for a brief moment so I could toss his designer shirt onto the floor. I rolled him onto his back and straddled him, planting kisses all along his chest and neck. I bit into my own tongue to draw blood and went to Aiden's mouth, kissing him.

Aiden responded eagerly, exploring my mouth with his tongue. I gently bit into his own tongue to draw his blood, and an explosion of passion erupted in our mouths. Our breathing picked up to keep pace with our growing desires. His hands wandered down to the bottom of my shirt and lifted it up. He didn't bother fiddling around with my bra, but instead just moved it up so that my breasts were exposed. At least he didn't rip this one off me, like the one that was probably still floating in that lake somewhere.

His big hands were as soft as silk, caressing my left breast and toying with my nipple which was perked up in response to him. I moaned out softly as we continued the deep, bloody kiss. He gently rolled me off of him to lie beside him on the bed. Before long his hands explored even lower, as he found the bottom edge of my skirt and slid a hand underneath it, rubbing my clit softly through my panties. I began to gyrate my hips in pleasure, as the panties got soaked with my wetness.

He slid them aside and inserted two of his fingers into my wet fold, and I squealed out softly in delight, trying to remind myself that there were vampire ears who could hear us. We tried to be as respectful of each other's privacy as possible, but it was still weird getting used to it. Aiden began pumping his fingers inside of me faster and faster as he broke away from our kiss and took one of my nipples into his warm mouth.

I arched my back in excitement as he bit into my breast drawing blood, licking it off my nipple as it flowed over it like a tiny crimson river. I moved closer to his neck and sunk my fangs into it, letting his warm blood flood into my mouth. Sipping it down like a fine wine, I came closer and closer to my orgasm as he inserted a third finger and rubbed my clit with his thumb. At this point I didn't care who heard me, the wave of ecstasy came over me and I screamed out in pleasure with it.

Taking a second to catch my breath I put my mouth back to Aiden's neck and continued to drink his blood. He did the same to my breast, until our mouths met again and we mingled our blood together with our tongues once more.

Not to leave him hanging I unbuttoned his jeans and he adjusted himself so I could pull them down. No underwear as usual. It made for easier access, as I grasped his erect manhood in my hand and began to return the favor he so graciously gave me. I secretly couldn't wait until tomorrow, while all of this was wonderful, I really just wanted to go that extra step and feel him inside of me.

We lay together on the bed after we had both been thoroughly pleasured, cuddling and occasionally nipping each other and lazily licking up the blood that was drawn. Hours had passed and it was closing in on the evening at this point, so we hopped in the bath together, and afterwards shared two hot mugs of blood like it was the most normal thing in the world.

Aiden threw on some black cargo pants that had a lot of pockets for his vials of silver and weapons to conceal, and a black turtleneck sweater over a plain burgundy t-shirt. Designer of course. I dressed in the same clothing I had worn last night, and tied my long hair up again in a bun. I didn't want my hair to be one more thing to worry about, someone could easily grab it because it was so long, and bring me to the ground. Satisfied with myself, I took one last look in the mirror through my crazy purple eyes. It didn't seem like they were ever going back to normal, and at this point I had gotten so used to them it didn't really phase me anymore.

We left the room to head downstairs and see who was ready, and saw Fiona in the hallway. It was quite awkward to run into my fiancés mother face to face not even a half hour after I know she heard us together, but then I reminded myself how many times I have heard her and Christian fucking like rabbits down the hall from us, and the guilt faded.

She greeted me with a warm smile, never letting on that she may have heard us. She was still dressed casually, with her beautiful wheat-blonde colored hair in a ponytail that was just messy enough to still look fashionable…which I am sure she did deliberately, and it probably took her twenty minutes to create the effect.

"Christian is going to stay back tonight with Arabella, I was just about to grab my clothes from the dryer downstairs and get changed. I'll just be a couple of minutes," she informed us. We nodded at her and followed her down the stairs and had a seat in the living room.

Lucius had come back with the van, but didn't seem to be in a better mood. Arabella was still whining and sobbing here and there. I knew he was still on the fence about her, even after the interrogation. But he was dressed up and already strapped with his weapons for tonight's stakeout.

The Divine Assassins who were patrolling the grounds for the possibility of Jack being out there for the night started portaling in just after dark. Ridley came in shortly after they did. Lucius was antsy to get out of the house and get on the road to get away from Arabella's crying.

So we all piled into the van once again, minus Christian who stayed behind, and headed to the spot once again...never possibly knowing what we were about to face.

Chapter 21

When we got to Argyle Square, we cautiously headed into the alleyway behind the buildings. As we approached the spot that we had found the body in last night, we came across another note that was placed on the ground, with a small rock over it to keep it from blowing away. All that was on it was an address. It was in Jack's handwriting though, so we assumed it was meant for us. After a full sweep of the area, we headed back to the van. Whoever took care of the body did an excellent job of cleaning up, because I didn't see or smell a drop of blood.

Once we were in the van, Lucius pulled up the address on a map. It wasn't too far away, so now we needed to decide how to proceed. I wondered what we were about to walk into.

"This is most certainly some sort of game that Jack is playing with us. The question now is, do we take the bait and head to the address, or wait things out and hope to catch him in the act again?" Aiden asked from his spot next to me in the van.

"We're heading there, no question about it," Lucius replied without even having to think about it.

"Do you think we need to let headquarters know about this?" I asked Ridley, not wanting to get into any trouble with the Divine Assassins.

"Wouldn't be a bad idea, extra help is never a bad thing either," he replied. "You want to call them?"

"Sure," I said as I reached in my coat pocket to get my phone. I dialed my grandpa, not only was he one of the leaders, but I knew him best and was more comfortable talking to him...even if he was a grouch most of the time.

It rang three times before he finally answered, "Hello, Skyy," he said.

"Hi Grandpa. Ridley and I thought we should let you know that we have a lead we are following here in London. We're heading to an address that was on another note that Jack left for us in the alley that we found the murdered woman in last night," I said.

"Who do you have with you?" was his reply.

203

"It's me and Ridley, Lucius, Aiden, and Fiona."

"Alright. Get to the location, and scout the area before making any decisions. Send us the address so that we have it in case we need to get there quickly. Call us once you've assessed the situation," he ordered.

"It's probably just him toying with us. I doubt he'll even be there. My guess is we'll come across another victim or body. I hope that isn't the case, but he isn't stupid enough to actually meet up with us. But we'll let you know what the situation is once we get there," I assured him.

"Be careful, Skyy. We'll wait for your report," he said and then hung up. I sent him the address in a text message.

I gave the thumbs up sign to Ridley from the back seat. "All set, we need to call them once we get there and assess the situation." He nodded at me as we pulled out into the street and headed towards the address.

Everyone was pretty quiet on the ride over there, and I got lost in thought daydreaming about what kind of ceremony the Radiant fae would perform for us tomorrow in The Lucent. And what I would wear, how to do my hair…it was going to be low-key and quick, but I still wanted to look nice. Aiden broke me out of my trance by gently rubbing the back of his pointer finger across my cheek. I looked up and smiled at him, and he bent down to give me a kiss.

I felt the van jerk around as Lucius pulled off of a paved road and onto a dirt road. I hadn't even noticed that we were out of the major part of the city until now, in what looked like a really bad area. The dirt road went on for about a quarter of a mile before we pulled back onto a small street that had some warehouses on it, and a few small houses littered here and there. All of the warehouses looked old, run-down, and abandoned. The houses didn't look much better.

Lucius pulled over onto the side of the road by one of these warehouses. "The address should be just up ahead. Make sure you've got everything you'll need ready, who knows what we will find," he said as he looked at us in the rearview mirror.

We nodded, and did as he asked. Once everyone was ready to proceed, he pulled the van back onto the small road. We didn't get far when my heart jumped into my throat. I couldn't believe what I was hearing…Bathory's voice, along with a male who could potentially be Jack the Ripper.

"Stop!" I yelled out to Lucius as I unbuckled my seatbelt and flung open the door to the van. "It's Bathory! Call it in!" I barked out to Ridley.

I heard the male voice laugh sinisterly, "Perfect timing. Sorry I can't stay, Elizabeth." Ridley had made a super quick call to headquarters before we all jumped out of the van and headed towards the house the voices were coming from.

I heard Bathory scream out in rage, "Jack! You son of a bitch! You'll never be able to hide from me!" her voice was trembling with anger, and it sent shivers up my spine.

We encountered dark fae who were on guard outside the home. They were in their tiny light forms as we approached. The deep, dark blues, purples, and crimson of their forms quickly transformed into humanoids, with teeth bared as they came flying towards us.

All of us had weapons drawn by then, I had my fire sword out which was illuminating the darkness around me like a torch. Lucius had already taken out five dark fae before any of us had even touched one. Bathory had come out of the house, clearly caught off-guard by our arrival. She was yelling out to two dark fae to get into the house and open up the tear to The Gloom. Her long, silky, jet-black hair was up in a loose bun, and she had on a simple long black cotton dress you might lounge about the house in. Her feet were bare, and as soon as she laid her eyes on me they turned into two slits as she glared at me.

"Skyy," she hissed out through her teeth. I was taken back to my time I was captive in her castle, instantly intimidated. But I had to muster the courage up to face her again, and hopefully finish her off.

Her disgusting excuse for fae wings that she had grown while experimenting on herself with dark fae DNA were trying to spread open. The bony parts were trembling as they tried to open up, but sections of them were cracked or wilting towards the ground instead of supporting the feathers, which were also trying to grow.

Just like last time I witnessed this bizarre event, the "wings" would grow and sprout feathers that would wither and fall off, like dead leaves slowly falling off of a tree in the fall. There were thousands of them growing and shedding at once it seemed. They were mostly jet-black just like her hair, but glowed a dark blue color faintly on the edges...which was probably from the dark fae DNA.

Her eyes were burning brightly, glowing and changing colors by the second. I thought my crazy purple eyes were odd, but hers took the prize here. Whatever kind of magic or experiments she had toyed with throughout her life had certainly changed her.

Even though she was terrifying, I could see that there was some fear on her face. She wouldn't come out any farther than the front porch of the house. "Open the tear now, get over here!" she barked out to the closest dark fae to her.

I was reaching into my pocket for a vial of the silver dust. It might paralyze me too, but it didn't matter...we had Bathory here in front of us caught off guard, we had to take this chance to stop her. Aiden was right by my side running with me. Lucius and Fiona were a blur, teleporting around taking out the dark fae so quickly that you could barely even see them. They were tossing out the iron dust that paralyzed the fae to assist with the process.

"Where the fuck are the Divine Assassins!" I heard Ridley yell out as he battled a dark fae.

Aiden and I were almost to the front porch where Bathory was standing, but seeing that her dark fae were obviously preoccupied she had to do something to buy her some time. I had expected her to flee from us, but instead she stood her ground, and began chanting in a strange language.

Glowing pale red light began to emanate off of her hands, and then it grew into electrical charge, which grew into pale red lightning that was shooting off her hands now towards us. I just barely had time to dodge it, and could feel my shoulder stinging from the little bit that had grazed it.

Trying to get close enough to her now to toss the silver dust out would be a challenge. I didn't even notice the dark fae who was coming up on my left, but Aiden saw him and took his head off with ease. They were definitely a lot weaker here in our dimension than in The Gloom. Sparing a quick glance around, I noticed there were only three dark fae left, and they wouldn't be here for long.

In that split second I took to look around, Bathory teleported off the porch to the curb behind us. Her entire body was surrounded by the odd red lightning like a shield now, but it was flickering as if she were having trouble keeping it going. My guess was that teleporting and trying to keep her spell running were taking a toll on the severely drained Bathory. She wasn't used to not having infinite power now that her book of souls was destroyed.

Aiden and I shot over to where she was in an instant, careful not to get too terribly close to her just yet. I popped the topper off of the silver dust vial, and the second I saw the lightning shield on her flicker for a moment, I teleported towards her and tossed the dust.

She screamed out in agony, and the lightning started to fade away again back into her hands. Oddly enough the silver didn't instantly paralyze her like it did to a normal vampire. She was most certainly hindered, but she was still able to move slowly.

Aiden was right next to me though, and he tossed another vial of silver dust onto her. She collapsed to her knees finally, as her freakish wings wilted to her sides touching the grass. Out of the corner of my eye I could see that the Divine Assassins were portaling in. They needed to get inside that house and look for Jack the Ripper, and I heard Ridley say just that thankfully.

Fiona and Lucius had taken out all of the dark fae, and were now standing tall beside Aiden and I. Bathory was panting and moaning on her knees in front of us now, with her head hanging. Her hands were in the grass supporting her, and the grass under them was glowing with that pale red magic that she conjured the lightning with.

Aiden and I had managed to avoid the silver dust blowing our way, and were still mobile. "Look at me, you bitch!" I yelled out to Bathory. I should have just taken her head off and been done with it, but I wanted her to know that I was the one ending her life.

With great effort, she managed to lift her head and look at me. There was no begging or pleading from her, just pure hatred glowing in her eyes as she looked at me. If she had been standing she would have held her head high, I was sure of it. She was still panting in pain though as she started to laugh at me.

"You didn't get the best of me, Bathory. You should have run instead of trying to fight us. You're finally getting what you deserve, for all the pain you've brought to others for so many years. Now you get to join them in death!" I yelled at her.

None of the other vampires tried to take my moment from me either. They knew I needed to be the one to draw my sword and do it. I took it out of its sheath once again, and it lit up the darkness for one final glimpse at her.

Just as I swung it to take off her head, I heard her choke out "That's what you think," softly. I put all my anger and sadness I had gathered over the last few months towards her into my sword, as I sliced through her neck and watched her head fall to into the grass with a soft thump next to her body. Her hands stopped glowing immediately, and then her body slumped down next to the decapitated head.

I felt relieved, and I couldn't believe it was finally over. Tears started to stream down my face. Lucius gently took the sword out of my hand as I turned into Aiden's arms and sobbed hysterically. I was happy that she was dead, but I couldn't control my emotions thinking about the time I went through at her hands, and about of all her victims in the past.

I only sobbed for a brief moment, but Aiden and the others stood by me silently and let me cry it out. I got ahold of myself, glancing again down at Bathory's body before asking, "Did they find Jack? Was he in the house?"

"No sign of him, your men are sweeping the area though. If he is here still we'll find him," Fiona told me as she smiled at me. "I am so proud of you Skyy. You finally got Bathory!" I moved over to her and she embraced me in a warm, assuring hug.

"I am sure it will sink in eventually, right now I am still in shock!" I said, still sniffling from my cry.

My grandfather had come in with the Divine Assassins at some point, and had made his way over to us. "Good work Skyy, this could have gone horribly wrong. I am sorry we didn't send backup in with you, we didn't think it would turn out like this though," he said as he rubbed the side of my arm trying to comfort me.

I shook my head to discard what he said, "Nobody could have known. And who cares…we got her! Finally!"

"This is a deserted area but we can't let this mess sit out here for long either way. Our men are already gathering up the bodies, but there are a lot of them. Aiden, would we be able to access the incinerator back in Scotland?" he asked.

He nodded at Grandpa, "Sure. I can either go with you and your men, or give you the keys to get in," he said.

"You can stay with Skyy. I am sure she'll need you. We can portal over to your castle and get it finished, and then I'll have Ridley return the keys. By now we know how to get the thing cranked up and running," Grandpa said in a rare show of humor. We sure had put a lot of bodies in that thing.

Aiden fished in his pocket for his keys, and took three off of the ring and handed them to Grandpa. They shook hands, and Grandpa thanked him before he went to join the others to gather up all the dark fae bodies.

"So what do we do with Bathory's body?" I asked.

Lucius gave his opinion on the subject, "If it were up to me, I'd chain her crazy ass in silver, and put the head in a silver bag…just to be sure. Then burn her. The body will have to be burnt either way."

We all laughed at his suggestion, but it might not be a bad idea. None of us could touch her body because it had silver dust all over it, and getting too close to that would paralyze us. The Divine Assassins would need to take care of her.

I decided to find Ridley and let him know about the silver chains. "I don't think we have anything like that sitting around headquarters, but we'll take her body through the portal first and get her cremated first to be sure there isn't any chance of her regenerating or something nuts like that," he offered.

I nodded, "I wouldn't waste any time then, get a portal open now if you can, and do it. I have no idea what she is capable of. And she made an odd comment just before I killed her. When I said that she'd be joining all the others she had murdered, she said 'That's what you think'. I sure hope that was the final end of her," I said as I crossed my arms over my chest and sighed.

"You and me both, girl. You did great tonight though Skyy. We'll face whatever problems might arise from this later when they happen, but for now let's celebrate this as a win," Ridley said as he gave me a high five.

"I would if it weren't for Jack disappearing during all this. We still have him to deal with," I reminded him.

"If we got Bathory, we'll get him. Just a matter of time. Why don't you guys head back to the house for now? There isn't much else you can do here, our men will handle all the dirty stuff," he said as he smiled at me.

I let out a breath of relief and thanked him, "Sounds good. We'll meet up with you later on at the house then?"

"Yep, I am sure we'll have to go into headquarters at some point for a debriefing but I'll let you know," he said before walking off towards the growing pile of bodies. Moments later four men went over to Bathory's decapitated body and picked it up along with the head. I saw them open a portal and walk through it with her.

That would hopefully be the last time I ever saw Bathory, in any form. I gathered around my vampire family, and we walked back to our van that we had flown out of in a hurry. Lucius had left the keys in the ignition, and none of us had shut any of the doors. The lights inside were blaring and the warning bell that informs you that you're a dummy was dinging like crazy.

We piled in the van, and I felt like a huge weight had been lifted off of me. "One down, one more to go," I said to the vampires.

"Looks like Jack is smarter than we thought. I suppose he had to be to survive this long without being caught. Hell, he had to be to survive Bathory for as long as he did," Aiden said as he laughed.

I laughed too, "No shit, with a temper like hers, and being a mental case on top of that, I am shocked she didn't kill him long ago. I wonder what their relationship was all about really."

"We'll probably never know. What the hell do two serial killers talk about I wonder?" Fiona pondered.

"I have no idea, but I don't think Jack was thrilled with Bathory judging from some of those letters I read that we found in her castle," I replied. "It doesn't shock me that he wanted her dead, and the snake was probably too scared to do it himself."

"It is obvious he had thought out what would happen there tonight, and planned it all in advance. Bathory was clearly shocked when we showed up. I'd say Jack is a lot cleverer than we had anticipated," Aiden said. Everyone agreed with that statement.

Once we made it home, we were all eager to clean up and get out of our bloody clothes. Ridley came back with Aiden's keys and let us know that all the bodies were cremated and thanked him once again.

By now it was almost dawn here in London, and Ridley let me know that the Divine Assassins needed me back at the headquarters for a quick briefing. I drank enough blood to hopefully get me through, before I kissed Aiden goodbye. I let Ridley open a portal and take me through with him.

It seemed like every Divine Assassin in the Order had gathered in the large room we held the meeting in. They all cheered at us when we walked into the room. Every single person in that room was somehow linked to Bathory. All of their families had suffered from her insanity at one point in history or another. So seeing her brought to justice was something they had been waiting a long time for, as bitter-sweet as it was.

People I didn't even know were patting me on the back and thanking me. How quickly I was being accepted into the ranks now that I had dealt the final blow to Bathory, when up until now they all regarded me like I had the plague because I was a vampire. Assholes.

Ridley and I had to relay what little information there was to them about the events that led up to us coming across Bathory. Once that was over, Grandpa and two of the other leaders asked to speak to me in private.

I followed them into a small room and had a seat. Grandpa was the one who spoke, as the other two just observed. "How have you been feeling, Skyy? Ridley said you're doing much better in the field."

I nodded at him, "I have been doing better, at least that is what Aiden keeps telling me," I said as I laughed.

"Well, you certainly did a good job tonight, and we have been thinking that it is time to give you more training and responsibilities here. We have more learning potions for you, if you're willing to take them. I know your eyes have never adjusted back to their normal appearance, but there doesn't seem to be any other symptoms from taking the potions either. It will be your call, you can either read the books manually, or take potions," he offered.

I shrugged my shoulders, "I'll take the potions. I feel fine, and it's a lot faster than reading. I don't have much time for reading anyway."

"Since you and Ridley were the main people on the case in London with Jack the Ripper, we'd like to see if you'd be willing to stay out there for a while longer and keep at it. If you need some time off to go back to see your parents or to have the wedding, we'll accommodate you of course," he asked me. I was shocked that he wasn't telling me, but instead giving me the choice.

"I don't see why not. He needs to be caught as well, and I am willing to stay out there and see what leads we can get."

"Great news, Skyy. Please just let us know if anything changes with you though. If you feel like it is too much to handle, let us know," he said in a concerned voice.

I assured them that I was alright and thought I could handle it. "What are the plans for the Order if and when we finally catch Jack?" I asked, thinking ahead to the future.

Grandpa looked over at the other men, then back to me. "We might not be as busy as we have been on the search for Bathory, but I am sure there are still plenty of threats out there that need to be dealt with. I am certain that some of our men will be parting from us and going their separate ways. Some of them were only here to find and eliminate Bathory. We'll figure it out as we go," he said and offered a smile.

I nodded at him, and then took my leave. I was happy as ever to be back with Aiden again. After a long and exhausting night, both physically and mentally, we were both ready to settle into each other's arms and relax in anticipation of our exciting plans for the wedding in just a few short hours.

Chapter 22

Jack couldn't wipe the smile off of his face. It went better than expected. He had figured that Bathory would kill them all, but as it turned out she was weaker than she had let on. Although it would have been ideal for her to kill a few of the vampires before they took her out, he couldn't complain. She was gone! Finally! No more manipulation, no more of her vampires following him around. No more fear of what she might do to him if she ever had enough of his retaliation. He wouldn't miss anything about her. Jack had been dreaming of this day for centuries, and it had finally come.

It was obvious to Jack that he couldn't stay in his beloved London any longer though. Not with the Divine Assassins on his trail. He had arranged transport on a boat to New Orleans with some immigrants that would be entering the country illegally. They didn't ask a lot of questions, which was exactly what Jack was looking for. With the right amount of cash, they agreed to let him stay under deck at all times, and not bother him. He wouldn't risk flying, because if he got caught with a layover in the daytime he'd be in trouble.

Jack had heard Elizabeth speak of New Orleans several times. It seemed like a city where anything goes. It had a lot of tourists, people always coming and going, and a lot of partying and alcohol which meant people made poor choices. Prostitution in the city was also very high. Jack would have a lot of variety to choose from, and some new scenery might do him some good.

He knew he couldn't push his luck by staying in London, and that he couldn't go up against those vampires with their numbers. The two older ones would kill him in an instant. He had to stay one step ahead of them. Sure, he could stay here and keep taunting them, but it would get him nowhere. Jack was out of ideas. Maybe after he dropped out of sight for a while, they would stop looking for him. They weren't even after him to begin with, they wanted Elizabeth.

But Jack didn't know as much about the Divine Assassins as Bathory had. They would never stop looking for him.

Chapter 23

It was pointless to even try to rest. My mind was going a million miles per hour, and Aiden could tell that I was restless. I should have been happy, thrilled, walking on air, thinking about our wedding in The Lucent. But I couldn't get Bathory out of my mind. Those last words she spoke just before I killed her had me on edge.

We knew there was a possibility of phylacteries being out there, and if they worked like we thought they did, then that meant that Bathory could be resurrected. The Divine Assassins had sent people out to all the locations that the ghosts knew of looking for anything that could resemble a phylactery. But what if it wasn't enough? What if there was a location they had missed?

It was almost too much to handle thinking about it. I hated Bathory with every fiber in my body, I wanted her death to be final. Nobody should ever have the amount of power she had gained over the centuries. Even at her death, she was more powerful than any vampire that any of us had ever seen. The silver dust slowed her down but it didn't lay her out like it would to a normal vampire.

Not to mention we had no idea who her allies were. We knew she had vampires working for her, but who they were or where they lived was anyone's guess. She had centuries to build up a small army, build homes in every continent on the planet, and hone her dark magic skills.

It pained me to think it, but we could never truly let our guard down.

And then there was Jack. That little spineless shit had set us all up. My guess was he thought he would come out on top no matter who was left standing. Some of us would get killed, and he'd have that much less to worry about. We walked right into his little trap too. Not that I was unhappy that we had managed to kill Bathory, but what if one of us had lost our lives in the crossfire?

Jack had to be stopped. Unless he was also working with the dark fae, I didn't think he'd try another ambush like that.

And we certainly wouldn't be walking into another one like we did last night. So where would we go from here?

It was all too much to think about. I owed Aiden more than this. He was thrilled to be getting married to me, and I was lost in deep, dark thoughts, so I tried to shake myself out of it. We were in our bedroom in the rental house in London, which looked like it would be our temporary home for a while now. I was laying on my back, and sat up in the bed to face him as he lay stretched out on his back. Crossing my legs, I put my hands on his stomach.

"When do you want to get Dreamer here to take us into The Lucent?" I asked him, putting on my best smile.

Aiden sighed, as he took my hand into his. "Skyy, I can tell your mind is troubled. We don't have to do this today you know? We can wait until you're in a better state of mind," he said as he gently kissed the back of my hand.

"Aiden, I have been waiting for this day for a while now," I said. We couldn't go into too much detail because the others would hear us. "I'm sure once we get to The Lucent everything will fade away and it will be wonderful. Let's get ready, I'll only need about a half hour, and then we can get Dreamer here."

I stood up off the bed, and reached out for Aiden's hand to lift him up off the bed. He took it and I pulled him up with little effort. Smiling at me, he wrapped his arms around my waist and kissed my forehead. "You're going to want to tell Ridley or someone at headquarters that you won't be available for a day or two."

"Oh? And why is that?" I replied to him with a sly smile on my face.

"You need to get out of here and relax for a while, that is why. Doctor Carrick's orders, milady," Aiden replied.

"In that case I will let Ridley know that he is on his own for a few days," I said as I reached for my phone on top of the dresser. I sent Ridley a message letting him know, and the reply was: Good. You need to relax. Have fun!

Once that was taken care of, I began sifting through my limited wardrobe for something to wear. I generally didn't wear much white, because it looked terrible on me. Even before I was a vampire, I was pale because I am a natural redhead. White just makes me look washed out. I figured it'd be fine on a wedding dress, but for today I just picked out a simple light blue tank top, and some slim fit jeans. I knew we'd be flying with the Radiant fae, so a dress wouldn't be practical anyway.

Once I changed my clothes, I went into the bathroom to put on a little bit of makeup and try to do something with my hair. Aiden usually commented that he liked my hair down instead of up, so I plugged in my curling iron and got out the hairspray. I put some big, loose curls into my hair, and tossed on a little bit of mascara, blush, and lip gloss. It wasn't anything fancy but I felt pretty enough.

I slid on a cute pair of sandals and let Aiden know that I was ready. He had packed two small carryon suitcases for both of us, which were laid out on the bed. I lifted my eyebrows at him, in a silent question.

"It's a surprise," he said, and winked at me. I had to trust him, and hope that he had packed the essentials I'd need for our mini vacation.

"Well, I am all set if you are. I can get in touch with Dreamer any time now," I said as I sat at the edge of the bed.

"I let Lucius know we were going to be in The Lucent, in case he needed anything while we were gone. And told him we'd be gone for a day or two," Aiden informed me.

"Good, I was going to suggest that we let someone know we'd be out of reach while we were there," I replied.

Not long after that, I got the pink crystal out and called Dreamer. She wanted to take us into The Lucent from an outdoor location on the property, so we followed her outside and we met up with another of our Radiant fae friends, Holland, who was there to help Dreamer take us through the tear into their beautiful realm.

Dreamer took me, and Holland took Aiden, and within seconds we were once again in The Lucent. It was just as amazing as I remembered it. We came in from a different location than before, but it was not any less stunning than the last time. Bright green, soft grass was blowing lazily in the breeze on gently rolling hills for as far as the eye could see. Beautiful wild flowers were scattered in various colors all over the hills. The sky was bright blue, and we saw the rainbows that defied everything we knew on our dimension crisscrossed in the sky. They went in every direction you could imagine, creating beautiful pictures.

I realized that I was once again standing with my mouth hanging open in awe when Dreamer giggled, breaking me out of my trance. "You should see your faces! So adorable!" she squealed out in delight. I blushed as I smiled at her.

Holland was also smiling at us, and just as I suspected, my dreary mood began to lift. How could you be anything short of ecstatic here in The Lucent? And with the company of Dreamer and the Radiant fae, there was no way that I could stay down long.

We were going to have to be "dusted" again, which is the process of the Radiant fae scattering their fae dust all over our bodies, enabling us to fly with their assistance. Holland and Dreamer shrunk down to their tiny light forms and began to whiz all around us, sprinkling us with their magical dust. Before long I felt my feet lifting off the ground, and Dreamer went back into her humanoid form to take my hand. Holland took Aiden's hand and then we were lifting off higher in the sky on our journey.

Holland flew Aiden up next to me so that we could hold hands while we soared through the beautiful sky. I was so busy looking around at the landscape that I didn't notice Aiden was looking at nothing but me. He had a huge grin plastered on his face, and I could tell that he was beyond happy. I squeezed his hand in mine and smiled back at him.

We flew over landscapes that would never exist in our dimension. One area had flowers that retained the shape of a flower, but were transparent. They shimmered all the colors of the rainbow at once inside, and had light emanating from the center of them. We flew over a field of sunflowers that had insects that looked like giant bees pollinating them. Small balls of light bounced back and forth between the flowers and would then shoot up in the air, exploding in small showers of water.

As fascinating as our flight was, it was relatively short and soon we started to descend to the shore of a beautiful lake. The colors in The Lucent were so much more vibrant than those on our plane. It was an explosion of color, and the water in this lake looked much like the water in an exotic reef would, bright greens and blues, and it was crystal clear.

We gently landed on the soft grass near the lake, which was littered with tiny, brightly colored flowers as well. There were several Radiant fae in their light forms all around the area, flying up and down throughout the flowers. The individual colors of their dusts mingled together and formed beautiful colors. I noticed a small arbor that was constructed just near the shoreline of the lake. Made out of woods that were native to The Lucent, it was simple and beautifully crafted. The wood itself gave off a faint shimmer of light. Everything in The Lucent was gorgeous.

The Radiant fae had decorated the arbor with growing vines that had flowers blooming all over them. From the middle of the arbor hung a large, clear crystal that caught the light from a million different angles. It shone more brilliantly than any diamond I had ever seen.

Dreamer and the other Radiant fae all went into their humanoid forms, and I could see there were a lot more than a few of them there now. Close to two hundred of them, maybe more, gathered in the grass on both sides of the arbor area. They left enough room to form a walkway to reach the arbor, and twenty Radiant fae, ten on each side, lined up along the walkway. They each represented a different color of the rainbow, and some colors in between.

Dreamer was smiling from ear to ear, as usual. A male Radiant fae walked up beside her. He, like Solara, represented more than one color. His garb was aqua blue and simple, just a tunic that went down to almost his knees, and plain pants of the same color. His eyes were the color of the lake behind us, sparkling aqua blue, but his wings and hair were blue and a vibrant color of yellow. He smiled and bowed before us.

"Greetings, Skyy and Aiden, my name is Laguna. It will be my pleasure to unite the two of you together in a life-bond. Although the ceremony is not the same as you would have in your culture, I would like you to understand that we expect you to honor and uphold your joining here today as you would a wedding back on your plane. In fact we believe very deeply that once you are bound together in a life-bond, that you will remain together both through life, and after death. If you both understand that we do not take this ceremony lightly, and agree to honor both one another and the life-bond, then we can begin," Laguna said in a gentle, yet authoritative manner.

Aiden took my hand into his as we both looked at each other. We smiled, and then nodded to Laguna that we understood. "We can't thank you enough for giving us the honor of coming into The Lucent for this ceremony. Both of us understand the terms you have laid out before us, sir. We are ready to begin whenever you are ready," Aiden said to Laguna.

He smiled at us again, and gestured towards the arbor with his tiny hand. "Very well, I will take my place under the Branches of Unity. Once I have prepared the ceremony, you will be prompted to walk along the pathway up to the Branches of Unity."

With that being said, he lifted off into the air and flew over to the arbor. Dreamer motioned for us to walk beside her, and we followed. We stopped at the beginning of the pathway. "Once he is ready, he'll motion for you to walk forward from here,' she said. She kissed each of us on our cheek before taking flight and placing herself in the crowd of Radiant fae. I noticed she was up close to the arbor, hoping to have a good view for the ceremony.

My heart was beating fast now, realizing that Aiden and I were finally going to make our relationship official. I squeezed his hand, and whispered softly "I love you," to him. He whispered it back to me, and kissed the top of my head.

A band of musician Radiant fae flew down from above, each carrying a tiny instrument in their hands. All of them looked to be crudely made from wood. They took place outside of the arbor on both sides. Before long, soft music was floating on the breeze.

We watched Laguna anxiously as we stood waiting on him. After a few moments he made a gesture with his hand, and all of the Radiant fae that lined the pathway held their hands up, palms out, towards the fae that was directly across from them. Then, an explosion of colors formed an archway all the way down the path. It was a rainbow tunnel, shimmering with wonderful colors. I gasped out loud and covered my mouth in awe. "It's so beautiful," I said softly, getting tears in my eyes.

Just then, Laguna motioned for us to walk down the pathway. Hand in hand, we walked slowly down the rainbow path. The light gave off a warm, soothing heat that made us feel safe, happy, and protected. We stopped at the end of the pathway, under the arbor standing just in front of Laguna. Once we were under the gorgeous crystal, it projected its multicolored light all over our skin, much like a prism would back on our dimension.

"Much of what I say will be in our native tongue, and you will not understand it. I will prompt you at certain times in English when I need your reply," Laguna began. We both nodded at him. He smiled back at us and began to speak in their native language. It was soft and light on his tongue, very pleasant to listen to. His eyes would close for a few moments, and then would open again. He would lift his hand over one of our heads, then the other while speaking.

"With your permission, we will place a crown upon each of your heads, representing not only the life-bond, but also your bond to the earth, and light that surrounds you," Laguna said, waiting for our reply.

Unsure what to say, we both nodded at him silently, giving our permission. A male Radiant fae came from Aiden's side, while a female came from my side. They stood before us, and asked that we bow down so that the crowns could be placed on our heads. They were made from delicate vines, and had tiny flowers scattered throughout. Very simple, yet beautiful, just like everything in The Lucent.

Once the crowns were placed, Laguna went to each of our heads and chanted verses in a sing-song voice in his language. He then went back to his place under the arbor. Reaching into his pocket, he pulled out several stands of what resembled ribbons, about two feet long each. Each of them were a different color.

He went on to explain them, "Next we will unite you together, using the Strands of Understanding. Each of these represent a specific trait or quality that we believe essential to life, and the bonding of two individuals. They have been infused with special magic that will be absorbed into both of you as I weave them together with you," he said.

"Skyy, please place your hand with your palm facing up into Aiden's hand," he instructed. I did as he said, placing my hand in Aiden's. The first Strand, or "ribbon" as I liked to call it, was red. He spoke words in their language, as he wrapped the Strand around Aiden's wrist, then wrapped it around my wrist, and then set the end of it in our outstretched palms. "This Strand represents the reason we are gathered here today – Love. Without love the world would be a dark and miserable place. You will struggle throughout your life-bond with your partner, no doubt, but never forget that you two were destined to be together, and bound eternally by Love," he said in English.

The next Strand he placed was orange, and this one represented Respect. Laguna wrapped it around our wrists just like the red one. Then came yellow, green, blue, indigo, and violet. The primary colors of the rainbow.

They represented Communication, Trust, Faith, Family, Care, in that order. He explained briefly that we should always communicate with one another, and always trust one another. If we ever doubt that trust, we fall back to the communication to work things out. To have faith in one another, and in the earth and life around us. That family, both blood, and those that have proven to be as close as family, are always important. That we should always care for one another's feelings and always take the time to listen, and lastly that we will always physically care for the other at all times, in sickness and in health.

Once we had all of the Strands wrapped around our wrists, he spoke again in his native language. The Strands looked like ribbons, but had an ethereal feel to them. They were solid enough to feel, but not quite an inanimate object. Just as I looked down to inspect them closer, they began to move gently, twirling around our wrists slowly.

"All of the Strands values are now embedded into your consciousness, and into your life-bond. They are the base for which your relationship will grow from," he explained. "Now they will shower you both with their love and knowledge.

As he said that, the Strands began to move upwards, off of our wrists twisting together into our palms before shooting up into the air above us like a firework. We were showered with multicolored rain as the Strands fell upon us. The sparks of rainbow colored light were warm on my bare shoulders as they touched my skin and they felt good.

"Next I shall ask that you hold both of your hands out in front of you, with your palms up," Laguna said. We did as we were told, as the sparks of color still floated down from the sky above us.

He spoke in his native tongue once again, then spoke to us in English. "Next we must pay our respects to the world around us, for without it we wouldn't have life…or love for that matter," he said with a chuckle. "Please stand very still, as we infuse you with the knowledge of Earth, Air, Fire, and Water," Laguna said.

I watched in wonder as Laguna's hand hovered over my left palm. Soil appeared in it, hovering just above my skin. A small seed sprouted from the soil and slowly grew into a flower. "Without earth we would have no food, no shelter. It is fertile, it is stable. It nurtures us," he explained.

Then he went to Aiden, and in his left palm a small tornado appeared. I could see the wind blowing his shirt around softly. "Air also brings us life. Without it, our plants would not grow, our lungs would not fill, and we would not exist. It carries away your worries, and calms our minds," Laguna said as he smiled.

Laguna hovered his hand above Aiden's right palm then, and a small flame was lit just above it. "Fire can both create and destroy life. We would not have warmth from the elements without it, nor would we have the means to create several of the tools that we use on a daily basis. Fire lends a powerful balance to nature," Laguna said as he walked away from Aiden and stood back before me.

A miniature waterfall, flowing into a small pool of water appeared above my right palm. "Water is essential to our very existence. Without it we would wither and die. It hydrates us, it cleanses us, it delivers nutrients to our bodies. Without water our plants could never grow."

"By respecting, and living alongside of these elements, your lives will be prosperous. Your relationship will be nurtured by the elements. Keep this knowledge close to your heart, and you will live happy lives," Laguna said before waving his hand over our palms. The elements disappeared as his hand passed over each one.

Some more chanting and singing in their language went on, and then Laguna spoke to us for the last time. "I understand in your plane, that your wedding ceremonies are sealed with a kiss to unite the couple as one. Our life-bond ceremony does this as well. It would be my pleasure to introduce you as a bonded couple. If you accept all that has been presented before you in this life-bonding ceremony, you may kiss one another to confirm your bond," he said.

Aiden took both of my hands into his and pulled me towards him. We were both grinning from ear to ear. He bent over and placed his lips on mine, softly kissing me. It may have been my imagination but it felt like energy of some sort was flowing between the two of us. As if the Strands and the elements were forming the eternal bond between us, officially.

Roars of applause erupted from the crowd of Radiant fae that took witness to our ceremony. Aiden and I broke away from our kiss and embraced each other in a big hug. We then turned to the excited crowd, joining our hands together, lifting them into the air to show we were joined as one. More cheers from the fae.

Dreamer flew over to us, with tears streaming down her face. "I hope those are tears of joy, Dreamer?" I asked her.

She nodded her head quickly, "Oh yes! Yes, yes, yes! Of course they are! I am so happy for you both! What a beautiful life-bond ceremony!" she said in pretty much all one continuous word in the same breath.

I laughed at her, "Good. I would be worried if you were crying in a bad way at our wedding!"

"Come with me, you have to see the banquet that was prepared for you!" she squealed in delight and she stood between us, taking one of our hands in each of hers.

We walked through the throngs of people who were observing, to an area just outside of the arbor where we got married. I hadn't noticed this when we flew in, maybe it was set up while the ceremony took place, or maybe I was just too excited to have even noticed it. But there were several tables lined up with plenty of food on them, and small tables and chairs for the guests to sit at.

I covered my mouth again in awe. "Oh Dreamer! You guys didn't have to do all of this for us! It is more than we could have ever imagined! Thank you, from the bottom of my heart. It's wonderful," I said as I hugged her. The musician fae had moved over to the celebration and began playing more of their lovely music.

"Let's eat and celebrate!" she said, as more of the Radiant fae cheered. She sat us down at a table that was way too small for us. We felt like adults sitting at the kids table for a holiday dinner with the family, but I wasn't about to let that bother me. Radiant fae began to bring us plates of food, and goblets of drink. I noticed there was no meat, only fruits and vegetables, prepared in different ways.

I glanced over at Aiden, unsure what to do or say. As vampires, we didn't need to eat "human" food anymore. We survived solely on blood. Though we could technically eat the food they brought us, we wouldn't get any nutritional value out of it.

He smiled and winked at me, leaning over to kiss my cheek and whisper in my ear, "Just entertain them, this is how they celebrate, it won't kill you to have a bit to eat and drink," he said. I nodded at him, and picked up one of the glass goblets they had placed before us. I put it to my lips to taste it, and found that it wasn't too bad. Some kind of honeyed wine, very light and sweet to the taste.

I popped some of the fruit in my mouth as well, pretending to enjoy it. It did taste very good, better than I remember any fruit on our dimension ever tasting. We stayed with the Radiant fae for a few more hours, celebrating and chatting them up. All of them gave us their blessings for a wonderful marriage.

The sunset in The Lucent was breathtaking. After asking for permission to have a walk together, Aiden and I excused ourselves from the party to walk in the meadow along the lake and witness the sun setting. The sky turned deep purples and vibrant pinks, it was the perfect ending to the perfect day. Aiden leaned down to kiss me once again, this time with nobody watching. Our kiss began to get deeper and deeper, and before long I found myself moving down to his neck.

Breathing hot and fast into my ear Aiden whispered, "We should excuse ourselves and see if Dreamer can take us back to our plane. I want to be alone with you, milady."

I nodded at him, as he took my hand and we walked back to the banquet area. Now that the sun had gone down, we could see various different bugs illuminated all around us, buzzing from flower to flower. Like fireflies on steroids, they were beautiful to witness. I asked Dreamer if she could take us back through the tear into our plane, she went to grab Pacific, and before long Aiden and I were saying our goodbyes, thanking the Radiant fae for a wonderful time.

Before we left, Laguna came up to us, handing us a piece of parchment paper rolled up and tied with a rainbow colored ribbon. "This is our version of your marriage certificate. You won't be able to understand it, but it is physical proof of your life-bond that took place here today, for you to cherish," he said as he bowed before us.

"Thank you, Laguna. It was truly wonderful, a day we will never forget," I said as I gave him a quick hug. He returned it and then flew off into the night sky.

Dreamer and Pacific dusted us, and took our hands as we also took off into the sky towards the area they would send us back through the tear. The night sky in The Lucent was breathtaking. There couldn't possibly be a place back home that looked like this...the stars were so bright and vibrant, sparkling like diamonds in the sky. You could almost see and touch every single one.

A short flight back to the tear, and I was hugging Dreamer and Pacific saying goodbye. "We'll be in touch soon, Dreamer. Thank you again for everything!" I said as I gave each of the little fae a hug. Aiden did the same and then the tear opened up.

We were finally back at our rental home in London. Aiden ran inside and grabbed the two suitcases he had packed for us, and ran back out to me. "Now, we have two choices milady. We can fly in our private plane to the location, or I can tell you the location and you can open a portal to take us there."

I grinned at him evilly, "Well, they said I need to keep practicing my portal skill, so are you up for it?"

Pretending to be scared, Aiden cringed away from me. "I don't know, will we make it there in one piece, with all of our limbs in the right places?" he joked.

I scoffed at him, "I hope so. At least I hope the important limbs are in place," I nudged him as I winked. "I'll need latitude and longitude coordinates to a location at least near where we are going that we could teleport into privately," I said to Aiden.

"I don't think you'll have to worry about anyone seeing us. Let me get the information for you," he said as he pulled out his phone.

He still didn't tell me where it was, but once I was handed the coordinates, I opened a portal and we took off. We landed on a tropical island, with beautiful blue waters as far as the eye could see.

Chapter 24

The sand we were standing on was pure white like sugar, and the sun was shining brightly. I had to shield my eyes with my hand over my brow to see. I turned around and saw lush green trees off in the distance. Over to my left, out on the water was a long dock that led to a decent sized bungalow.

"Wow, where are we Aiden?" I asked him in awe.

He rubbed my back with his hand. "This, milady, is your own private island. I bought it for you. Built the house for us, equipped the island with plenty of fun things to do. Jet Ski's, a boat, some horses to explore the island on, water ski's, you name it," Aiden said as he smiled down at me.

My mouth was hanging open in shock. "Umm, did you just say you bought me an island?"

He chuckled, "Yes, I did. It's all yours. Well, it's all ours…if you'll share with me," he said as he winked.

I jumped up and threw my arms around his neck. He lifted me up off the ground as I wrapped my legs around him. I kissed him passionately, and came up for air long enough to say, "I love you, Aiden. Thank you!"

"Let's go check out that bungalow, what do you think?" he asked.

I nodded as I continued to kiss his neck. We weren't even on the island more than ninety seconds before I wanted to jump his bones. Of course I was excited that my husband had just bought me my own freakin island, and wanted to explore it…but we had plenty of time for all of that. Right now I had one thing on my mind, and it wasn't waterskiing.

Aiden teleported us in a flash to the front door of the bungalow, and opened the door with the greatest of ease. It seemed quite cliché that he was carrying me over the threshold as his new bride, but it also felt pretty damn awesome. He set me down long enough for me to take a quick peek around. The entire floor of the bungalow was made from plexiglass and you could see right down into the water below!

As I was standing there in wonder for a split second, he had flashed back over to get our bags and was already back by my side. "This is amazing Aiden," I said, still soaking it all in.

The bungalow wasn't huge, but it was a decent enough size with plenty of room. It had a living room, two bathrooms, and three bedrooms, along with a spiral staircase that led to a loft up above the living room. There was a back patio with a hot tub built into the deck, and a ladder leading down into the gorgeous ocean below us.

Wasting no time, we got to exploring to find the master bedroom. It was towards the back of the house, facing the west so that we were sure to get some amazing sunsets. There was a small deck off of it with lounge chairs as well. The room was very open and airy with plenty of windows. We walked out to the small deck, and Aiden wrapped his muscular arms around my waist from behind.

"I hope you like it Skyy, it's my wedding gift to you. A place we can come and relax together, and leave all our worries behind," he said as he kissed my neck.

I turned in his arms to face him. "It's beautiful Aiden, more than I could ever dream of. I can't believe how much my life has changed in such a short time. But meeting you has been the best thing that has ever happened to me, even if we've had a hell of a time."

"None of it is your fault Skyy. I just want to be here for you, and to support you, in whatever fashion that may be," he replied sincerely.

I kissed him, with tears in my crazy, purple eyes. Aiden used to comment on them from time to time, but hadn't said anything in a while, so I guessed he got used to them. My kiss quickly turned into a make out session, as they usually do. Except this time we could go as far as we wanted. And I planned to do just that.

My hands wandered down to the buttons on his shirt, and I undid them one by one before sliding it down off his shoulders, rubbing my hands across the strong muscles in his

229

upper arms. He lifted up my tank top almost as soon as I had his shirt off, tossing it onto the wooden deck.

Our lips never broke free of our kiss, as his hands went behind me to fiddle with my bra hook. I reached back with one hand and unhooked it for him to expedite things.

I sighed in pleasure as his large hand cupped my left breast, and deepened our kiss. My heart sped up, and my breathing got heavier as he toyed with my nipple. My hands reached down for his belt buckle and I fumbled around with it until it was finally undone, then unbuttoned his jeans. He was already kicking out of his shoes to make room for the pants to come off.

I slid them down his hips and he kicked them off to the side, and he was totally naked before me…finally! Our kisses were fast and desperate now, and I craved not only his lips, but also his blood. I was about to go into a frenzy, and needed to taste him immediately.

As he began to unzip my jeans I slid my tongue from his lips all the way down the side of his neck. I nipped him softly at first, drawing only a tiny drop of blood, but once that hit my tongue I lost control. I heard him moan out in pleasure as my fangs sunk deep into the vein in his neck. He yanked my jeans down off of my hips in a hurry, as I kicked them and my sandals off, all the while feeling his salty delicious blood pump into my mouth.

Now, both naked, he pressed my body up against his, skin to skin. He then sank his fangs into the side of my neck, which electrified my body with pleasure. It felt like every nerve ending in my body was sighing all at once. We drank deeply from one another's neck and I began to slowly walk him back into the bedroom as we did so. The back of his legs hit the bed, and he sat back softly on it. I sat on his lap facing him with my knees on either side of his body. I could feel his huge erection against my soft skin.

I broke away from his neck and forced my lips back onto his, smearing the blood all over our cheeks. Our tongues met once again, the salty essence of our blood intermingling with each other's. My heart was beating out of my chest by now. I was in a bloodlust, and lusting for sex at the same time. Aiden moved his mouth to my right nipple and took it into his mouth, as I took his erect penis into my hand. He toyed with it in his mouth, flicking it about with his tongue, setting me more and more on fire.

I heard him groan out in pleasure as I softly stroked his penis with my hand. He bit into my nipple with his fangs, drawing blood. My body once again tingled with pleasure. I couldn't take anymore, and had to have Aiden.

I gently pushed him back farther on the bed, straddling him with my own body. I looked him in his beautiful green eyes, which were glowing on fire right now, and said "I love you, Aiden. More than anything in this world."

As I put my lips back to his, he said it back to me, "I love you too, Skyy. I've waited my whole life to find you." I could feel my wetness dripping down from me at this point. I was soaked, and more than ready for him. To finally be with my husband, as his wife.

Sliding my hips down, I didn't need any help at all from my hands to get his hugely erect penis into my soaking fold. I moved slowly, trying to take him in and enjoy every second. Once he was about halfway in I slid the rest of the way down on his shaft, taking him inside of me completely. Aiden screamed out in pleasure at this, grabbing my hips to hold onto me. I glanced down at him, and his eyes were closed, his head was thrown back, and he had a look of sheer pleasure on his face.

I slid back and forth on top of him, slowly at first, then faster and faster…forgetting everything around us until I found myself screaming out in the ecstasy of release. Aiden wasn't long after me. I looked down at him and smiled. Blood and sweat was covering his neck and chest, but he had a huge smile on his face.

He rolled me off of him and laid me by his side, caressing my cheek softly with his hand. "That," he said and paused, "Was AMAZING," he finished.

I laughed out loud, and kissed his cheek. "Yes, it was!" I replied.

We lay there in each other's arms for a long while, lazily kissing and biting at each other, before I finally sat up and stretched. "Well, we've all but ruined these sheets, hope there are spares here. Want to go for a swim?" I asked.

Aiden nodded and got up to stretch. Since we were all alone on our own private island, there was no need for swimsuits. We dove into the crystal clear water and enjoyed a nice swim. Since we could hold our breath much longer than a human ever could dream of, we got to go on our own snorkeling adventure, minus the snorkel. There were beautiful fish swimming all around us. After our swim, we watched a beautiful sunset on the deck as I laid between Aiden's legs on one of the lounge chairs.

Over the next two days, we explored the island by land and sea. There was a lush tropical rainforest on it, with two beautiful waterfalls. We explored some pretty creepy, yet amazing, caves. We went boating and jet skiing, and rode some horses down in a small valley, then up the side of the one and only mountain on the island. And we had sex at pretty much every single location we came upon. It was amazing.

When the time finally came to head back to reality, we were both sad to leave. But I knew that this gorgeous place would always be here for us to come to when we needed some alone time to relax.

Once we were back in London, it was back to the grind trying to figure out where Jack the Ripper may have gone. Ridley portaled in as soon as he heard we were back. There had been no sightings of him, and no murders since the showdown with Bathory that he had set us up for.

We weren't sure if that was good or bad, but one thing was for sure: we weren't ever going to let our guard down, or stop looking for him. Ridley and I spent the next few weeks scanning every single television and newspaper in the world for any kind of sign or signal that Jack may have fled to a new location. There were plenty of murders, but none that fit his style. Thankfully the Divine Assassins had access to quickly scan these outlets, or else we'd have gone crazy.

In the spare time I did have, I started to plan my "real" wedding with Fiona. The one to please the masses, as I liked to call it. Since it was important to my family to be present, we had decided to go back to Massachusetts to have the ceremony, and settled on an orchard on a huge piece of farmland. Fiona wasn't thrilled with it, but with the right decorations I was sure that we could make the most out of it. I didn't want it to be in a huge public place, because some of the guests would be vampires, and I knew not all of them loved being around humans. There was a historic barn that the landowners had converted into a reception hall for events. I left ALL of the decorating and catering options up to Fiona, as I honestly had no desire whatsoever to get involved in it.

I portaled back to Massachusetts a few weeks before the wedding to go dress shopping with Cate and my mom. I hoped and prayed that my contact lenses that Ridley had made for me worked and stayed in place. I could only imagine what they would think if they saw my purple eyes. We had also planned a family dinner with Aiden, so my family could meet him before the "big day" and he had Ridley portal him in two days after I arrived.

Since Bathory had been disposed of, we were pretty certain that Aiden's mansion which was down the street from my old house would be safe to stay in for the short time we were planning on being there. I met him over at the house the night he arrived. It was weird to be back, where it all started. It seemed like so much time had passed, with all the crazy stuff we had both been through since we met.

I ran into his arms to greet him. He lifted me up and into a kiss. "I missed you," he said.

"Missed you too," I replied. He set me down and I looked around the mansion. He had paid a maid service to come in once a week to dust and keep things clean, like he did for all of his houses he was not currently living in. "To think, this is where it all started. You and me, I mean. In a graveyard no less," I chuckled.

Aiden kissed my forehead, "I am sure people might think it was quite odd how we met, but I am glad it's our story. I am glad I met you."

"It feels weird being back here, seeing my parents and Cate, after so long. I also hate having to lie to them about Grandpa. Well, it isn't really lying, so much as keeping my mouth shut. My whole life, to them, has to be a lie," I sighed.

"I know, sweetheart. But it's for the best. Just enjoy the time you have with them, because you won't be able to always see them, and in the blink of an eye their time here will have passed," Aiden replied in a somber tone.

"I know. Well, I hope tomorrow goes well. My parents are very normal I suppose, but they are also very religious. Cate will love you, no doubt about it," I said, hoping for the best.

And it did go very well, all things considered. There were a few awkward moments when my parents asked questions that were too deep, but Aiden bounced back quickly with a made-up reply. My mom thought he was handsome and charming, and my dad thought he was a knowledgeable businessman who was wealthy and would take good care of his daughter. Of course Aiden was all of those things and more, but they didn't need to know that.

Cate was secretly swooning over Aiden, she couldn't stop staring at him, and every time we were alone she went on and on about how handsome he was, and about how lucky I was. She came to the dinner with John, who was Christian's old boss, and I wondered how her actions made him feel. Next to Aiden, he was just an average guy.

We left the next day with blessing's from my parents and Cate. The wedding would be in just a few short weeks, and I kissed and hugged everyone goodbye promising to see them soon.

Once we got back to London, I was back on the hunt again. I was depressed to be back in London, and sharing a house with other people. I wondered why we had to stay here, if we weren't even sure that Jack the Ripper was even in the city still. Since we could portal anywhere in the world, I was going to ask if Aiden and I could at least head back to his castle in Scotland while we wait for something to pop up.

I went to the Divine Assassin headquarters to talk to my grandpa about it. He was happy to see me but busy as usual. Although we temporarily won the fight against Bathory, there were still plenty of other vampires out there that weren't like us. We were still trying to hunt down her army and allies, and since a decent chunk of Divine Assassins left once Bathory had been slain, they had to pick up the work of the ones who left.

"How were your parents?" he asked me as he skimmed through a large book.

I sat down in a metal chair that was in the room we were in, crossing my legs under me. "They are good. They really liked Aiden, but I could tell my mom was pushing for us to move back to Massachusetts," I said.

He nodded as I talked, and I wondered if he was even listening to me or focusing more on his book. "Speaking of which, I came here to ask you about the living arrangements in London," I said cautiously. I never really knew what would set my grandpa off these days.

He peeped up from his book briefly, "Oh? What about them?" he replied, then put his eyes back to the book.

"We have been actively searching for weeks now for Jack, and I honestly don't think he is in the city anymore. And if he is, he is staying under his rock for now. I wondered if Aiden and I could head back to his place in Scotland. We can always portal in anywhere we need to be at a moment's notice," I asked.

He was silent for a few seconds, but then nodded his head all the while keeping his eyes on the pages of his book. "I suppose that would be alright, but I'd like you and Ridley to still work together on a daily basis on the case," he said sternly.

I smiled at him, "Of course. Ridley can portal in, or I can meet up with him, it's no big deal. I just hate London to be honest. And Aiden and I want some privacy too."

"Understandable. Go ahead and make your arrangements. You'll have to make sure someone continues to watch over your new vampire girl though. Just keep me informed, and keep on the job," he said.

"I will, Grandpa. I am sure Fiona and Christian can watch over Arabella for a bit," I said smiling. I did wonder what would happen to her in the long run, especially since Lucius had scared the living daylights out of the poor girl.

I stood up to thank him and hug him goodbye. As I was about to portal out, he called my name. "Skyy?" he said. "I wish I could be there, at your wedding, with your parents. I miss them both terribly. I'd love to see you walk down the aisle. I know I gave you and Aiden both a hard time about the vampire thing, but I really do like the lad, and think he is great for you."

I wasn't expecting that, not from him anyway. It brought tears to my eyes. "Well, couldn't you still manage to come? Couldn't we make you invisible somehow?" I brainstormed.

Grandpa's eyes lit up, as if he had never thought of the idea, "You know Skyy…that isn't a bad idea."

I left the headquarters with a huge smile on my face. Things were looking good, for the immediate future at least. I wasn't being held captive and tortured, and we weren't running from a madwoman. One psychopath serial killer was dead (for now) and the other one was on the run. I almost felt guilty that I was enjoying myself so much lately.

Two weeks later, my dad was walking me down the makeshift aisle in the apple orchard. It was a night time wedding, just after sunset, as some of our vampire guests didn't have the sunlight protection spell. A decent amount of people were there, both human and vampire alike. My mom and dad insisted on inviting every single person from my life who had ever met me, and Fiona invited a whole bunch of vampires I had never even met before. She was so excited her son was finally getting married.

Cate was my maid of honor, and Lucius was Aiden's best man. Aiden had hired a marching Scottish band for music, and they had made a grand entrance before we walked down the aisle. As Dad walked me down they played "Flower of Scotland." Although we had already been secretly married, I couldn't help but get tears in my eyes and smile as I saw Aiden waiting for me at the end of the aisle. It also touched me to know that Grandpa was here somewhere, secretly watching.

He was smiling at me, looking amazingly handsome in his tuxedo. Our colors were silver and teal, and there were lanterns and candles lit all around us, giving the wedding a soft and romantic feel. There was a small gazebo at the end of the aisle that had white lights strung up on it that the ceremony was performed under.

I took my place by Aiden's side as I handed my bouquet to Cate. I glance over at Lucius and saw him give me a quick wink and smile for reassurance. Looking back over my shoulder at the crowd did make me a little nervous, there were more people here than I had previously thought. And all eyes were on us. I wondered what the humans thought about Lucius, and some of our other "huge" guests, like Constantine.

The ceremony was basic and quick, nothing fancy. Before long Aiden and I were sealing our vows with a kiss, and this time a "legal" marriage certificate. We went on to the reception in the renovated barn, and Fiona spared no expense. We had a huge cake that we cut and pretended to eat and love, catered five star dinner service, a DJ and dance floor, you name it and we had it. The best part was when I tossed my bouquet, she was the one who caught it. I gave her a high five and a huge hug. It would be great if she and Christian were next to be married.

We ended the night with a bang, literally. There were professional fireworks on display, and a limo waiting to whisk Aiden and me off to our hotel she had booked us for the night in downtown Boston. We hadn't planned on a honeymoon, since we already took one of our own. I used the work excuse, and Fiona bought it, but made me promise that Aiden and I would take a nice long belated honeymoon in the future.

Later that night, after Aiden had stripped me out of my eight thousand dollar wedding dress that Fiona insisted was the "one" for me, we lay in bed snuggling after hours of sex. Having to be careful not to get the hotel sheets all bloody was annoying, but we managed.

The next day we were teleporting back to Italy to get Cupcake from Lucius' villa where she temporarily stays when we can't watch her. After that it was back to the castle in Scotland. Finally, it was just the three of us. Our small, but happy family. I knew for sure this wasn't where I wanted to put my roots down but it was better than London, and it was our private sanctuary. In the future Aiden and I could decide together where we wanted to call home. And the best news was, we were free to travel anywhere we could imagine, in the blink of an eye.

Aiden and I stood in one of the castle turrets watching a lovely sunset. Hand in hand, for the moment without a care in the world. I smiled at him, telling myself for the millionth time that day how lucky I was to have found him. "I love you, Aiden Carrick."

He smiled at me and kissed my lips softly. "I love you too, Skyy Carrick."

Epilogue

Unbeknownst to Skyy and the Divine Assassins, Jackson Ripleigh stepped off the boat and onto the banks of the Mississippi, breathing in the hot and humid air of New Orleans, Louisiana. And, unbeknownst to Jack, a vampire by the name of Claude was sitting in one of Elizabeth Bathory's homes in that very same city, fondling a tiny garnet gem ring that he held in his hand. Inside of that ring was Bathory's spirit, waiting to be resurrected.

Jack's first order of business was to find a place to stay. He had to act quickly before the sun rose. Heading down to the world famous Bourbon Street, he wandered the French Quarter for a bit, taking in the sights, sounds, and smells of a city that never sleeps. 'Oh yes, this will be fun indeed,' he thought to himself. There were hordes of people wandering the streets and dark corners of the city, most of them drunk. It would be easy to feed, at the very least, and hopefully to find his new victims. But first he had to establish a safe and secure place to hang his hat.

Jack asked a few store owners along Bourbon Street where he could find a hotel. He checked into the Hotel Monteleone for now. It was close and high class enough that he didn't have to slum it. In the days to come, he would look for a house to purchase. Only being able to do so by cover of darkness would make it more difficult, but he had found in his long life that there wasn't much money couldn't buy. Even a real estate agent who would wander out to show houses after dark.

The next few days shocked Jack, as he got settled into the new lifestyle in New Orleans. He soon found out, anything goes here. He could even feed, in public! Twice now he had fed on a victim who was more than willing to come with him, without mind persuasion, once in a dark corner on the patio of a bar, and once right on Bourbon Street! Afterwards he had to wipe the victim's memories, but he could not believe what people could get away with right in the public eye in this city. He was falling more and more in love as the days passed.

The residents and guests in the city both had some odd fascination with vampires. There were shops that catered to and sold "vampire" items. What a joke, he laughed to himself. Humans would dress up, complete with fake fangs and contacts, and walk the streets of the French Quarter. People would congregate in cemeteries and locations around the city for ghost walks. If they were looking for terror, he would surely deliver.

Once Jack had acquainted himself with New Orleans enough to feel confident enough to map out a kill spot, he began to feel more like himself, and less like a tourist. Weeks had passed, and he now owned his own house in the Garden District which was only a short distance from the French Quarter. Blood was free for the taking on any given night on Bourbon Street, but he wanted more…he had not killed in a very long time.

Now he had to decide how he wanted to make his grand entrance. Should he go big, and elaborate? Or something small to start? There were so many small alleys and dark corners of the French Quarter, it reminded him of back home. Plenty of places to hide, and plenty of places to escape from if need be.

His plans were in place. He had lined up a "call girl" as they liked to be referred to here in the States, and arranged for her to show him a good time in the French Quarter. He pretended to be an out of country businessman here for work. They were to meet in Jackson Square, and then proceed to Bourbon for some partying, before heading back to his "hotel" for a nightcap.

Jack was almost shaking he was so excited to finally be killing again. He watched the woman walk up to him, dressed in a short, tight black dress, and high heels. She was young, and still attractive, and had no idea her life was minutes from ending. Though it would be bedtime for most people, twelve a.m. was still primetime for New Orleans.

She smiled and walked over to him, meeting right under the Andrew Jackson statue as planned. "Hi, I'm Bethany," she said as she extended her hand out to greet him.

Jack took it gently into his, and kissed the back of her hand, which made Bethany blush. "Pleasure to meet you," he replied. She thought she caught his eyes glowing for a moment, but convinced herself it had to be a reflection.

"Shall we be off to Bourbon Street then?" she said and batted her eyes at him, trying to be flirtatious.

"Yes," Jack replied with only a word. He purposely led her to the right side of the Saint Louis Cathedral, down Pere Antoine Alley. It was the lesser used of the two alleys that went alongside the church, and he needed it to be at the church. It HAD to be at the church.

Since she was being paid to be his escort, and since the city was so laidback, he didn't think anyone would notice or care that he would kiss her in public, in a dark alley. He took her into his arms, pretending to kiss her. Instead he moved her against the wall, with his back to anyone who would pass by. At this hour there weren't many people in this particular area, they were all on Bourbon Street.

He used mind persuasion to take her vocal chords away, but wanted to keep her mind aware of what was in store. This was always his favorite part, and he wanted them to be fully aware of what was happening.

He had on a long, leather trench coat. He slipped a knife out of it, first slitting her throat. Bethany's eyes became wide with terror as the blood spewed from her windpipe. Since she was wearing such a short and flimsy dress it didn't take much to get up it. First he cut off each of her breasts, and then he sliced her open from her sternum to her uterus. It was a quick and messy job, not like he would usually do. But he was nervous and excited at the same time. He didn't want to get caught so he made it quick. He ripped her intestines out and wrapped them around her neck. By now she was dead, and his work was done.

He giggled like a mad person might as he made his escape, teleporting out faster than any human could see. There would be no evidence of him on camera. He traveled this way all the way back to his house in the Garden District. Once inside he spun around once in joy, putting his bloody fingers into his mouth to savor the flavor of his kill.

He went to bed that next morning a new and refreshed man. Jack the Ripper had just been reinvented, in a city that had so much potential.

Being the egotistical and self-loving maniac that he was, the thought never crossed his mind that someone, somewhere, could possibly put the pieces together and figure out it was him. But when Ridley scanned the worldwide news and television reports for the next day, his alarm bells went off.

"Skyy," he said as he portaled into her castle in Scotland. "I think we may have discovered Jack's location," he continued as he handed her a newspaper. Her eyes got wide as she read it.

"Aiden, I think we might be making a trip to New Orleans," she said after she had finished.

That same afternoon, Claude had finished the reanimation spell to release Elizabeth Bathory from the phylactery. She stood before him, in a weakened state, withered and shaking. "Claude, I need you to tell me where Jackson is. We have to pay him a little visit once I am well again," she said, anger permeating from her voice.

Stay up to date with upcoming books in the series, and see what's new at www.hollyhudspeth.com

You can also follow me on Twitter @SkyyHuntington and on Facebook

If you liked this book, please leave your thoughts on Amazon! It only takes a few moments of your time, and you'd make my day!

About the author

Holly Hudspeth is a best-selling author living in Texas. The Skyy Huntington series is an epic, fast-paced series that features five books: The Lie, The Countess, The Pursuit, Guided by Moonlight – Lucius' Story, and The Portal. One Small Detail is a medieval fantasy romance novel.

She takes pride on the fact that her series has something for everyone. There is magic, fantasy, alternate worlds, horror, undying love, plenty of action, and numerous supernatural beings...some of which are her own unique creations! It will keep you turning the pages wanting to find out what happens next.

Holly's passion for literature began from the first moment she learned how to read. She enjoys writing fantasy, paranormal, romance, and horror stories, and has also created short stories based on avatars she played in online video games such as Everquest and World of Warcraft. Holly also likes to put her own fictionalized twist on historical figures in her books!

In her spare time, Holly likes to play mmorpg's, collect comic books, go to renaissance fairs and comic cons, travel, garden, and spend time with her family and friends. She and her husband currently reside in Fort Worth, Texas with their young son Gavin, and their four dogs which are spoiled rotten.

Stay up to date at www.hollyhudspeth.com or Twitter @SkyyHuntington

www.ingramcontent.com/pod-product-compliance
Lightning Source LLC
Chambersburg PA
CBHW031948240626
47153CB00003B/905